Awful People

AWFUL PEOPLE

a novel

Scott Mitchel May

©2024 Scott Mitchel May

ISBN: 979-8-9874654-5-5

Cover design by Tex Gresham.

Published by Death of Print.

The Death of Print colophon was created by Tiffany Belieu and Craig Rodgers.

Printed in the United States of America.

I would like to acknowledge and dedicate this book to Alan Good, Axel B. Kolcow, and Tex Gresham. I don't know much, but I do know that no author is promised another book in this world and that this book would not have happened without them. Beautiful weirdos the lot of them.

Chapter One

Excerpted from Interpersonal Interrogation and Statement Aggregation of one Michael Amadeus Greene: **/**/2019

MAG: "I mean, like, I knew Molly, way back in the day, before all the bullshit, and she was just like this party girl. Crazy personality, hyper sexual, but like, you know, she wasn't trying to fuck around on Frank, you know?"

UNKNOWN: "Was there any indication that she was unstable at all? Anything about her that seemed amiss, then?"

MAG: "You mean did we know what was coming?"

UNKNOWN: "Not exactly. I mean was there any indication that she was capable of doing something *like* what happened, not *exactly* what happened."
MAG: "Ah, gotcha. Did she show any signs that she could do a violent thing, like, if required to? Did she seem capable, or whatever, that sort of thing."

UNKNOWN: "Yes. What primarily interests us is how deep she was in, how far she would go to protect her interests, and how the stress of her lifestyle manifested itself leading up to the incident in question."

MAG: "Look, Molly once told me she had an ongoing sexual relationship with one of her Father's friends while she was still in high school, but she presented it as if they were in a relationship, not that he was taking advantage of her. Another time, she told me she jerked two boys off at once while sitting on a couch in between them, which she called "going skiing," because she had a cock in each hand like ski poles, get it. I don't know why I am mentioning this now."

UNKNOWN: "Because it speaks to the way she was. The hyper-sexual personality type she adopts when talking to male friends. Are you attempting to address what you perceived was her mindset... at the time?"

MAG: "Yeah, that. She also told me Frank didn't suck her titties the way she liked, he was too timid with them or something. We were alone at the apartment when she told me that. I think she wanted me to make a move, say something foul so she could get the rush. But I don't think she would've actually let me fuck her. You know?"

UNKNOWN: "She got off by getting close, showing power in that way, exerting her control. Does that sound right?"

MAG: "Yeah, kinda, I guess. At parties, we'd all chip in for cocaine, but Molly had to be the one to dole it out,

Inviting people to her room in groups of three to take their lines. She had to be the one to control the even distribution of the drug to ensure that it lasted, and everyone got their fair share. Of course, she was doing lines and bumps and numbies with all the groups so she essentially got three to four times as much as anyone else. No one minded though."

UNKNOWN: "How frequently did Frank and Molly have these parties? How often was there cocaine use?"

MAG: "I mean, like, not that often, full-fledged parties with coke and dancing until all hours that is. There were small gatherings, partying, almost every night. And Christmas, Christmas was fucking nuts. You know Molly loved to wear thongs back then, and low-rise jeans, she liked to wear black thongs that showed over her jeans. She even wore a black thong underneath her white wedding dress. It showed through the whole day. I think she likes the black thongs because she had a larger-than-life ass, she had small tits, but her ass was really something. I think she thought if she wore the visible thongs, people, men and women, would focus on her ass, and not her face or tits. Not that she had a displeasing face, she didn't, just that, I think she thought her ass was her best feature."

UNKNOWN: "And when the incident occurred . . .?"

MAG: "Right, Christmas '09. It was cold and snowing, and everyone had tracked some slush onto the kitchen floor where we all took off our shoes and boots. Molly and Frank cleaned out a room in the basement for overflow and there was a dartboard down there."

UNK: "The same dartboard mentioned in the report?"

MAG: "Yeah. But there was another one upstairs in the boys' room."

UNK: "That's not mentioned anywhere."

MAG: "No, it's not, but it was there and I can tell you for certain which dartboard was *the* dartboard. Like, it all happened, and then the cops asked everyone what happened, and everyone was pretty consistent about *a* dartboard, but no one bothered to mention that there were actually two dartboards."

UNKNOWN: I see . . . go on."

MAG: "It was hot in the apartment and Molly was wearing that super-clingy green dress that went down to her ankles that she sometimes wore, but it was like a tank-top on top. The kind with the super-skinny straps. I remember her nipples were poking out because she wasn't wearing a bra. I caught her tweaking them, her nipples, at one point after she did a line, and then she just smiled at me. Weird."

UNKNOWN: "Is this relevant?"

MAG: "I don't know what's even relevant anymore."

UNKNOWN: "Okay, go on."

MAG: "The party was in full swing and it had to be like two, or maybe three in the morning. My wife, I was married, did I mention her before? My wife? Helen? That was one of the reasons it was weird that Molly was always being inappropriate with me. Her and my wife, Helen, were close, real close, like they were always together. They worked at the same restaurant, The Antiquated, and Helen was always over at Molly's, like in between parties and get-togethers. Helen and Molly would just be hanging out, smoking weed, drinking, watching *Criminal Minds*, shit like that. So, that's also why I would never take Molly's bait. There was the thing where I didn't really think she wanted to fuck me anyway, just got off on seeing men's reactions, how they'd stiffen around her. And then there was the thought that Molly was just trying to trap me, get me to say something like 'If Frank won't suck those tits then fuck you proper, maybe I will,' or something equally gross, and then go off and tell Helen that I tried to fuck her. Because, and you should really know this about Molly, she is a constant shit-starter. Fucking professional pot-stirrer and shit-talker."

UNKNOWN: "This seems tangential."

MAG: "It is."

UNKNOWN: "What's the relevance to Christmas night '09?"

MAG: "It illuminates her mindset, speaks to character, and gives insight into how she liked to operate."

UNKNOWN: "Proceed, but know, if this goes further off the rails, I'll have to bring you back to the topic at hand . . . what we brought you here to talk about."

MAG: "If I think Molly's been rehabilitated?"

UNKNOWN: "Yes and no. We just want you to remember what you can from that night. We want to collect all the recollections of the aggrieved."

MAG: "To try and keep her here?"

UNKNOWN: "That's irrelevant. Please, continue."

MAG: "Like I said, Molly couldn't be trusted, which was why when she would start talking to me about her sexual exploits, or history, or she would tweak her nipples at me, or bend over and expose her thong, or whatever, I couldn't take the bait because next thing I know she . . . wait come to think of it, she wouldn't even tell Helen, that wasn't her style, she'd tell like Arthur, or Caitlin, or Jose, or Jed, or like maybe she'd get drunk and just let it slip casual like when me and Helen weren't there, but the rest of the group was. Yeah, that's what she'd do. And then they'd all spend the night running me down, before deciding that Helen just had to know, and Molly would make it seem like she didn't mean for that to happen, that she was sure I was an okay guy, but she just had to tell someone because it was eating at her. Then they'd call Helen and Molly would confess and I'd be fucked, and she would look like the good guy. That's how she operated. Also, and I know this for sure, she would shit talk anyone who wasn't currently in the room. Like in the friend group. If you weren't in the room at that moment, at the apartment I mean, she'd gossip and backstab you. It's just how she was, still is maybe, I don't know anymore."

UNKNOWN: "She was catty and manipulative?"

MAG: "Yeah, that's one way to put it, but I really think that that was just a means to an end."

UNKNOWN: "Which was?"

MAG: "She fed off the discord and chaos that pitting people against each inevitably caused. It was a way for her to assert some control over a life that I think was rapidly getting away from her. She was watching her friends blossom after college, some in grad school, others starting real careers, and she could talk all that shit about loving the way she lived, the choices she made and all that, but it had to be hard to know that certain things, from way back, made you the way you were and that the behavior you exhibit, your whole personality, is just a manifestation of having had real, intense, childhood-ending trauma. Molly wanted control. That's what I think Christmas '09 was about."

UNKNOWN: "So, the dartboard, the one from the basement that is."

MAG: "Yeah, Frank was downstairs in the basement with Arthur, and Molly was upstairs tweaking her nipples and dancing in the living room to Rusted Root or something like that. I was going between all the rooms because I was like a floater at parties back then. I liked to just kinda wander around, picking up snippets here and there, jumping into conversations when I felt I could contribute and then ducking out again. Helen was on the three-seasons porch smoking and cooling down. Now you have to understand, while the events of the night are sort of tattooed on my brain, I can't really be sure what is a genuine memory and what has just become part of my story over the last decade because I've heard everyone's story and internalized their narratives."

UNKNOWN: "I understand the complex nature of memory, how it can become fused with the recollections of others. We're just trying to get the gist, a synopsis of the event."

MAG: "God, it's been ten years already. It's fucking weird how time just moves on and everyone goes on to do what they do and Molly has just been in stasis. At least in my mind, just in a holding pattern . . . waiting, I suppose."

UNKNOWN: "She has been in treatment, and they say she's made incredible progress."

MAG: "Like I said, with Molly, no one knows."

UNKNOWN: "Please, continue."

MAG: "I remember going down to the basement after walking through the living room because there was no one there I wanted to talk to. Molly was dancing in that way girls sometimes do where they hold the hem of their dresses in their hand and sort of pull it up around their knees and thighs, and you sometimes can get a small, fleeting glimpse of underwear. I remember pausing and looking for a moment, and she seemed to see me and she pulled her dress a little higher . . . it was Dave Matthews! That's what she was listening to. Tripping fucking Billies! Anyway, I remember she was wearing a black lacy thong, she flashed it at me and I shook my head and went downstairs."

UNKNOWN: "Then what?"

MAG: "Frank and Arthur were drinking and not really playing darts, but more like having a heart-to-heart while throwing darts at the board. I got the impression they were into some heavy topic because they kinda shut up when I came down, and then started talking about something trivial . . . I don't remember. But I want to say what they were talking about before I came down, was what Arthur was going to do when his fiancé came back from training at corporate in Des Moines . . . if he was going to tell her about the cup-cake on the side or not. Turns out, as we know now, that Arthur had more than the one cupcake on the side. So, I was in the basement when it happened, the actual thing, I was right there, front row center."

UNKNOWN: "What was that like? Any aftereffects?"

MAG: "Fucking terrible is what it was like, and yeah, I had nightmares for like three years. Even now, I just get an eerie sense of disquiet that I can't place, and then I remember, and it's all back just like it was, then. All fresh in my mind, all new, like it's being placed there in real-time as it's happening, again. And it takes months for the aftershocks of even the recollection to recede and I can forget about it again. But I never really all the way forget, like it's an omnipresence in my history. But, other than that, I'm pretty much fine."

UNKNOWN: "So, what happened? To your best recollection, I mean."

MAG: "Molly came down, like almost right on my heels, and she looked crazed, eyes wide. This is where fused memory comes in because I would swear on a stack of bibles that I saw her dose like a half-sheet of acid right before the party started, but I can't remember what room that was in, or when exactly I saw her do that, or if just Helen, or Baker, or Jed, or one of the randos told me that. You know?"

UNKNOWN: "A half-sheet is pretty consistent across the recollections."

MAG: "Anyway, she goes, 'What are you guys talking about' and gives Arthur this sideways glance."

UNKNOWN: "Then what?"

MAG: "Then nothing really, nothing that would set her off. She didn't even wait for someone to answer her, she just walked calmly to the dartboard and grabbed a dart . . . they were the old type ones, heavy and metal, and then she stabbed Frank right in the fucking neck. He could've lived if she didn't get him right in the vein there — the jugular. Anyway, fountain of blood. Then all hell breaks loose, and she starts screaming, 'The Shed! The Shed! The Shed!' and she was stabbing him over and over in the face and neck with the dart. Fucking wild."

UNKNOWN: "Thank you, that's all."

Two kids are all right

At 4:25 in the afternoon on a Badger Saturday in 2007, her apartment was empty save for the two children who were playing video games and eating a Jack's Supreme Frozen Pizza in the living room. The boys (Pullman and Phillip Novinsky) heard something that sounded like a person trying to break into the back door of the apartment. They both froze with the kind of fear that only children can feel. That unknown and outside-of-your-control fear. The kind of fear that makes your skin tingle and your blood go cold because you know that if the thing you suspect is happening is happening then you are too small to prevent it, and you will likely die. They both felt it and looked at one another. Then a voice, an angry voice, a "Motherfucker!" said loudly, though muffled through the walls. Pullman was first to break his paralysis, looking at Phillip and then pointing to the kitchen, trying to get his brother to go take a look through the back window at the three-seasons porch. Phillip began crying, tears falling off his blunt and rounded chin. His lip quivered and his face turned red; "I don't want to," he said, in that halting cadence children make when genuinely upset.

"Fine," said Pullman, taking his first steps, Philip grabbing his hand trying to get him to stay. On the tippiest of toes, Pullman made it to the kitchen in silence, and then over to the window. He pulled back the curtain and looked out on two men completely immersed in their own business. One of them was holding a baggie containing about a quarter of an ounce of marijuana and the other was holding his cell phone out in front of him in a see-just-look-at-this-right-here kind of gesture. Pullman listened and watched from his curtain-obfuscated spot.

"See, asshole . . . I got the text right here. From Molly: 'quarter is clocked P/U 4:30.' The shit's for me."

"Look, and I'm sure that's what it says, and I got the same message on my phone, but I also got the weed, and I laid the money, and like, possession is nine-tenths or whatever, so it's mine."

"Dude, come on, don't be a dick . . . let's just do this, let's split the shit. I'll give you $50 and we can re-up with Molly later. That way neither of us leaves here empty-handed and pissed off."

"Only an eighth is for me, my brother-in-law wanted the other half."

"So?"

"So, I took money off him, and I really don't want to have to go back and explain why I don't have his shit. I don't see how any of this is my problem. This isn't on me. Your beef is with Molly."

"Dude, don't make me beg, c'mon."

"I said no, motherfucker!"

"No need to get ugly. I'm just saying have a heart."

"I said fucking no!"

"Fine. Be that way."

The man with the baggie stepped past the man with the phone, nudging him with his shoulder as he did. Pullman heard the man with the phone say "Dick" and the man with the baggie, wordlessly, turned around and laid one right on the phone man's jaw, knocking him out cold. Pullman was once again paralyzed with fear and wet himself right there in the kitchen. Hours later, Frank Novinsky came home to find his boys hiding under their bed, there was no sign of either man from the porch and it was weeks before Frank and Molly got the story from the boys' mother, Frank's ex-wife, which was not ideal, like at all.

Molly's system

There was a broken wall clock on a table inside a three-seasons porch on the west side of Madison, WI, and under that clock, a person could find anywhere from an eighth of an ounce of marijuana to a half-ounce of marijuana, or the requisite money to buy anywhere from an eighth of an ounce of marijuana to a half-ounce of marijuana. Very rarely was there more than that, Molly preferring to handle larger transactions in person. Molly was also a server and a cocktail waitress, which means she worked all sorts of odd hours. So the clock was just the best solution she could come up with for a logistical problem that was impacting the amount of marijuana that she could sell on any given day. She would leave the weed, send a text, and the customers would pick up the weed and leave the money. Simple. There was of course an obvious flaw with the whole system — a risk. Anyone, at any time, could come by and swipe either the weed or the cash. She'd understood this as a risk when she had come up with the solution to her weed-selling bottle-neck, but she felt that she had mitigated that risk in two ways: first, she only offered this stash-and-go option to her most trusted customers and friends. And second, she scheduled the pick-ups in advance so only the person/people needing the weed knew when the weed, or money, or both would be present. And since she was a relatively small-time player, there was never more than like $300 worth of product left out at any given time. She trusted her people, and they all understood that they had a good thing going. One thing that anyone who's ever bought illicit marijuana will tell you is that the shittiest part of the whole exchange is waiting to hear back from your dealer as to when you can go and meet up and pick up the marijuana in person, and then pay the person in person, and it is generally understood that you are always on the dealer's time, which let's face it, is usually found to be wanting in the expediency department. Everyone had a good thing going with Molly Duch.

Explaining herself

Molly Duch was short (under five feet two inches) with a snaggle tooth and long, frizzy (not curly) auburn hair steaked with white, and a tiny waist that ballooned at her hips. She worked at the Antiquated Brewing Company and she made excellent tips, being as that she was exceptionally charming when she wanted to be. She was friendly enough, but wry, which gave her an edge. She was also funny and outgoing. Sexual in an undefined, but obvious way. She had had two DUIs, but those weren't that big a deal in Wisconsin and the court let her keep her license for work. Between the weed-dealing and the money she made serving she was in the high five figures per annum. She had her degree, a B.S in the study of infectious diseases in India (she was sort of allowed to make up her own major), but she never wanted to go to grad school, or get an office gig doing the nine-to-five thing. Her Father told her this kind of life wouldn't last and she knew he was right, but she and the friends she surrounded herself with all wanted to keep the party going, and it's not like office jobs or post-grad programs were going anywhere. On her left foot, there was a tattoo of a tree, and that was the first thing her boss noticed about her way back in the day when she was new and even younger. He left his wife of ten years for her. He and his wife (at the time) had two pre-K children. The kids, in 2007, were nine and eleven, respectively. They stayed at Molly's house with their Father every other weekend and for three weeks during the summer. Sometimes, unsupervised.

They were, by all accounts, good kids. Frank Novinsky married Molly Duch only six months after his divorce was finalized (the shortest time allowable by Wisconsin law), and he fit in well with her circle of friends, which was quite a testament to him as a person, considering he was ten years senior to all of them. It was like he picked twenty-four up right where he had left it, though the lifestyle didn't suit him particularly well this go-around. The parties. The drinking. The drugs. He participated because he loved his (new) wife, and he did have some fun, just not as much as her or anyone else. For him, the fun always crescendoed early on in the evenings and he spent the small hours of a party's dwindle wondering if he made the right choices, and knowing he both did and did not. The apartment in which they lived was the bottom half of a single-family home, and it was where the group of friends gathered most days to smoke weed and drink. There wasn't a party every night, but there was partying every night. Frank managed the closing shift at The Antiquated and came home most nights to some kind of substance consumption in medias res. Molly was twenty-four in 2007.

Chapter Two

Her gift is exposed

IN JUNE OF 1989 she moved a #2 pencil roughly 7-8 inches using nothing but her own supremely focused concentration, and try as she might, she has never been able to do it again, purposefully — until today.

The FPPIB: lay of the land

Stainless steel. Concrete floors. Exposed but neatly organized wiring running the length of the corridors' ceilings. Suited men and one suited woman. They still let you smoke inside. There are no windows — not even topside. The Air Filtration System is top-notch. Meeting rooms with numbered doors. Long steel tables with stools attached in The Mess. Elevator banks on both the east and west sides of the subterranean compound. Mucho gov bucks to construct. 5G capable. Private encrypted servers. You better have Q clearance or better just to shake hands down here. Little is known. Much is whispered. No sunshine here let me tell you. The men still Brylcreem their hair and wear hats that match their suits, when topside. The woman acts like the men act. She thinks she has to. It's the culture. When asked by other Agents in other Agencies what a typical day in the FPPIB is like They always, without fail, say there are no typical days. Their coffee comes from giant, silo-style, stainless coffee urns and is kept unusually hot throughout the day and is drunk black by all FPPIB Agents — even the greenhorn newbies who still have to ask where the copy paper is kept. The copy paper is kept on floors -10, -12, -14, -16, -18, and -20 and is always three doors down to the left once you exit the elevators. Copy machines are kept on floors -11, -13, -15, -17, and -19. This is never explained to the Agents of the Federal Paranormal/Psychological Investigation Bureau but was done as sort of like an entry-level psychological experiment for the then newly created agency. To date, only sixteen Agents have ever asked if the copy paper can be moved from the storerooms on even-numbered floors to the copy rooms on odd-numbered floors and each one of those Agents has made rank at an accelerated clip. To date, no Agents have put this together including the Agents who've made rank at an accelerated clip. All Agents are told that the FPPIB is a meritocracy. It most certainly is not. No Agent has ever made rank through nepotism. All agents that have made rank, thus far, except of course for The Bear, who has been The Director since the FPPIB was created under President Regan at the urging of his wife Nancy, have made rank either through some experiment devised by The Bear or through filling out the requisite paperwork that corresponds with the requisite years of service as outlined in the Official FPPIB Guide and Rule/Regulation Book's Official FPPIB Promotion and Paperwork Timetable found on Page 12,275 Addendum J to SS 72. Bill Stevens, and Steve Rodgers, and Rodger Roberts, and Bob Helens, and Helen Abelmen, and Able Wojciechowski have all made rank. All FPPIB Agents call

The Director The Bear. They spend the bulk of their days chasing bogus claims and talking to crackpots and lunatics. There are typical days. On Tuesdays, The Mess serves fried chicken so good that there is a line of Agents at the double doors by 10:30 A.M., as They once ran out by 11:45 A.M. and some Agents didn't get any and were left hungry and angry and it was a real downer. The Bear is tall. He has an extremely slight build. He has all his hair still. He uses Brylcreem. He smokes Winston Cigarettes. He still polishes his shoes himself. He does this every morning. It has been so long that no one remembers anyone ever calling him by his name. His name is Winston Hargrove and he was old when Regan appointed him. No one knows how he is still alive, let alone so spry. His hair is still jet black. In his youth, when he played leather-helmeted football, his teammates called him The Bear. He once took a dump in Regan's personal bathroom in the middle of a meeting with Ronald and Nancy. He kept talking on the way to Regan's personal bathroom. The President and The First Lady followed and they continued their meeting. Something interesting has happened. Helen saw it with her own eyes and told Bill and Bob, who she found smoking near the elevator banks on -13. All three of Them ran it up the flagpole to The Bear. He wanted answers. She wasn't giving anyone any answers. Helen is asked to see her. She refuses but in a way that is acceptable, for now, to The Bear. They table the discussion and say They will revisit, afterward. It's decided. They must bring everyone in. Nothing can escape the compound. No information can get out. No one can leave once they've come in. Some things move and some things don't.

That one guy does that thing that those one guys always do at parties that no one enjoys, ever

Baker Thomas played acoustic guitar at parties, and he only played originals, which made everyone at parties super uncomfortable and unable to enjoy themselves.

Chapter Three

Jed Lucas fucks a girl who killed a man

IN OCTOBER OF 2001, Jed Lucas was spending insomniac nights on the corner of State and Gilman. Madison, WI, was cold at night and he liked the bite in the air. He had a place he could be, he wasn't homeless, and he had a job at which he worked steady hours, and he didn't want for much. He didn't have much either, but he was A-OK with that. The point was he was doing just fine for a high school dropout. He worked as a cook at The Antiquated Brewing Company located on the corner of State and Gorham. Jed was a grill and pasta man, and it was a big responsibility for him. He wasn't homeless but he spent a lot of time with the homeless. Not like the *real* homeless, but more like the gutter-punks — the traveler-kids — the ones who go from place to place and just live like that. Last night he slept with one of them. A woman, maybe twenty-two to Jed's eighteen, who was named Jodie Jane Johnson. Nicknamed Grody Jodie on account of her sporadic bathing habits. She'd left New Orleans in a real hurry about a month and a half ago, having got into a rough bit of business down there. She only told him about it after she let him fuck her on his couch. She said "You can fuck me if you want" and he did. Afterward, she told him about the rough business. Jed wasn't sure he'd have fucked her if she'd told him about it before-hand. She painted him a picture of herself sitting on a bench on the Riverwalk next to The Mississippi there, and it was late at night or early in the morning, depending on how you view time and your thoughts on when nights end and mornings begin. She was drinking. Had been all night. She had a half-drunk bottle of Olde English that she was working on, and like four empties of the same down by her feet. She wanted to see the day break over the river, was waiting for it, and that's where her concentration was — the river. Never mind she was facing northwest. She told Jed that she didn't hear anyone approach, but someone had, and that he was familiar to her, one of the other gutter-punks she ran with on a regular basis. His name was Chester Raymond Blithe, but he went by Cheese, as he, like Jodie, was originally from Wisconsin. She let him sit next to her on the bench and she told him about her plan to watch the sunrise and he pointed out she was facing the wrong direction and they both laughed. They sat like that for some minutes and she thought he had fallen asleep. She thought she would fall asleep. She told Jed she didn't remember what happened, but she was pretty sure he had digitally penetrated her before she knew it was happening. Then, the next thing she knows, she's standing there with the neck of her Olde English bottle in one hand and Cheese is laying on the Riverwalk twitching with a fractured skull. At least she was pretty sure she fractured his skull. She didn't stick around to find out. She left him there. She said she had no idea what happened to him. She thought he was probably dead. Jed had not been able to stop thinking about what she'd told him since she'd told him. He thought he was now some sort of accessory after the fact. On the corner of State and Gilman, he decided that she was lying about the incident, that it had never happened, and that he would forget all about it. That was how he decided he could live with it, the knowledge.

Jed hadn't been drinking, just sitting and smoking, and he knew Jodie was sleeping back at his apartment, but not in his bed — on his couch. A car pulled up around 3:45 A.M, an old beater, and a man who looked to be in his early thirties leaned out the window and asked Jed if he wants to do some Xan. "Sure," said Jed.

"Get in."

"Your car?"

"Yeah."

"Why?"

"My wife's back at the motel, we'll take the shit now, then go back there and drink."

"Sure," said Jed. He got in the car and was comfortable with the position in which he'd placed himself. He was a big six feet three inches and he'd had to hold his own before. He was not scared. Also, he knew what Xanax looked like and he was smart enough not to take any unmarked pills. The man handed him a full Xanny-bar and told him it was his to take. Jed ate the whole thing before they left the corner of State and Gilman.

Cuckoldry gone awry

The pay-by-the-hour motel was somewhere on the east side, and Jed had never been further than the far end of the Isthmus so he had no idea where they were when the man whose name he could not recall parked the car. They walked together through the parking lot and up some exterior stairs to the second-floor rooms which were only accessible from the outside of the building. The lobby was not on their side of the building, so no one saw them pull up and enter the room. Jed was aware that he was feeling quite hazy.

The room was a standard-issue motel-type affair: queen bed, dresser with television perched atop, mini-refrigerator, night table with no bible, and a small restroom. The woman that the man referred to as his wife was lying on the bed and the man presented Jed to her; he said, "Honey, this, this is Jed, and he says he likes to party." She shook her head and Jed thought that he felt the room go tense and dramatic. Silent, but dramatic. He didn't recall anything else that was said. Anything else that happened. He had no idea how much time had passed.

In the car, on the way back to State and Gilman, the sun was bright through the passenger window and Jed was silent. The man didn't speak. It occurred to Jed that he was unsure of himself, like, it crossed his mind that he'd browned out at some point and he was un-aware of exactly what had happened. The sun was up. He knew that. He couldn't recall when he went to sit and smoke on the corner of State and Gilman, how long he was there, or what time the man picked him up. He'd thought he was going to fuck the man's wife — he remembered that.

The man dropped him off on the corner of State and Gilman and then drove away. Jed walked the block and a half to his apartment.

Jodie was up and waiting for him when he got home.

"Where were you?"

"The east side."

"Why?"

"I don't know."

"How'd you get there?"

"Some guy."

"What did you do?"

"I don't know."

"Come to bed."

"Okay."

Four hours later Jed woke to the sound of his digital alarm clock, and he allowed himself exactly three minutes to consider the worst thing that could've happened the previous evening, and then he touched Jodie's arm, kissed her there, and got out of bed. Fifteen minutes after that, he was standing in the kitchen of The Antiquated Brewing Company and he was prepping his mise en place and he wasn't thinking about anything except for the inevitable rush that was forthcoming in less than an hour. He stocked his cold drawers with burgers and steaks and chicken breasts and cubed chicken for pasta, he prepped LTO set-ups, chopped parsley and scallions, and he folded three towels into neat squares and placed them on the metal ridge under his burners. Baker Thomas came in twenty minutes late for his shift, and Jed followed him out back to go smoke. They both sat on milk crates.

"What did you get up to last night?" asked Jed.

"Played my guitar at bar time and made like fifty bucks. Rhodey came by at like 3:00 and we took what he said was ecstasy, but was actually a crushed Oxy, I think. You?"

"Me? Fucking nothin'."

"Jodie is still at the house."

"Yeah."

"That going to be a thing now?"

"I don't know."

"Well, if it is, you should tell her that she should put on some clothes before she comes out of your room in the morning. Tay flipped her shit when she saw her. Said I was staring at her bush. I don't need that headache."

"Yeah, I'll tell her."

"You okay? You seem off."

"I'm fine, don't worry about it."

"Saw the new girl on the way in, she said she's having a party tonight, she invited all of us."

"Who? Molly?"

"Yeah."

"Cool."

"Cool."

Chapter Four

A passive-aggressive key fob

THE ELLIPTICAL WAS A FRUSTRATINGLY STUPID MACHINE and the more Michael Amadeus Greene pumped his arms and his legs the more he hated Helen for not so subtly hinting at the fact that he had gotten fat since they married back in '06. He wasn't fat, he thought, but he did recognize that he had put on like twenty pounds around his mid-section, and he was aware that his face had taken on a very moon-like quality. She (Helen) had attached a key fob that gained Michael access to the Princeton Club Fitness Center to Michael's keys one morning before he woke up, and she'd left him a note explaining that it was to be considered an early Hanukah gift. One she hoped he would enjoy while she was at work and he had his nights free. He hated the elliptical and he hated Helen for always pointing out his failings. He'd hated Helen when he married her too. He'd hated her for so long that he'd forgotten exactly when he began hating her, and he was sure that he had made her grow to hate him too. She wasn't coming home immediately after her night shifts at the restaurant anymore, and with her working her day-gig (gaining her requisite hours for Wisconsin state certification in psycho-therapy) he rarely, if ever, saw her. She was going to leave him. Probably after the holiday season. Most likely after Molly's annual Christmas party, and he was going to make sure he was fuckable before that happened. Michael wasn't fit before he put on the weight, he was just skinny. But now he *had* to get fit, ripped. He wanted to show her that her nagging only served to get him prepared to say "so long, baby" when she inevitably asked him to work on himself (personality-wise), or brought up the idea of a separation, or even divorce.

The locker room at the Princeton Club Fitness Center was expansive and cavernous and it had a dozen or so neat rows of stacked half-lockers with larger full lockers distributed within, a large restroom, private showers, and a private door to the steam rooms and pools. He didn't change since he came in his gym clothes, but he stopped in the locker room to weigh himself (228) and take a piss. There were always too many people at the gym. The ground floor had a large open area for free weights where men with visible definition in their arms, legs, chests, and backs did bench presses, dumbbell curls, squats, and deadlifts; it was always super packed. Michael watched these men in their tank tops, grunting and pushing weight, and he thought that their bodies looked really uncomfortable to have to live in, like to have to spend the day in. He saw women there too — all loose tops over sports bras, squatting in power racks with medium-weight on barbells slung over their shoulders. It was a place of definition, he thought, a place in which he'd have to eventually end up if he wanted to get ripped. Up the industrial-chic metal stairs, on the second floor, Michael picked out an elliptical that was way away from anyone else using the machines. There was no question that he was going to perspire in a rather unpleasant way, and he didn't want any of the women up there to be closer than a two-elliptical measure from him when that happened. He was sure no women were actually paying attention to him but he couldn't shake the feeling that all women were always paying him their closest attention, and that all the attention he was being paid was negative attention. He noticed the women, of course — paid them attention. They were all in those tight black pants that show panty lines and highlight the shape of their asses and sometimes the cleave of their vaginas, and in that moment, Michael thought about exactly how the Camel Toe sub-category on PornHub.com came to be. He pictured some seedy amateur porn producer, somewhere in California, deciding to get defined — ripped. Maybe he'd (the seedy producer of pornography) gone a little soft around the middle, Michael thought, like me. While the smut-man's legs churned in Sisyphean struggle on an elliptical much like the one Michael was astride, three young and attractive and unobtainable women walk past him in their tight and form-fitting pants. Sweating profusely, this man thinks to himself, that every man at the gym is only doing the work necessary for making one's self a desirable sex partner. The gym is an obscenely horny place, he concludes, and everyone here just wants to fuck. But the idea doesn't stop there. "Why does every man want to fuck at the gym?" he asks himself. "It's the toe," he whispers, inspired. It's the faint sketch of an outline, colored and completed by the imagination's gaze. It's the excitement of getting an idea of something you're not supposed to have any intimate knowledge of.

Michael imagined our smutty friend bursting into the by-the-hour-motel-room where they're shooting the latest production of Dorm Room Dirty Girls and shouting to the talent "put these on!" and tossing a pair of black fitness pants to the women on the bed, "hike em up your crotch as far as they'll go!" And that day, that man, left his mark on the world. Twenty minutes had passed while Michael contemplated pornography, and just as he expected he was sweating like a beast, his shirt a mess of wet, and also just like he expected, the women around him were focused on themselves and had not so much as glanced his way, but now he couldn't help but let his eyes wander to their crotches as they walked past his machine, and he couldn't help but feel like he was one of the world's bad men.

Chapter Five

Frank's wife finds out

HE GOT THE CALL around twelve noon on a Sunday — Logan Frederick was super-duper pissed, and what's more, it was super understandable that Logan was super-duper pissed. For one thing, Molly and Logan used to be a thing before she decided that he was just a little too boring for her and she left him, breaking his fucking heart for real and taking with her, from his home, all of the things that he had bought for her over the nine months that they had been together and she had lived with him. And for another thing, Logan was having to deal with the very real fallout of Frank's wife finding out about Frank and Molly's late-night liaisons in the manager's office. Frank had no idea that Logan knew about him and Molly, and Frank certainly didn't know that his wife knew about him and Molly. He still didn't know who told either of them and why his world came down around his ears, forcing him into a life that looked nothing like what he had envisioned as an undergrad at Tulane studying business administration. When his phone rang, he was playing with his eldest in the yard and when he saw it was The Antiquated Brewing Company calling, he thought about not answering, but then he felt a sense of obligation, as General Managers are wont to feel, and he took the call. That call went like this:

"What's up?" Frank's customary way of greeting.

"Frank."

"Yeah Logan, what is it?"

"Your wife's here and she's fucking pissed. And frankly, Frank, I'm pissed too. I got two screaming women in my dining room, and one of them is holding a small child and screaming at the other about wrecking homes and being a 'stupid fucking whore.'"

"I see."

"Oh, you see, well let me tell you something that you don't see, you just threw your life away on a twat who, by the way, is going to either leave you when she gets bored or absolutely burn your shit to the ground."

"Logan, you don't get to talk to me that way."

"Look asshole, I just thought you should know that your wife and your girlfriend are about to kick the shit out of each other at your place of business, so, if I were you, I'd expect a call from Tom. Because Frank, and I say this relishing the fact that I get to do this, my next call is to him."

"I'll be right there."

Underwear parties are not as fun as he imagined they would be

Molly Duch made their apartment up for the occasion and the place looked like it could've been a cabana off white sands somewhere. She had inflatable palm trees, beach chairs and towels laid down in the living room, and had cranked the heat up to ninety degrees. Outside it was a frigid Wisconsin winter night, negative fifteen with the windchill, but inside it was Tampa. The emailed invite read:

UNDERWEAR PARTY!!!
FRANK NOVINSKY TURNS 40
ACCEPTABLE ATTIRE INCLUDES
BOXERS
BRIEFS
PANTIES
BRAS
&
TANK TOPS
PARTY STARTS AT 9:00 P.M.
BE THERE!!!

She told Frank the theme of the party about twenty minutes before the first guests were set to arrive. It was a special surprise for him. She gave him a white wife-beater and a pair of Superman briefs which he put on, looking sheepish and uncomfortable. Molly took her pants and top off and Frank was somewhat relieved and thankful to see she was wearing full-bottomed underwear for the night. When the party started in earnest everything would be a blur and he knew that, but he was confident that he could keep his new wife under some sort of control. Of course, he was wrong.

The events after 1:00 A.M., to the best of Frank Novinsky's recollection, went something like this: Frank felt wildly uncomfortable seeing most of the waitresses who worked for him in nothing but their underwear, and he felt even more uncomfortable seeing the cooks in their briefs and boxers. Jed wore a robe over his boxers, and when Molly objected, he let her take it off of him — this also made Frank wildly uncomfortable. Baker Thomas brought his guitar and was playing originals in the basement while the people around him flirted and got themselves all horny. Molly and Helen and Michael did cocaine in Frank and Molly's bedroom and Frank, himself, wondered just how long he had to keep drinking before he could sneak away to the bedroom his sons slept in when they slept over. But nevertheless, people had come and it was decidedly less sexy than he thought it would be, but they *were* there for him, so, he decided he would try and have as good a time as he could — considering. He drank and he did the odd line or two, and he smoked some weed, and then, around 4:00 A.M., having long since lost track of Molly, he headed for his sons' bedroom, where he found Jed Lucas taking his new wife from behind on the bottom bunk of his sons' bunk beds. He closed the door slowly. Neither of them noticed him and he never said a word about what he had seen.

Chapter Six

A comic is not that funny

TRYING ON A NEW PERSONA, Jesse Lee Robinson was telling his jokes on stage and it was not going well, like at all. The persona was something that he'd been workshopping for quite a while now. Over eight months. He desperately wanted to be the next guy to make it bigish by being the guy engaged with what was really going on in the world in a truly topical and political and satirical and witty way. He wished he was wry. She was wry, but not funny, not really, he often thought. He wondered about her, when she wasn't around him, which was almost all of the time. She smiled his way though, and that had to mean something. What was topical and political in his corner of the world was that Wisconsin had just banned gay marriage in its constitution and the United States was at active war in Iraq for the second time. His friends (back home in N. Illinois) had all joined the army out of a sense of patriotism, and obligation, but also because they all wanted some sweet revenge too. But he did not because his Mother communicated to him that that would be a stupid decision and that only stupid little boys make childish decisions based on pure emotion. War is lousy with emotion, after all, is it not? she had communicated. "I think Republicans are a lot like homosexuals," he began to the silent room that somehow seemed much larger and more cavernous than it ought to have any right to be, "you know, because they say people are just born gay, and I can't see how anybody chooses to be a Republican." He held for applause, but none was forthcoming. This appearance was his first appearance at The Comedy Club on State, and he'd been given a generous five minutes. Before this gig, he'd only done Open Mics where he was the lone comic among musicians and poets and he really, really needed this to go well. Performing and all that goes with it is lousy with emotion, is it not? The silence was broken with a cough that he was pretty sure was the club's manager clearing his throat. "I mean think about it," he continued, plowing ahead, "as a Republican, you have to go up to people every day and introduce yourself, 'Oh *you're* Bob, nice to meet you, I'm evil. Now, if anyone needs me, I'll just be over there burning a cross and kicking a baby.'" Jesse heard the hiss of a bottle of beer being opened at a table that seemed too far away and there was a single laugh, which to the comedian's ear is much worse than if there were no laughs at all. The room now felt very cold to him, but he was also perspiring. It was an odd kind of chill he felt, a humid kind of cold. As if his blood had become frozen peat-bog smoke rolling off low embers on a Scottish morning. His bowels both roiled and clenched painfully in alternating waves of discomfort, and he had to suppress what he was sure would be, at the very least, an epic fart, which he gave a moment's thought to loosing audibly as if it were his schtick. "I mean who in their right mind would ever sign up for that life, willingly." The last word was drawn out dramatically and for effect. "It's a wonder how they get to sleep at night. Oh, wait, no it isn't, they sleep fine on pillows stuffed with your money!" A smattering of awkward applause that sounded meek, like leaves blowing on concrete in fall. He looked to the back of the room and the manager was standing there, but he was not waving the candle and Jesse was realizing he still had like four minutes left. He pulled the microphone from its stand and adopted a more relaxed posture, pacing calmly back and forth and breathing deeply as if he was thinking really hard about the state of things, but then he decided he'd sit on the stool that he had not noticed before with his knees wide and his back slouched drastically, and with both hands gripping a microphone that swung low between his knees because he's a fan of a comic who does the same thing too and he thought it looked hip and cool and disaffected and detached from it all. Like the posture itself was social commentary saying I'm so affected by all this shit that I'm now numbed to it, but really, I'm not numbed to it, just so supremely affected that I feel it so deeply that I can't even sit up straight, that's how exasperated and over it I am, join me, here, where I am. He breathed deeply once more, this time directly into the microphone, and he began a joke he thought of as his strong material. He conceptualized it as a humorous political rant where he'd forgo the traditional setup/punchline framework and instead deliver the goods with self-awareness and an ah-ha moment of enlightenment. "Look, it's not as if I haven't somehow benefited from the inherently unjust and racist foundation upon which our entire society has been built and have come out ahead because of the implicit biases that most white people, Democrat and Republican alike, just carry around with them. I know I'm the 'suburban' — (ironic air quotes form a visual parenthetical around the word suburban for the audience, letting them know that he believes both them and himself get it, and know exactly what he is speaking about because almost everyone in that room shares the experience of having lived a very white, suburban adolescence) — white kid talking about fairness while enjoying the benefits that systemic unfairness affords me. But believe me, I've had a fucked-up life too. Well to be completely fair, I've had a white people fucked-up life. You know, like, where you are allowed to make all the mistakes you want and still have everything just kind of work out . . . and then at the end of the story you aren't beaten by the cops in the streets while some asshole films it instead of, like, you know, pulling them off you." The manager was now flicking a blinking red light in the back of the room while at least one person in the crowd began to boo in a very loud and persistent fashion. Jesse got up from the stool and placed the mic back on the stand and sighed deeply. I just want to leave you with this," he said, but the MC took the stage before he had the opportunity to finish his thought. The old hook had cometh. At the bar, just outside the main room, he heard the night's MC say, "Okay, well, that was a thing we all just saw. And now please welcome to the Comedy on State Stage, Martin Henn!" Jesse Robinson ordered a shot of Jameson and a Spotted Cow and he sat and he drank through the next six acts. The club manager never came over to speak with him, and neither did any of the other comics. He believed it was because no one wanted to get the stink on them, but the reality was just that Jesse wasn't the kind of guy that was easy to be around. He wasn't the easiest person to talk to, especially while occupying bars that would rather see him leave than watch him count out his loose change for beer and whiskey.

At 2:30 A.M. Jesse was hammered, and when he got back to his apartment his girlfriend (Amber with the big tits as she was called behind her back by some of the cooks at The Antiquated Brewing Company where she worked as a bartender and hostess) was waiting up for him and she had cold pizza and beer. "So?" she asked.

"I fucking killed it."

A comic goes to work and has an observation

The next day Jesse reported to The Antiquated Brewing Company at 5:30 A.M. and was dog-shit tired. He was the first to arrive, coming in before the managers, and was met by a person who both had a key and knew the code to the security system. This person made coffee and sat at the empty and closed bar while Jesse worked. There was no trust in this world he knew, no trust at all. The person was neither male nor female to him, just an amorphous blob that sat and drank coffee and did not trust. He hated the blob, he thought. He spent his first hour making pizza dough, his second and third hour cleaning and polishing the dining room, and when the cooks arrived at ten, he waved hello and pointed to the coffee the blob has made and asked if they'd like a cup. Baker and Jed and Michael, the opening server, didn't speak to him or acknowledge him at all, like he didn't count, but he didn't mind; they were, after all, very busy people. He knew they went out together almost every night, and he knew they took some of the female servers with them, and he knew this resulted in at least some of them having sex with the servers that went out with them, but they had never invited him to come along even though he had gone out of his way to mention when he was hungover from partying himself so that they know he, too, partied, and would welcome the opportunity to party with them as well. After mopping around the feet of the blob, which the blob refused to pick up for him at the bar, he went outside to smoke on an upturned pickle bucket. Behind The Antiquated Brewing Company, on the corner of State and Gorham, in Madison, Wisconsin, the sky was cloudless and the summer's morning was hot. He lit a Winston and he sat down on his favorite bucket. The last time he had a favorite bucket it was thrown away, so he had written "Jesse Lee Robinson's bucket" on this bucket. He pulled out a notebook from the back pocket of his jeans and he began to write the start of an observation. He wrote: "Smoking when it's hot outside is the absolute fucking worst. Like, first of all, you know it's bad for you and that the whole act itself is just a long and cowardly way to off yourself without leaving behind an awful mess for your loved ones to clean up, but also, when it is hot outside, it is just really uncomfortable to smoke. Like, physically uncomfortable. You can actually feel the heat in your lungs and it makes you acutely aware of what it is exactly that you are doing to yourself, and you hate yourself for doing it, and you begin to sweat but you can't stop yourself from doing it anyway because you are addicted, you are an addict, and with each and every puff you are just saying to the world, 'See I really am a piece of shit.' Smoking when it's hot outside is like smoking when you have a cold. Like, a head cold. It's an act done out of pure addiction and nothing else. There is no enjoyment. Only obligation." After he wrote the word obligation, he made a note in smaller print in the margins that read: "punch this up" and, "I think we got something here, Boss." Then he put the small notebook back in the back pocket of his jeans, flicked the butt of the Winston at Logan The Day Manager's Audi, and went back inside where it was nice and cool and everyone left him alone and he could feel both grateful and profoundly upset that no one besides the blob ever made him feel as if he existed at all outside the confines of his own skull.

A comic is slightly funnier than before

The Liquid Lyrics Lounge on S. Park Street hosted an Open Mic Night every Monday and Jesse hadn't gone for the last few weeks, but now his super-hot girlfriend was insisting that he go try out his new stuff. She had heard him practicing in their bathroom mirror when she was supposed to have already left for work, and she told him that his mood got too dark and he got weird when he wasn't doing comedy; and she was right, of course. He had been in a dark way since the local showcase night at Comedy on State. Before

47

that, too, if he was being honest. He hadn't even tried to get up anywhere since that night. She said he should go, he should do his stuff, he should have a few drinks, let loose, and then get some shitty Chinese Food and that he would feel better for it, and after, they could couple, sexually. She also said she needed a night at home with her thoughts and that when he got home, she would also be in a better space, mentally.

The bar at the Liquid Lyrics Lounge was sparsely stocked so he ordered a Jack Daniels instead of Jameson and paid with the copious change he had in his pockets. He had three drinks before his name was called. He was following a poet who was also named Jessie, but with an ie and was female, and was, in Jesse The Comedian's estimation, a real Debbie Downer. He started his set by making a mean joke at her expense. He stared at the people from an odd angle, like he was seeing them from the side rather than straight on, which didn't seem particularly odd to him at the time, and he began, "Everybody put it together one more time for Morticia the Depressed Poet. We get it, lady, your high school boyfriend was an asshole and you're pretty sure you caught the clap from the feral cat you tried to fuck last night. We've all been there sweetheart — (he hit the sweetheart particularly hard and condescendingly) — but you don't hear the rest of us bitching." Yet another persona that was a not-quite-right fit for him, personally. Some in the crowd laughed and the rest, probably some of them her friends, shifted uncomfortably in their seats. One person, a man, booed. "What are you, her boyfriend!?" he continued, "Look pal, I get it, you got to stick up for your lady an' all, but let me give you some free advice, fucking run. Run now. Because, and I really mean this, that one's gonna shave your head while you sleep and burn her name into your scalp with a brand she fashioned from a coat hanger. And your hair will never grow right in that spot ever again and you'll have to like grow it out extra-long just to sweep it over the worst mistake that you ever made in your fucking life." More laughs; no boos. "Anyway, I'm Jesse, no relation to whatever that was we just saw. I'm twenty-three and I'm seriously considering just like really settling into my own mediocrity. Like, just like really owning my own mundane, less-than, never-gonna-happen life. Like, really owning the fact that I'm fucked in the head, crazy-insane, and that no amount of effort on my part will change the fact that I'm probably going exactly nowhere. Don't laugh, assholes. Because guess what, you're all probably going nowhere too." This was not the material he'd practiced in the mirror. A few people got up and headed to the bar for drinks. "That's right, go get a drink! Hell, get me one, because like Morticia there pointed out, this life is fucking miserable." Four young men began laughing and clapping, though it seemed too far away to be in the same room, and he smelled urine, but couldn't place from where it was coming, and he assumed it was just how this place smelled sometimes. Jesse had no idea what about his performance they were enjoying. "Here's a thing," he flipped open his notebook, "Smoking, right? I like to smoke when I have a head cold because I fucking hate myself." Jesse then abruptly put down the microphone and left the stage, muttering incoherently to himself and feeling the night air well before he hit the door.

Excerpted from Interpersonal Interrogation and Statement Aggregation of one Jesse Lee Robinson: **/**/2019

JLR: "I'm starting to regret ever agreeing to help you people, you know that. You like really make it hard on a guy to like, just do the right thing."

Floating Head haloed by light against a room of obsidian: "I think our relationship has worked out well for you since the incident."

JLR: "Yeah, it has, but like I don't know why she's still here, still asking for me. It's not pleasant, you know?"

Floating Head haloed by light against a room of obsidian: "Look, Jesse, just do us this one solid, this one last time, and I swear, and The Bear agrees and has signed off, we'll never pull you up again. Not for this, not anything related to Molly, not for anything ever again."

JLR: "I felt it, you know."

Floating Head haloed by light against a room of obsidian: "I assumed you may have."

JLR: "Is it getting bad?"

Floating Head haloed by light against a room of obsidian: "She's herself now, and she is more."
JLR: "What are you hoping that she'll do once I am in there, with her?"

Floating Head haloed by light against a room of obsidian "We're hoping that she'll calm down and focus."

JLR: "On Frank?"

Floating Head haloed by light against a room of obsidian: "On what happened to Frank, yes."

JLR: "Look, I want to help. I want to be that guy for you, Bob."

Floating Head haloed by light against a room of obsidian: "Jesse, and I really don't want to have to continue to be the guy who brings you down, but I gotta tell you, that if you sit here and make this any harder than it needs to be, then I have been authorized to pull your card permanently and accommodate you in a room with her for as long as she wants, and we can take the gloves off, and The Bear, though he is pained to do so, would personally sign off on that too. You have to do this, man. We are at our wits' end with her."

JLR: "But man, it's not as if I don't know what she is capable of, more than most I suspect. You can threaten me, that's fine, but I have to wonder, is it better to submit and face what is potentially a psychologically annihilating type event, as like my own choice, or, to be dragged to it against my will?"

Floating Head haloed by light against a room of obsidian: "If it helps you, Jesse, we only place it at like a 40% probability that she has become catastrophically un-stable."

JLR: "So, what, if that's the case she does her thing to me, and then what, after having blown off some serious steam, she becomes pliable again?"

Floating Head haloed by light against a room of obsidian: "Look . . ."

JLR: "Has anyone else gone in there? From back then?"

Floating Head haloed by light against a room of obsidian: ". . . . ."

JLR: "I'll take that as a yes."

Floating Head haloed by light against a room of obsidian: "Jesse . . ."

JLR: "Fine, fuck it, whatever."

Floating Head haloed by light against a room of obsidian: "Great, that's just fantastic, we, I and The Bear, really do appreciate you, Jesse. And in the interest of transparency, Michael did get sent in there and it didn't go well, but he had also talked some pretty bad shit about her that she happened to catch, so we don't think that will happen again in your particular case. Also, you won't be alone, with her I mean, and time is of the essence here. We have to get you to the staging area."

JLR: "God, what happened to him?"

Floating Head haloed by light against a room of obsidian: "Not a concern."

JLR: "That's reassuring."

Floating Head haloed by light against a room of obsidian: "Look . . ."

JLR: "Do you guys even know what happened to him? Like, do you even know what she did to him . . . psychically?"

Floating Head haloed by light against a room of obsidian: "Oh, we know what she did to him, but not like the *how* she did it, but that's why you are here too. We feel, I mean it is the general feeling in the FPPIB, that she likes you, and will maybe open up if you are in there with the rest. This whole thing is moving fast now, we have to get you to the staging area and you need to lead the rest in there, you need to guide the whole McGilla. You are likely key to the whole thing, Jesse. You are likely chosen. Do you comprehend what that means? Special beyond anyone's ability to even imagine. You are the one. The one who can save everyone from all threats, from without and within. Jesse, the world needs you in there, with her. We, nobody really, could do this without you. You are the magic-boy, the archer most gifted, the one who can tame wolves and vampires alike, the only one who can turn it all around and make it all right again. Jesse, we need you. Your country needs you. And, *he* needs you. But for any of that to happen, we need you first to understand that she is in a fragile state. You must be the person she wants to see, the person she remembers. The person who lives in her memory, her past. Not this guy that you are now. This absolute disaster."

JLR: "This persona is not the *me* me, don't worry about that. It's one I can slip on and off at will. I can be in my twenties again. That's not an issue."

Floating Head haloed by light against a room of obsidian: "A lot is riding on you performing. The One *always* performs. Always comes through, in the end. It's dire, but you know that, and we are confident you are chosen and here because you will perform."

JLR: "Can I see her now?"

Floating Head haloed by light against a room of obsidian: "Very soon, everyone's already waiting at the staging area, but we need to clean you up, cut that hair, bathe you, a good delousing at the very least, and get you in some period-specific clothes. You are more now than you were then, and she'll notice that for sure. We can't have that, Jesse. You are chosen, but she is too. We need you clean, clean, clean. Otherwise, the death will come from the pits most deep and lay this place to crater-holed doom in a hellfire most extreme. And that, my man, is something none of us wants . . . right?"

JLR: "Too true, and right you are, of course, but what am *I* supposed to do then when I leave here? This is how I make my way, out there. The hair and the clothes and the stink, they're all part of it. My fans' expectations of me are rigid, I'm afraid."

Floating Head haloed by light against a room of obsidian: "Look, if this goes well, just, I dunno, shave yourself completely bald and say you were in Mendota on a seventy-two-hour hold, and that They shaved you from your nuts on up, and gave you ETC or some shit, I dunno. Look, I'm not going to tell you your business, but c'mon, chosen one or not, you gotta work with us here."

Chapter Seven

Performative vindictiveness

He felt vertigo in his head turn to nausea deep in the pit of a stomach that ate nothing but gin-olives the night before. He knew he was probably too late, but he wobbled unsteadily on his feet anyway. It was hard to get up off a mattress not elevated by a box spring, especially in his condition. Anywhere but here. He'd done it here before and it was truly unpleasant. Also, there was no one around anymore to place a helpful bucket or small trashcan sans bag next to his side of the bed. He had appreciated that but was unsure if he'd ever expressed that appreciation. Such a dick. He touched his soft belly and tugged at the bottom of his jean jacket; he was confused. The attire was unexpected. He slept nude even when blacked out. He looked down at his mattress on the floor and he saw there was a blood stain where his face slept. He touched his cheek and it was impossibly swollen. He realized he couldn't open his left eye. He rushed to the bathroom just then and barely made it to the toilet. It was upon him. He puked in painful dry heaves which produced only a stabbing hurt in both his face and his guts and, eventually, only the scantest of thick yellow bile-heavy vomit. It was viscous and ropey and it clung to his chin and didn't fall in the toilet. There was no water to be found anywhere in his system. He was sick and needed to keep vomiting but there was nothing in his well except for regret and pain. He wiped away the obscenity hanging from his chin with the back of his hand. He did not look in the mirror to get an accurate assessment of the damage he had sustained. He knew it was significant.

The thermostat on his mostly empty living room's wall was not lit up in that vaguely computerized and digital green, there were no numbers of black telling him the temperature of the room, he had to go by feel alone and he felt that it was at least ninety degrees in the apartment at this early and hurtful hour. The layout of the place was such that the kitchen flowed into the living room without a wall separating the two spaces, only a breakfast bar, and off the living room was a space for a home office which could be closed from the rest of the apartment by shutting two large pocket doors. There was one bathroom and the bedroom was down a short hallway. There was a balcony, too, but Michael hadn't used it since Helen left because he smoked inside now. The whole place smelled like stale Camels and old beer. There were takeout containers littering the counter space and the dishes in the sink were so old that they'd stopped stinking and the food remnants on them had solidified to the point that Michael figured he'd just have to throw them away, eventually. He pressed a few buttons on the thermostat before giving up. He winced at a sharp pain in his cheek that didn't fully recede but instead radiated heat as it dulled back to a constant but manageable ache.

His affected cheek felt slightly moist in the way only a trauma injury in the very beginnings of healing felt. The kitchen lights didn't respond to switch flipping and the inside of the refrigerator felt warm and smelled slightly sweet from the rotting milk that was already some weeks past its expiration date, and now, in the warmth, had begun to really bloom. He shut the door. His cell phone was almost dead —10% life. He called Helen and the phone rang twice before being sent (not went to, but sent, and he knew the difference) to voicemail. "Helen, I hope *your* day is schtarting off wonderfully," he mumbled awkwardly through his teeth due to the cheek which wouldn't let his jaw quite open to its normal angle, "becaushh I'm here with rotten food shhitting in the fucking dark! We had a goddamn deal! You dechhided to leave thishh apartment without shho much ashh a weekshh' noticehh. You dechhided to have your *Daddy* pay for a vacation from your responshhhibilitieshh — from your life. We agreed that the only way thishh would work, ishh if neither of ushh got shhcrewed over. I'm responshhible for two-thirdshh of the rent and the cable bill . . . you're responshhible for the reshht and the electric bill. I fucking told you when you moved out that I didn't want to have to chashhe you down for money. Call me back!"

The electric company wasn't interested in Michael's situation when he called them. They explained it would be $263 to turn the power back on and a convenience fee of $5 to do it over the phone. Michael read the customer service rep the number on his debit card and she told him his power would be back on within the hour. Still naked from the waist down, he sat crisscross applesauce on a leather loveseat and he waited for the power, his leg and ass skin sticking most uncomfortably. Less than an hour later the AC and all the lights popped back on all on their own. The morning's ordeal took less than forty-five minutes to solve. I'll say it took two hours, thought Michael, I'll say I was late for an important call . . . and I missed out on the biggest opportunity of my career.

Benny Moskowitz explains it all

The little office in which she practiced family therapy was off Odana Road in a shitty complex of buildings designed to look like other cities. She was in the New Orleans. Helen and another twenty-something shared the space, both having hung their own shingle after finding it completely difficult to get picked up by one of the going family therapy concerns in Madison, WI. Hours for certification by the Wisconsin Department of Professional Services could be hard to come by in that economy so Helen Abelmen took clients on a sliding scale, and, as a result, made next to no money at the practice and had to moonlight to make ends meet. Sitting behind her small desk, Helen Abelmen looked at her appointment book. Benny Moskowitz at 11:00 A.M. She had painted her office a dull cream and her furniture was of brown leather. She had a small couch for her clients and only an office chair on wheels for herself. It was cozy but nice. She had invested some real money in making the place not look slap-dash. Benny Moskowitz was a Mexican who was adopted at the age of two by a nice couple living in the Nakoma Neighborhood on Madison's west side. His Mother paid Helen's full rate. He was a referral through friends of her Father. Two paintings hung in her office: one was of a pasture with a red barn off in the distance and the other was of a tree in winter. Molly painted the tree in winter and sold it to Helen for $200 — Helen knew she overpaid. Helen was sure that her life was going in the right direction but she couldn't say the same for Molly, and with her allowance, and what she brought in from her night gig, she could afford to pay what Molly asked. She loved Molly and Molly loved her too. There were unspoken conspiracies alive in every brushstroke of white and gray.

Benny rang the bell in the outer office that buzzed an intercom in Helen's suite. She stood, smoothing her slate-gray skirt and puffing her blouse as she did. She placed her rolling chair in front of the couch with only a small wooden coffee table in between. Opening the door, she motioned for Benny to come inside. Mrs. Moskowitz was sitting next to him in the waiting area. "I'll just be out here," she said. "Whatever," he answered. When Benny sat, he slouched deeply and put his feet up on the coffee table in a posture that was as if he was lying down but propped on a stiff pillow: his chin on his chest and his face looking at his navel in a disinterested way. Neither Benny nor Helen said anything for a few minutes. Helen was not trying to get Benny to speak first. She had no issue with opening a conversation in the therapy setting, it was just that she'd found in working with Benny, especially after he'd had an incident, that if she went in with a full head of steam he would shut down immediately and the session would be lost. She picked up her tea, which had been steeping on the coffee table, and took a sip.

"You leave the bag in?"

"I feel it gives it a deeper flavor; less watery."

"Mom takes the bags out and she puts them in the sink. Then after she's done, she throws the bags away. She says it's so she doesn't drip tea on the floor."

"She's careful with her house."

"Yeah, she's careful with the house."

"It's probably because it's a nice house, she wants it to stay nice."

"We have a lady who comes twice a week for that."

"You think you shouldn't have to be so careful when you have someone who will come clean up after you?"

"Fuck it, right? It's not my fucking house."

"Or your car."

"Fuck that car too."

"Benny, we've been over this, I know you, I know when you are posturing. Why did you take the car?"

"Look, the other kids, the ones at school, they don't think I'll do what I say I'll do, so I gotta fucking show em that I always mean what I say, and if I say I'ma take the old bitch's car, then, I take the old bitch's car. If I say I'ma pop their fucking mouth, then, they best believe I'ma pop their fucking mouth, know what I'm saying?"

"We've been here before Benny. The question isn't if you will do the stupid thing, or are willing to do the stupid thing, we've established that you are certainly capable of doing any number of stupid things, the question is why, still, after all this time, are you compelled to do stupid things to impress people who you yourself have said 'don't matter for shit.'"

"You, and that bitch out there, you don't get shit about me. You think I *want* to be some fucked up Jew-Mexican living in some dumb-bitch-widow's mansion? I never got a say in this shit. I never got the option. I got told I was a Jew. I got taught Jewish shit. Then I went out there and I got told I was a spic. I got taught hard what being a spic was. And now you want me to sit here and tell you that I know I don't have to do stupid shit. Lady, I have to do stupid shit because otherwise those other motherfuckers, they'll fuck with me all damn day. This way, right now, no one fucks with me. I pop their mouths and they shut the fuck up. It's that simple."

"But why total your Mother's car?"

"Cause fuck that car."

Sometimes a gift is just a gift, but, sometimes, it's also not

Helen Abelmen's boss would sexually harass her all night at the upscale wine and tapas restaurant where she began moonlighting after she opened her practice, but it never got physical, just off-color remarks. She made too much money to raise a stink; though at the end of every shift (usually around 2:00 in the morning) she was exhausted both physically and mentally and all she wanted when she got home was for Michael to be waiting for her, on the couch, with maybe her favorite movie (*Casablanca* or *Fight Club*) all queued up and a bowl of fresh popcorn on the coffee table.

She walked through the door of their apartment and Michael *was* on the couch, he was asleep sitting up and the PlayStation was on and the controller was in his hand, there was a half-packed bong and an empty bottle of Kirkland-brand Vodka on the coffee table. The place reeked of Camel Lights and dank weed. She was holding a Thai Chicken Flatbread Pizza. Michael had texted her about ten minutes before her shift ended requesting it. She'd thought he'd had plans for them when she got home, and she'd canceled plans to go to O'Grady's with the other servers for a nightcap. She could've used a night to blow off some steam too. She shook Michael's foot. He did not stir. She slammed the pizza down on the coffee table. He did not move. She lit the bong and took a long pull and exhaled it in his face. Again, nothing. Michael's keys were on the breakfast bar that separated the kitchen from the living room. She dug through her purse and found the fob attached to the gym membership she had set up for the two of them and she attached it to his keys. She took a moment and wrote "Happy Hanukkah Babe! Now you'll have somewhere fun to go at night. Love you" on a sticky note and then she went to bed, too exhausted to try and wake him again.

The next morning she had her first client at 11:30 and her alarm woke her at 10:00. She got in the shower and washed off the grime of serving the night before then dressed and did her makeup. She texted Molly asking if she could help with the Christmas party in any way and signed the text XOXOXOXOXO. When she walked into the living room Michael was still there and snoring and it was obvious that he'd got the small trash can from under the kitchen sink sometime during the night and vomited in it. She did not attempt to wake him. After she locked the door behind herself and was safely down the hall she called her Father. It rang twice and when he picked up she said, "Daddy, I can't take this anymore and I need your help."

"Anything you need, you know that."

"I need you to help me find a place to stay. I need to leave Michael; I need a security deposit and like three months' rent."

"What happened?"

"It's not one thing, it's everything."

"When?"

"He gets weird at Christmas. After the holidays."

"I'll set it up. I'm so sorry."

"All I need is time. All I need is some time to sort this all out in my head."

"Just try and have some fun. I could tell you this will be easy now that the decision is made, mentally I mean, but it won't."

"Molly's Christmas party is in a couple of weeks. I got that to look forward to."

"Just don't act out. It's tempting to act out, but that'll cost you in the end. I acted out and look at what happened to me"

"She's still my Mother."

"And you're still the best thing about her."

Chapter Eight

A move to Antigo without warning

HER DAD (a giant of a man originally from Ashwaubenon, WI) found employment in the year 1988 in Antigo, WI, and up and moved him and herself the ninety-one miles without so much as preparing poor Molly (who at the time was only 5) for the eventuality of having to say goodbye to the friends she had had since she could remember remembering anything and she cried for a week straight when they first got to town. They lived in a one-bedroom apartment for over a year while her Dad saved up the scratch for a down payment on a modest single-family home. He — that is, her Dad and only caregiver since the tragic death of her Mother in a freak boating accident wherein she (Molly's Mother) drunkenly dove in off the back of the family boat (head first) after Molly, believing Molly's unorthodox swimming motion was her struggling to stay afloat and that she (Molly) was at risk of drowning, at the exact same instant that Molly's Father (Hank Duch BTW) was starting the engine, and Molly's Mother was decapitated upon entry (to the water) by the suddenly whirring propeller — worked building custom furniture out of locally sourced lumber, taking the whole product and slowly turning it into smaller and more workable pieces of wood which he then fabricated into rocking chairs and benches for porches and the like. His boss was a prematurely white-haired gentleman by the name of Kurt Hostetler whose family went back all the way to the founding of Antigo in 1876. Kurt and Hank were the same age and got on famously from the get. Also, as it was evident that Hank could use all the help he could get, Kurt and his wife Sherry sort of adopted the Duchs, and Molly went to the Hostetler house after school while her Dad was still on shift making furniture. She spent her afternoons with Sherry and her son Eldredge, who was three years younger than Molly, autistic and nonverbal, but a good egg and fun to be around. And that's how it went for ten years.

The Shed

The Hostetler House sat at the top-most bend of a cul-de-sac in a pre-planned residential neighborhood that was only 75% built-out with blank lots of green-brown grass in between some of the houses, giving the whole development the look of a mouth that had taken a beating and lost some pearly whites. Driving through the neighborhood gave Molly a feeling of lonely space and a longing to leave. The Hostetler House itself was a two-story single-family with gray vinyl siding, white trim, and a red door with a sign reading Welcome, which Sherry would change with the seasons. It was the fall, so the Welcome sign hung from the door resplendent with faux acorns, faux leaves of brown and sienna, and framed in faux twigs.

The driveway where she'd (Molly) parked had an oil stain on a blacktopped bump-out on its left side. Usually, Sherry's Explorer was parked over the spot but not today. Molly parked over the stain and sat in her car for another few minutes while a song she particularly enjoyed finished on the radio and she only got out after the song's last note faded into the DJ's saccharine radio voice.

The Hostetler house sat on a half-acre fenced-in yard with a recently constructed shed on its southwest corner. The shed was one of those double-wide sheds that could fit a riding lawnmower and a workbench and tools with enough space for a fully grown man to work. Kurt Hostetler kept no lawnmower or tools or workbench. Kurt Hostetler had constructed a bar complete with dartboard and stools and kegerator and neon beer signs and an old leather sofa on which to lounge, and a television with rabbit ears that could pick up the local affiliates so he could watch The Packers and The Brewers. She knocked on the double doors of the shed and received no answer, so she entered. The switch on the wall was one of those that sticks off the wall because the switch was encased in metal housing and had the wire to the switch running on the outside of the wall. She flipped the switch on the wall and an overhead light came on, bathing the room in bright; and also, two Miller neons (one Highlife, one MGD) began to flicker before illuminating fully and settling into their dull buzz and hum. She poured herself a tall beer and began idly tossing darts at the board. She mostly hit the meat of the board, towards the inner rings, but there was no pattern in the darts as she was not aiming. Kurt came then. He didn't talk to her. He didn't pour himself a drink. He took the last remaining dart from her hand and tossed it towards the board and missed completely. She allowed herself to be taken on the rough floor of the shed and when he was finished she asked him for a cigarette, which he gave her. Before he left to go back to his furniture business and her Father, he told her she could stay as long as she liked but that Sherry would be home at 5:00 P.M. sharp, and that she should probably be gone before then but should feel free to return should she want to eat supper with the family that night. Molly said she'd like that and asked when he planned on telling Sherry that he was leaving, and he answered only, "Soon."

Antigo High School (where Molly was a sophomore) serviced roughly 800 students in toto. Just small enough so everyone would be aware, in a general way, of everyone else's business. She had two close friends with whom she shared everything, including what'd been going on with Kurt Hostetler. They were concerned. She was not. Britney Schultz's family was native Antigoian and her Father knew Kurt Hostetler quite well, and she told Molly that her Father would be appalled to know what his longtime bowling buddy was up to in that shed of his. Molly told her that Kurt was going to leave Sherry for her and that Sherry had been fucking her Father on the sly for the last two years anyway so it all worked out in the wash. They both agreed that it would get messy, eventually.

Molly and Britney were late for second period but they were in no real hurry. Their history teacher was in his mid-twenties, had longish hair, and was still trying to be the cool guy. Molly said, "I think I'll fuck Mr. Diedrich to show Kurt I'm serious," and then said she had to pee and ducked into the ladies' room before Britney could respond. Britney yelled, "I'll wait," through the door. The four stalls of the ladies' room were all closed but Molly saw there were no feet underneath. She went in the furthest one and pulled down her pants and her almost neon-bright white cotton full-bottomed underwear and she sat and she made no water except from her eyes, which she managed to produce silently. When she finished, the girls walked silently on, never addressing Molly's comment about Mr. Diedrich, and they entered a History Class already in progress.

Burning down the house (party)

If Antigo High had about 800 students, then about 650 of them were at the Clifford Farmstead on the outskirts of town on the last Friday night of the school year. Some kids stood around a giant bonfire burning on the northwest corner of the property and made frequent trips to the barn where the kegs and other booze were stored. In the barn, the faint musty smell of old hay and animals long since gone lingered in the night. The kids hopped up on the buzz of hormones, mid-grade marijuana, and cheaply obtained booze noticed nothing but themselves. Music played over a boombox that had been dragged from Billy Clifford's personal bedroom in the farmhouse proper. Boys grouped together noticed girls grouped together. These were underclassmen and they were still nervous about sex and relationships. They obsessed over questions like does he like me? and will she say yes? and what if I touch it and I don't like it? Molly, Britney, and Jennifer (a tangential associate and not Molly's second-closest friend) each had a bottle of Boone's Farm they were drinking from. "Let's go back to the fire," said Molly. "Everyone's so cliquey in here."

Outside in the sticky new-summer Wisconsin air the headlamps of Dylan Carney's completely redone eighties-era IROC Z broke the dark between the bonfire and the barn, and Molly stopped to watch him get out, light a smoke, and go in the barn. It struck her as somewhat sad, but ultimately cool, that he was alone and without friends. Herself and Britney and Jennifer (again, these girls didn't like Jennifer that much but she'd caught them right as the bell was ringing on the school year as a whole and had asked them to hang out and it would've been rude to say no, that and plus Jennifer had mentioned that she, too, was going to Billy Clifford's Barn Party Bash and that she could drive them and then designated drive them home safely as she didn't particularly enjoy going much beyond buzzed and preferred not to get completely drunk or high in any way) continued to the bonfire but Molly made note to make an excuse to quickly need to get back to the barn. The fire made their cheeks tight in that way that felt like they were only slightly on fire. The smoke had already clung to their clothes. Molly loved the smell. Britney took a pull from her Strawberry Hill Boone's Farm and Molly gave her a derisive side-eyed laugh. "What?" Britney asked.

"You drink like such a girl. Here, like this." Molly upended her own bottle (hers being Apple Blossom) and finished it in a four-to-six-seconds chug. "I'm going to get more."

"You're going to see if you can talk to Dylan."

"Maybe I'm going to do both, you ever think of that?"

"Whatever."

"You need anything?"

"Like you're coming back anytime soon."

She walked slow and deliberate with an unpracticed saunter that was supposed to swing her hips but fell just short. The cool of the grass reached over the toes of her thongs and it tickled the tops of her feet. She moved like she thought she was strong and in control and knew everything that was going to happen from here on out. She was in the cutoffs and the tank top that made her most feel like a person who was in charge of their own sexuality. Outside the barn, boys leaned and smoked and called each other crude names demeaning each other's perceived sexual preferences. She asked them for a cigarette and was given a Marlboro Red and a match with which to light it. Her hair was loose around her shoulders and she took the stick of the match between her thumb and forefinger and with a practiced flick of her wrist she struck it against the barn wood wall and it alighted and Molly Duch felt, actually felt in her bones, how cool she must have looked to these boys (Dylan Carney among them). "Thanks," she said, tilting her head and putting the flame to the Marlboro. Her long hair flowed naturally with the movement of her head. She inhaled the first drag and the cigarette came to rest between her fingers with her hand cocked at the wrist in the style of an adept. "Dylan," she said. He nodded his head towards her and she thought she could just barely make out the beginnings of the kind of knowing wink that said we are going places tonight, you and me.

"Your head is on fire," he said, as the boys around him started laughing and doubling over and pointing at her head, which was, indeed, smoldering and smoking like the bonfire she had just walked away from.

"What?"

"Your head, it is on fire, Molly."

She felt the heat on her scalp and her face, and at first, it felt no different from the skin-tightening heat of the bonfire but then rapidly became the kind of heat that caused real pain and hurt and she began to scream. Really scream. Blood-curdling scream. And the boys (Dylan Carney among them) laughed about as hard as any boys could laugh and pointed about as pointingly as any boys could point, and Molly Duch began to run great ovoid laps while her hair's fire grew larger and more orange and flame-like. Her screaming grew with her pain and her panic and with every lap she picked up speed and air which caused more hair to catch and the flame of her head to grow larger. The laughing of Dylan and his friends and the screaming and nonsensical running of Molly, plus the now-strong scent of burning hair, caused the population of the barn, and the bonfire, to converge at the commotion, which, in turn, caused more laughter to ring in Molly's ears while she burned. Finally, after longer than it probably should've taken someone to take action, a beefy Varsity Lineman with a head like an oversized block of spam and a jarhead haircut text-book shoulder-tackled her into the dirt and used his

Letterman's jacket to cover the flames of Molly's smoking head and extinguished the fire. After some moments, when the laughter subsided and the worry had begun, the lineman removed his jacket to reveal a Molly Duch with badly singed and blackened hair that jutted out in all directions and of inconsistent lengths. The wounds to her scalp, however, were thankfully superficial and would heal in time and allow for the complete regrowth of hair. The wounds to her ego, however, were not.

Excerpted from Interpersonal Interrogation and Statement Aggregation of one Helen Bethel Abelmen: **/**/2019

HBA: "You talked to The Ex, then?"

BS: "Michael? Yeah, we talked with Michael about '09"

HBA: "You know The Ex can't be trusted to give any sort of honest assessment about anyone's behavior back then, mine included. He always embellishes. Tends to overblow things."

BS: "We found his statement . . . helpful."

HBA: "Oh."

BS: "This isn't relevant to why *you* are here."

HBA: "I know, it's, it's just that, I'd hate for you to have a wrong impression."

BS: "I think we have a pretty good impression, of what transpired that is, and why, also."

HBA: "Good. So long as you know that anything The Ex told you regarding the various personalities involved may very well be exaggerated."

BS: "We understand."

HBA: "I'm here to give my re-statement then?"

BS: "In a way, yes, but no, not really, more like we need you to reassure us of your position within the organization."

HBA: "Bill, this is what I am talking about, this is why I wanted The Ex left off the list of potentials, not to save my own skin, but because The Ex has a unique ability to poison wells. Now I will always have in the back of my mind that you, and Steve, and Rodger, and Bob, and The Bear will always view me as just some ditzy post-grad thing running around in her bra and panties at wild cocaine and sex-type parties."

BS: "Helen, c'mon, it is only protocol."

HBA: "No you c'mon, Bill. You know as well as I do that special exception is often made when a subject of interpersonal interrogation and statement aggregation is of relation or former relation to Organization Officials of C-Grade or higher. And, last I checked, I'm wearing a D on my chest."

BS: "Yeah you are!"

HBA: "Bill! This is serious."

BS: "It was just hanging there, Helen, lighten up."

HBA: "Fine, it's whatever, just get on with whatever it is you think The Ex's statement has brought up regarding my position here in the organization."

BS: "Well, Helen, first you can start by telling us about Frank's fortieth birthday party."

HBA: "What do you want to know?"

BS: "Question 1: What were you wearing that night?"

HBA: "Is this really . . ."

BS: "I assure you this is purely to put the evening in context."

HBA: "I was wearing a white tank top and boy shorts, is that what you want to hear, Bill?"

BS: "Did you ingest any substances?"

HBA: "I knew that this is what this was, you just want to hear me tell you a story about running around in my underthings, in my twenties, doing drugs and drinking, a sexy-type story, you want to know about my life with Molly on like a tabloid level."

BS: "We want to know when your life with Molly really began, yes, that is part of it, but we also want to know how much of your life with Molly colored your decision-making, back then."

HBA: "Like, was I planning on leaving The Ex for Molly after Christmas '09?"

BS: "More like was Molly planning on leaving Frank for you after Christmas of '09?"

HBA: "She never said there would be a quid pro quo."

BS: "You never discussed a mutual breakup situation then?"

HBA: "It was implied."

BS: "Implied only?"

HBA: "Yes, hinted at is really how I would describe it."

BS: "Describe the tank top and boy shorts for me, were you ever cold during that evening?"

HBA: "Fuck you, Bill."

BS: "Yeah, that's fair."

HBA: "If this is going to be turning into some kind of spank-bank situation for you Bill, I swear to god I don't care what The Bear has to say, I'll walk right out of here right now."

BS: "Helen, c'mon."

HBA: "I'm serious."

BS: "You'd scuttle your career? At this point?"

HBA: "I got my degree; I can go back to what I was doing."

BS: "It'll never be the same, Helen. Never be like this. Always dulled, always as if you are viewing your own life through a cheesecloth. Always knowing that nothing hinges exclusively on your word, not anymore, nothing can change, or stay the same, based on what you say, what advice you give, and what decisions *you* make. It'll all just be so many hours filling so many days making so many weeks and years until finally, you retire and you're just another fat-assed octogenarian tending to gardens that no longer bear fruit. No, you aren't going back to what you were before; you aren't going back to that life, ding-donging with the anxiety-ridden and the depressives whose lives are so banal and regular that you can only actually advise them that their issues all stem from the fact that they never did anything real and never dared to be anything more than they are, and that now it is *actually* too late and that tug towards self-elimination they are feeling is, in all reality, probably not an unnatural feeling because they already know that all this, their life, is all a big nothing for them. You aren't going back to feeling that way, are you, Helen?"

HBA: "No, I suppose not."

BS: "So then, tell me, when did you first develop feelings for Molly?"

HBA: "Since the day we met."

BS: "When did you and Molly first do something about these feelings?"

HBA: "Five days after Frank's fortieth."

BS: "Why then?"

HBA: "Because I saw her do something that I knew she didn't want to do with a boy she didn't want to do it with because she felt it was the only way for her to express who she was, and I knew that that expression of herself was not truth."

BS: "What did you do five days after Frank's fortieth?"

HBA: "I took Molly out to Indian for lunch and I told her that I'd seen her with Jed, and that I didn't judge her for it, but that I loved her in a way that was beyond friendship and beyond the sexual. That I loved her in a way that was so deep and wide that it hurt my mind to think about. That I saw her hurt, and the things that that hurt made her do, and that neither of us had to be a slave to our hurts anymore."

BS: "And what year was that, again?"

HBA: "Bill, you know the answer to that."

BS: "And what year was that, again, Helen?"

HBA: "2005."

BS: "And what year did you marry Michael?"

HBA: "Bill . . ."

BS: "Helen."

HBA: "I married The Ex in 2006."

BS: "You know what I am going to ask."

HBA: "Did you ask The Ex?"

BS: "No."

HBA: "Why not."

BS: "Because it was not relevant to his interview."

HBA: "Ask it then."

BS: "Why did you marry Michael Amadeus Greene?"

HBA: "Have you ever met someone who can be unhappy, like really *be* unhappy?"

BS: "Have I met someone unhappy?"

HBA: "No, that's not it. What I mean is someone that *can be* unhappy. Someone that can be unhappy, recognize that they are unhappy, and then just live in that unhappiness without having it escalate to despair, without having it grow bigger and stronger and turn clinical. Someone who can live in that psychological gray area between the blues, the real blues, and depression. Well, that's The Ex. The Ex can live and be content even when he is unhappy and discontented with his situation. And, he can brave-face it like no one I've ever met. He can, when he wants to, when he has reason to, will himself into being content in his unhappiness and make those around him feel more content and happy in knowing that he is sticking in there despite not being exactly fulfilled."

BS: "You married him because he stuck around despite not exactly being happy with the relationship? During the courting phase, I mean."

HBA: "No. No, that's not even doing it justice. It's more like, The Ex, he can recognize that he is unfulfilled, but like, gain a sense of fulfillment and contentedness from ensuring that the other in his life is contented and fulfilled despite the fact that he, himself, is not. But that's also the rub. He gains no contentment and fulfillment from ensuring that the other is contented and fulfilled if he himself is already contented and fulfilled and happy. It's a sacrifice thing with him. He ties himself into knots making the other happy and contented and fulfilled, while he, himself, is unhappy and discontented, and in sacrificing his own comfort for the comfort of the other, he becomes happy and contented because he feels he's done something righteous. But you see the problem, right?"

BS: "Not sure I follow."

HBA: "The Ex, right, having sacrificed his own personal comfort, happiness, and contentedness, has made the other, namely me, very comfortable and happy and content, and in doing so, has made himself comfortable, happy, and content through his acts of selfless service, which, in turn, makes his acts of ensuring the other, again me, is comfortable, happy, and content, no longer an act of self-sacrifice, and thus no longer an act that brings him any contentment or happiness, which then, in time, cycles him back to a deep state of complete unhappiness with his relationship; at which point he again feels he's making a grand sacrifice by staying with the other, me, and the cycle begins again. At first, he is so attentive and self-sacrificing that it almost forces the other, me, to fall in a *kind* of obligatory love with him, if not love-love. After a long while though, it sours for real, the relationship, and all he's left with is a mountain of bitterness that does turn rancid and into real depression-level unhappiness that manifests itself in truly self-destructive ways, but he still won't leave, still can never be the one to pull the plug. In an almost cruel trick, he forces the one he's with, the one, in his mind he's done so much for, to be the one to pull the plug on the thing. Makes the other, me, be the one to ultimately hurt him so deeply that he can just write them, again me, off as an ungrateful bitch who couldn't recognize when she had a good thing going."

BS: "And that's why you married Michael?"

HBA: "In a word, yes."

BS: "And what about Molly?"

HBA: "She wasn't nearly ready to accept any deeper truths about herself. She almost got there, though. It's a shame really."

BS: "Have you seen her?"

HBA: "You know I haven't. I haven't even stopped at her room's door's window and looked in as I pass it daily."

BS: "Why not?"

HBA: "Because I love Molly, right? But she isn't capable of having a single moment outside of herself. She can love. She can hate. But it's always through her own narrow lens. I was willing to accept that as just her being her. But I can't do that anymore. I am no longer capable of being near her and not feeling a profound and complete sadness and pity that I find repulsive."

BS: "Pitying another is repulsive to you?"

HBA: "No, pitying Molly, in specific, is repulsive to me."

BS: "The Bear is insisting."

HBA: "I know."

BS: "Look, I get it."

HBA: "No you don't Bill, but that's okay, you don't have to see, you don't have to understand. On some level, and it's not your fault, I don't think that you are capable."

Chapter Nine

Maybe there was no one there, behind the glass, after all; but, then again . . .

REMEMBERING THE EVENT NOW, how that day played out I mean, I feel blank in exactly the same way I felt blank then. I mean I recall feeling blank then too, and now, remembering, and speaking about it, or preparing to speak about it, I feel the exact same way. It's all there. That's probably the problem with my current situation, everything is accessible to me. My feelings, or, in this case, my lack of feeling. She was old when she died so it was like, you know, not a great big surprise. 102 I think, and I had to travel from Madison to Mauston, WI, for the funeral. My Father grew up in Mauston, but we rarely visited. We saw her maybe once or twice a year until I was like fourteen but then we stopped going altogether. I don't know why we stopped going, if there was something that happened, or if we as a family just got lazy or stopped caring as much about making other people happy, and I was never the kind of person who cared enough to ask questions. I'm still not that type, I don't think. I was not told in advance that I would be seated up front, first pew along with all the cousins who saw her much more often and lived much closer by, or that I would be a pallbearer.

Her body lay in the vestibule of St Pat's and the coffin's lid was open and she looked like she always looked, but she also looked somehow false and fake and that's when, if I am recalling the memory correctly, I began feeling blank, like really feeling it for what it was. Though of course, I recognize now that it was always there, always present, but that I was just unaware that I was almost constantly feeling it because I had anesthetized myself to it — the nothing. It's hard to describe what feeling blank feels like as it's not exactly the opposite of feeling or the absence of feeling anything, but it's close, and all I can say is that it feels both grim and not, both frightening and not, if that makes sense. I didn't go into the thing with like the goal to completely shut down and feel nothing as like a coping mechanism, it's just what happened when I saw her body lying there. She was a short woman in life and the casket seemed maybe like it was ordered too big, like someone fucked up, casket-wise. Her cheeks were falsely rosy, far rosier than they were in life, and her poof of cotton ball hair, cut old-lady short, sat almost wig-like on her head. Like they had to recreate her hair for some reason and what sat atop her head was the best they could do.

My Father greeted me with a kind of all-business handshake that he thought better of as he noticed the whole family was in the vestibule with us visiting and chatting, but also looking at the two of us in specific, so he then used my hand that he had his grip on and he pulled me in for a back-clapping one-arm-over-the-shoulder like diagonal hug. The hug lasted a couple of moments too long to be natural and real. The hug lasted long enough for it to become apparent that he was counting the seconds and calculating just when it had been long enough so he could break free. Mr. Jedidiah Lucas Sr. is a bad hugger.

"You're helping carry the casket," he said after the hug.

"Okay," I recall replying. Though, and I am sure that you are aware of this, any recollection where I directly attribute specific words to specific people is going to be paraphrased at best, not exactly what they said, but more like the spirit of what they said, as best as I can recollect it, myself included. My stories are always like that.

We were still standing above grandma's body when this exchange took place and the air smelled vaguely of talc. Her face looked dull in that specifically powdered way, but I don't think they used talc on her face, maybe her body. Her face looked dull and blunted in that specific way faces look dull and blunted when too much foundation has been applied, and then the makeup that is built up on that foundation is just a touch heavy-handed. The talc smell smelled not exactly fresh, but more like what a person thinks of when they think of a fresh scent, the sense-memory of fresh, not quite the real McCoy. I recall having to walk away from her then after I was told I would be manning a handle and carrying her from St. Pat's and placing her in the hearse and then following with my Father (in his car as mine was deemed to be unfit for this task) in the funeral procession of automobiles to the Mauston City Cemetery where I would again man a handle and lay the old Gypsy to rest. This was all on December 22nd or maybe even the 23rd of 2009.

The crowd gathered for my Grandmother's funeral was massive because all the Lucases and the Winikes were home for the holidays. The Liturgical Mass lasted like an hour, maybe an hour and a half, and after mass when I got up to man my handle, I saw the wetted faces of people I did not recognize as family but who I knew were like second and third cousins of mine. Like I said, we didn't visit Mauston that often so any kind of relationship I had with my extended family, the cousins-something-removed I mean, was surface-level at best and I probably didn't even consider them to be family, more like acquaintances that I sometimes had to see. I have first cousins too, and them I do recognize as family because I did see them more often growing up, but that recognition isn't real in the sense that I feel, like in my heart, like they are family. Truthfully I am not sure what that feeling, the feeling of belonging to and really being connected to an extended family type situation even feels like.

Anyway, all the second and like third cousins are crying and their faces are red and tight from the salt in their tears, and they are wiping their faces as they watch us man our handles and begin to move grandma to the hearse for her final car-ride, and all I can think about is how these second and third cousins must've spent much more time with grandma than I did and how I had no idea that grandma spent time with them outside of family gathering type situations, and how maybe I'm feeling nothing, blank, because I only spent time with family at like sanctioned family gathering type situations.

I remember she had told me once about the first car she ever saw, a Model T, and how she was delighted when it had come down her road, kicking up dust and gravel, and how she chased it and it blew its horn which made a sound like ahhhh-uuuu-gahhhh, though she had conceded that that could've been a construction of her imagination giving color to her memory and not exactly accurate to exact events. Stories, you know? Wild.

We put her in the ground at like 12:05. I wore a suit I borrowed from my brother with a taupe/beige/light-brown top coat and fur-lined black leather gloves. My brother and Father were dressed similarly, and my Mother also looked nice for the occasion. Most of my family wore hunting gear or puffy winter coats of green and gold with the capitol G emblazoned helmet of the Green Bay Packers prominently displayed on their backs. After she was in the ground we all went back to St. Pat's where they had ham sandwiches and hotdish and cookies and juice and coffee in the basement. I stayed for the minimum required time and left after making the rounds of all the tables and giving excuses about obligations back home. On the way out I shook my Father's hand and said, "I am sorry for your loss," which seemed appropriate enough at the time but now seems to me to be deeply emblematic of our whole relationship and feelings for one another. I remember he nodded at me curtly and then I left. The point here, gentlemen, is that feeling the blankness that I now recognized that I had probably been feeling for most of my life persisted after that, stayed with me through the events of Christmas '09, and, I think is still very much so there, even now, the blankness. Just less so. But, again, remembering all this now, the feeling is felt 100% again, and is really unpleasant. But I will endeavor to persist . . . if only for your benefit.

The thing you need to know, in specific, is that I was friends with the guys who worked at The Antiquated Brewing Company from '01-'09, but I wasn't like, like them . . . going places . . . Baker was the exception, friendship-wise, but of course, you know that by now. It's different when you come from the same place as somebody and grew up together. Geography matters. Me, at that time, I was lost and wandering and probably on my way to an early cerotic death, *until* like '09. I didn't even go to college until '05, and I didn't even graduate until spring of '09. Helen already had her master's by then, and Michael was doing something with money-people on the west side. Molly was Molly, making it all happen in her own way. I was really behind, is what I am trying to say. But this is jumping the gun a little. If you want to know where I was at, mentally that is, on December 24, 2009, then you have to know that I came from a very broken environment in the flatlands of Northern Illinois and that in the flatlands of Northern Illinois there is a like anxiety that permeates the whole area. It's in the land itself. I think it comes from the corn, grows in the corn, and it is constant for those who are in tune to it . . . on its frequency. You have to develop psychic scar tissue or it consumes you, and eventually, you step out in front of a train or something. You have to be blank to it sometimes. That's how that all began, I think. I drank it away from like 1997-2009. Back then, in like 1997, I can remember exactly how it happened, exactly where I was, exactly how good it all was. It's imprinted on me, the feeling that is. My awakening. What had happened was my friend had had this basement in a record shop that the shop owner let him use to practice his drums and generally hang out. The shopkeep was only like twenty-two himself, and very irresponsible. He would let us hang out down there and do whatever we wanted in exchange for some light cleaning work around the record shop and his apartment.

Anyway, the first time my buddy invites me down there he has like four forty-ounce bottles of Malt Liquor, King Cobra I believe, two for each of us, and we are just hanging out and smoking cigarettes and drinking this booze in this kind of dark and dank basement. It wasn't like lights out pitch-black, but like basement during the daytime dark if that makes any sense.

He's practicing drums and I'm drinking and smoking, and like maybe two hours pass and the Malt Liquor is gone and it's time for us to both go home and have our dinners with our families, and so we walk up the stairs and into the record shop and the sun is coming through the storefront in daggers of light, so bright and pure and warm, and I just remember that at that exact moment, for the first time in my life, the constant anxiety and distractedness was gone, lifted and all gone, and replaced by the only feeling I've ever felt that I never, ever, wanted to stop feeling. That was like 1997.

By 2000 I was a real mess, we all were, really. I had this buddy named Dickless Jones, and Dickless had a dick so big it was like he had no dick at all because girls would refuse to touch the thing after becoming acquainted with it and the novelty of seeing the thing wore off, and all that was left was the harsh reality of the meaty thing staring them down, expectantly, and the prospect of somehow trying to accommodate it inside themselves became a reality. The point I'm going to be driving at here is the booze and the drugs and where that all started for me in earnest and how that ultimately led me to the events of Christmas '09, and how I'm lucky enough to have escaped Northern Illinois without my name appearing on any arrest reports. Dickless' thing was booze and cocaine. He was a champion drinker but only a so-so coke-head. So, there was this older girl who was nineteen when we were seventeen, and she had a real shitty second-floor apartment over by the railroad tracks in downtown DeKalb, Illinois, just down from the Marathon Station, and she would have all of us over to party on like a nightly basis. She was tall, broad in a way that was solid but not big, and she had that kind of black hair that looked dyed but wasn't, which she wore in a standard goth-girl bang cut — Dickless called her Nae-Nae. Nae-Nae's boyfriend, Anatoli, was a writer and an artist, and him and Dickless got along famously, until they didn't, which all had to do with a bet that Anatoli made with Dickless when Nae-Nae was at work. Anatoli bet that Dickless could not break one of the top logs on the log fence over at the park two blocks away using just a karate chop. Dickless being a former tournament-winning Kjukenbo fighter (aged eleven) said, "Like hell, I can't," and they debated the matter for a long time while finishing off some Jack Daniels and about a case of Busch Ice.

Never minding the fact that Kjukenbo isn't exactly known for its training in breaking things, the fence was one of those fences put together with zig-zag offset stacked and pegged logs that were at least five inches thick. There was literally no way that Dickless was going to be able to break one, and Anatoli knew that, but he figured all that would be injured would be Dickless' pride. Mind you now I got this account sec-ond-hand and later, but by all recollections, this is what happened and is pretty much accurate to the best of either Dickless' or Anatoli's memory at the time. "Okay," said Anatoli eventually, "time to show me what's what." The stakes of the bet were such that Dickless would have to show Nae-Nae and Anatoli his penis (Nae-Nae had always been curious but owing to the fact that the two were so close she was always afraid of offending Dickless by actually coming straight out and asking to see the penis and Anatoli, himself being bisexual, was certain that he could con-vince both Nae-Nae and Dickless to get into some kind of three-way situation if only the circumstances were charged enough) and remain with it (the penis) out for at least twenty minutes while they all did lines of yak. So, off to the park they go. And that's where I come into this story.

I was just walking through the park, high as all get out, and buzzing a little off some Mickey's Grenades, and I had just been ditched by the rest of my friends because I had bogarted the joint a little too long, and so I yell out, "DICKLESS JONES," just as he's taking his chop, which I do have to say probably distracted his swing, but I'm confident that it did not have any ill-effect on the outcome of the chop. I'm pretty sure what happened next was always going to happen next. Just one of those things that are bound to happen when you mix Jack Daniels, Busch Ice, sexual desire, and the male ego.

The sound when his forearm connected with that log could be heard from at least two-hundred yards away and it was sickening, totally one of the sounds that you hear and immediately feel sick to your stomach because you know, just know, something has gone so horribly physically wrong with another person, and you can actually feel it yourself, actually feel the queasy pain, and I am not ashamed to say that I threw up when I got close enough to see Dickless' arm hanging limp and unnatural in the middle of his forearm with that shard of bone sticking jagged-edged through the skin like he was assaulted from the inside. But you also need to understand that what got to me wasn't so much the gore of it, it was Dickless' laughing and the sheet-white look Anatoli was wearing, if that makes any sense. The scene was all wrong. Backward. Incongruous. I lost it, right there on my own shoes.

At the time Dickless drove a late-eighties Caprice Classic, and after a few moments his face became red and he was screaming "Fuck!" and "Cocksucker!" and he was storming around acting like he wasn't hurt. Anatoli grabbed Dickless about his shoulders, careful of the arm, and he whispered something in his ear that I could barely make out, and what he said calmed Dickless, at least a little. He said, "It's okay, you are loved." The calm only lasted a few short moments before the hurt and the embarrassment and the extreme anger came roaring back and Dickless made the decision that Anatoli was just making fun of him, that no one could love him, and that his bone-exposed arm would heal better if he went to his own house where his parents and his sister still lived, but he did not, and went to sleep in his old bed and woke up in his old house and had his Mother cook for him waffles and eggs and bacon, and squeeze him some OJ like she did sometimes. "Fuck you, Toli! Fuck you, Jed! I'm going fucking home!" he screamed, then he ran faster than I thought a man with a dangle-arm could run. And we chased him. But it may have been the shock, or the adrenaline, or something neither Anatoli nor myself could understand, but something gave Dickless real speed, and we could not catch him, and he was in his late-eighties, maroon-red Caprice Classic with the key turned and the radio blaring before we could even reach Nae-Nae's apartment; and he was taking off; and we were left to make a decision: chase him down and risk our own selves, or wait it out and hope for the best. We gave chase.

Anatoli drove a 1992 Geo Metro convertible in a sun-faded red that was more than up to the task of catching the lumbering Caprice Classic, but Dickless was driving recklessly, and Anatoli was smart enough to know he was not trying to catch Dickless, just meet him at a red light and talk some sense, but Dickless increased his speed as we tailed him closely and he blew a red light that Anatoli then also had to blow. We are damn lucky there were no cops around, but then again, if there had been, who knows? Things could've been better, all things considered. Then, the swerving began.

The day had turned ugly, and I'm not ashamed to admit, very scary. I will tell you my pulse quickened and I was sweating in fear for Dickless' safety, and when I think about it, even now, I can still feel that fear, still conjure up the free-fall feeling of watching someone truly out of control. We were watching someone flee embarrassment and feelings of rejection so fast and recklessly that it could kill him through the windshield of a Caprice Classic, and it was both surreal and extremely sad. The thing was, and I believe this, though I was too much of a mess myself to see it at the time, what Dickless was doing that day, with both the karate chop and the fleeing and recklessness that resulted from it, was running away from the numb he indulged in daily. Trying to feel anything, even if that feeling was pain and pants-shitting fear. Some sense of real-life through death-danger. He was recreating something, some hurt, some maladjustment was manifesting itself in real-time. It all came to an end when Dickless' Caprice took one giant swerve to the right, and with another sickening sound, went headlong at 65 MPH into a telephone pole. We were about a football field behind and by the time we got to the scene Dickless was outside the Caprice, on his knees, frantically ditching empties that had been scattered during the crash, using the one good arm that he had left to him. He was crying softly to himself and whispering, "Fuck, fuck, fuck" under his breath. The telephone pole was shattered in half, the top hanging from strained lines. The Caprice looked like somebody had karate chopped the front end almost clear in half, lengthwise, but Dickless was unharmed except for the arm, which I can honestly say was probably disappointing to him. We drove past him slowly and kept going. It was all so far beyond us, then. We knew we couldn't help, and frankly, neither of us was prepared to deal with any of the consequences of the afternoon, not really. Anatoli and I never really discussed that decision. We just both knew. I'm pretty sure neither of us ever regretted it, leaving Dickless to face the consequences alone, or felt bad about it, it's just one of those things you have to do when you are Out There and still running like that.

When the sirens started to break the silence of the roadside, Dickless ran the rest of the way home and his Mother let him in. She called the police and turned him in after he'd fallen asleep while sitting up at the kitchen table. He was out after a seventy-two-hour hold and back at Nae-Nae's the day after that. I left Dekalb the next year because situations exactly like that kept popping up. Kept happening. Bad things going down all around me and I was in no position to keep pressing my luck, not there anyway. The people like me, with my issue, who stay in DeKalb, never do well. The problem was my problems followed me. No geographical solutions and all that. Anyway . . .

Hey, have you ever heard of a peritonsillar abscess?

Well, I had one in the spring of 2002. My Mother drove to Madison, WI, to take me to the Dr. to have it checked out because I had been complaining of a sore throat that felt like I had a golf ball lodged down there. So, she like kind of freaks out and drives down and wants to come up to see the place as she'd never seen my apartment, but I won't let her up because it's like a mess of beer bottles and overflowing ashtrays, and, every once in a while, we'd find like a hypodermic needle under a couch cushion. We were letting street kids stay and not pay rent if they brought beer and drugs. This, by the way, wasn't my bottom; this story I'm telling is not even close. Long story short, the Dr. confirms the peritonsillar abscess, which is like a puss-filled sack and bacterial infection at the back of your throat, near the tonsils, and he prescribes a course of antibiotics which my Mother takes me to go get filled at the Walgreens downtown. Both of them warn me, my Mother and the Dr., that I can't drink any booze while taking the antibiotics because they won't be nearly as effective if I do, and they may not work at all, and then more drastic steps would have to be taken. So, I drink the whole time I am on them. And now I am back for a second round of antibiotics which I also drink the whole time I am on, and when both my Mother and the Dr. ask if I've been drinking during these courses of antibiotics I lie and say I haven't. At this point, my throat's golf ball has grown to the size of like a racquetball ball and is showing no signs of slowing down, and the Dr. wants to see me again. My Mother is freaked now, as I have "not been drinking," and I am getting no better, peritonsillar abscess-wise.

The Antiquated did not provide health coverage, just as an FYI, and at that time there wasn't a non-employer-based option I could afford. So I end up back at the doctor and they tell me that the only course of action now is a minor surgery where they would, under normal circumstances, book an O.R., put me under with general anesthesia, and drain the puss from my throat's racquetball ball. I, having no insurance re-member, explain to the Dr., and my Mother, that that sounds very expensive and I can't afford that. So the Dr. presents me with the cheaper option of doing the procedure right there in his office using only a topical pain spray, which my Mother volunteered to cover. I agree immediately, not thinking it all the way through, but then again, it's not like I had any other real option. Right?

So, they sit me in a reclining chair and tell me to open my mouth, and then a nurse sprays the back of my throat with something mentholated and I feel it go blank back there, numb. The nurse holds both my forearms to the chair and was kind of looking me directly in the eye. Her eyes looked soft to me, kind, and also pitying. The Dr. put something in my mouth to hold it open really wide. I feel the metal of his scalpel ding against my teeth as it goes in. I feel my throat being slit from the inside and the pressure of the flesh there being pulled apart with some tugging of the other instrument held in the doctor's non-scalpel hand. I feel the opposite of blank. I feel pain. Pain like I can't believe. I am crying in front of the nurse and she is, if I haven't mentioned this before, very beautiful. The scalpel comes out and the taste in my throat is putrid. So is the smell coming from my mouth. I see the Dr. going in with one of those suckers like a dental hygienist uses to suck the excess water from the water pick they use to clean your teeth. I hear a horrible sucking sound and feel the racquetball ball shrink in my throat's back. I get one last whiff of the rancid smell of my throat's puss before it, too, shrinks and fades. I almost pass out but don't. When it's all over, I am prescribed nothing for the pain and told not to drink alcohol or smoke Camels while the throat heals. I do both.

In 2005 I was pulled over for drunk driving. There was this waitress who had worked at The Antiquated named Sandy McDaniel, who I called Sister Sandy. Sister Sandy moved to Yellowstone to be some kind of park ranger the year before and she was doing really well out there and she was loving her life. We talked regularly by phone. Also, I had a steady girlfriend at this time who I'd moved in with the year before. She was sweet. Her name was Florence. Can you believe it? Florence. I called her Flo, she was like eighteen to my twenty-two, and she wasn't in school because she was pursuing her art while working as a barista and because she came from a family of dirt-poor farmers who couldn't help her like at all and she was damned if she was going to be caught in the "debt trap of student loans." Like I said, she was a sweetheart of a girl and she could be counted on for her half of the rent. We'd only been dating for like two months before we got the place together, and for like five months when Sister Sandy called me to say that she was coming back for a visit. Sister Sandy had no family in WI, but her girlfriend, whose name escapes me just now, did.

So they were going to be coming out to visit the girlfriend's family and they were going to be staying with the girlfriend's family for something godawful like ten fucking days, and she asks me if we can schedule a hang for the seventh day of their trip so she can have some excuse to leave the girlfriend's family's home and have some time away from the girlfriend, and if she could possibly stay at my apartment with me and Flo for the one night so we can go down to The Caribou and drink like we used to and talk books and movies and whatever. I say sure that's fine, and it's whatever, and I tell her not to worry about Flo because Flo is a real sweetheart, and I think she and Sister

Sandy will get along, and also that Flo usually goes to the Open Mic at the Liquid that night and isn't usually home until well past midnight. But the only rub, I tell Sister Sandy, is that I have to pull a close at The Antiquated that night, but that she could come in around closing and I could bring a change of clothes and wash up in the bathroom sinks and we could be on our way to The Bou by like no later than 10:30. She says that'll work because she can spend the day with the girlfriend and the girlfriend's family and then not feel so guilty about needing some time away. So that's that. Three weeks later Sister Sandy is darkening the doorway of the kitchen at The Antiquated and I'm just finishing cleaning up for the night when I see her, and I drop my mop and I run over and I give her a huge hug. It was the kind of hug that I love to give. The kind of hug I give women who are like 5" 3' or shorter. The kind of hug where I pull them in high, hook under their arms and lift them up and spin them around. Anyway, so I clean up and we get in my car and we head to The Bou, which is like maybe two miles away, and I tell Sister Sandy about Flo and her comedy and I also tell Sister Sandy that I forgot my weed at home but that we can just smoke when we get back later. She tells me about the girlfriend and how she doesn't like when Sister Sandy is away from her for too long. I probably said something like, "Yeah, everyone's got their thing."

The Caribou is a dingy shotgun shack of a bar, if you are unfamiliar, but they do have really good burgers and it's our Local, or, at least it was when Sister Sandy was still around and I lived closer . . . before I moved in with Flo. So, we get to The Bou and it's not packed yet and we get two seats at the bar, which we hold down for a couple of hours, and we talk about the books we are reading or want to read, movies we've seen or want to see, and general life shit. I tell her about how Baker got drunk with Michael one night at Molly's place and how Michael got to talking about how he ran track in high school and how Baker challenged Michael to a footrace and Michael accepted, and how both Molly and Helen said it was a dumb idea, but that everyone went out into the street anyway. Molly and Helen went down the opposite end of the street, each taking up a position on opposite sides of the street and stringing a toilet paper finish line between them. Long story short, when they take off on Molly's word, Baker immediately turns his ankle in a sickening way and we are all pretty sure that he broke it, but he doesn't want to go to the hospital, so we just help him to Molly's couch and he puts his foot up on her coffee table and he puts a bag of frozen peas and carrots on it and keeps drinking.

He still kind of limps, by the way.

Every forty minutes or so we walk the length of the bar, past the crappy little bathrooms, and go out back to smoke. When we do this, Winslow the legendary bartender puts a little folded triangular sign over our drinks that reads "Out Smoking." On one of these smoke breaks, Sister Sandy starts telling me about how she loves her intimate life with the girlfriend whose name I have misplaced, but that sometimes she finds herself, and I'm not trying to be vulgar here but these are her exact words and I know that because they have stuck with me over the years, "needing some dick." I remember I asked if she and the girlfriend used like a strap-on, and she said they did, but it's not the same. Shortly thereafter she asks if we can go back to my place and smoke some weed and relax. I say we can. Honestly, I'm like 90% sure at this time that Sister Sandy and I are going to have sex when we get to my place as we both know that Flo isn't going to be back for a while because she hasn't even called to say she's gone up and done her set yet. Also, I'm like 90% sure that I really wanted to have sex with Sister Sandy. I did love her. When we get to my car Sister Sandy tells me I've forgotten to turn on my head-lights, and without thinking I turn the little switch on the headlight control stick jutting out from my steering column and we take off. We are only a quarter-mile from my apartment on the west side when the lights appear behind me and I hear the sirens. Turns out, and I'm totally fucking stupid for doing this but I think the excitement of what I expect is about to happen kind of got to me, I forgot I have automatic head-lights and when Sister Sandy reminded me to turn them on, I turned them off. Anyway, I'm made to take all the standard field sobriety tests, which I fail, then I am breathalyzed and arrested. I start screaming to Sister Sandy to call Flo as I had had the presence of mind to give her my cell phone before I got out of the car with the officers. Two hours later, after sobering up a little in holding, Flo bails me out and takes me home where Sister Sandy is waiting for me. Sister Sandy is sitting crisscross applesauce on the floor. I take a bottle of wine from the cabinet, open it, then go lay down with my head in Sister Sandy's lap and we pass the wine between all three of us and I pass out without knowing it. When I wake, Flo is gone to the

Coffee Hut and Sister Sandy has a bunch of missed calls from the girlfriend. We meet the Girlfriend in the parking lot of the Qdoba behind my apartment. After Sister Sandy leaves, I masturbate which gives me the spins and I puke on my bathroom floor. This is also not my bottom. It does, however, get me to finally get my GED and enroll in community college.

I only spent one year at the JC before transferring out to a private liberal arts school. They had me take a couple of entrance tests to see if I could test out of some of the more basic Gen Ed requirements. I ended up having to take remedial math for no credit. Math 98. It was embarrassing, but I didn't do what I always did up to that point when I got embarrassed with myself — I didn't walk away. I did, however, go to classes high and get drunk every night. I studied communications and literature because I found that I didn't have to study with those subjects. I could just do it. I sometimes wonder what my life would be like now if I had just buckled down and taken courses that I wasn't 100% comfortable with, then. If I could be in like computer programing or teaching; hell, maybe even nursing. Or maybe I could've transferred to the UW and tried to get into law school somewhere after graduation. But, like I said, it wasn't like I was slowing down my lifestyle, and, I was still working full time in The Antiquated's Kitchen, and I was now alone in the apartment that Flo and I had rented because after a while shit just kind of fell apart. That's a lie. Shit didn't just kind of fall apart. I cheated on her with Molly. But I am sure you all already know that. I don't know why I tried to downplay it just then. I guess I still just feel kind of bad about what happened all around. The real fucked up part is that I didn't have to tell Flo. She wasn't there. It's not like she was going to find out. She didn't come around my Antiquated friends a lot. I know Molly wasn't going to tell Frank, and as for Helen, she did catch us like right afterward but she mostly just gave us a stern look, and she and Molly were thick as they come then, so, she wasn't going to blow up anyone's life over it, but I just felt so bad, like, inside. I've done shitty things before while fucked up, hurtful things, things I am not proud of. But this was kind of different. When I say I felt bad it's not just that I had that guilty and regret pit-of-the-stomach type feeling. I did have that, don't get me wrong, but it's more that I was in pain, real physical pain. Morning-till-night-can't-really-sleep pain. I felt it in my bones and my ligaments. I felt the guilt and the damage I caused in my brain like a knife. It caused days and weeks of that waking-dream half-sleep that is completely unrestful, and it wasn't fading. Not in the least. It was staying put and driving me insane and making me lash out at Flo for the dumbest things, and even then, the lashing out in misplaced and misdirected anger only served to deepen the pain and prolong the whole experience of feeling the pain. It was like if I could just internalize the pain and localize the pain to just the guilty-gut feeling, then I could manage it, but each time I lashed out at Flo, or a waitress at The Antiquated, or my poor Mother when she called to see how I was, the pain found new places on my body to manifest . . . my fingernails hurt, my hair, the bottoms of my feet developed plantar fasciitis even though I didn't run as a hobby. I had fucking tennis elbow and I never even so much as swung a racket. I was dying. Falling apart. And Flo, she was still being a real sweetheart to me, figuring I was going through some kind of existential thing having just gotten myself my GED and was having to take classes at the Community College.

She would make dinner for me, or pack me a lunch, or I'd find two packs of Camels on the dining room table when I got up a few hours after she had to be at the Coffee Hut. Real sweet stand-by-your-man kind of stuff. That made the pain unbearable. I didn't tell her because I thought that she should know so that she could decide whether or not she wanted to be with a man who cheated on her. I knew her heart, and I knew in her heart that she didn't want to know if something like that happened, that she'd rather not know if it was a one-time mistake type thing, if that makes sense. But I couldn't stand my pain and misery at what I had done. Couldn't stand the physical manifestation of my remorse. So, one night, I drank a real good amount of gin while she was out practicing her craft and I waited for her to come home. The second she was through the door I just blurt out, "I fucked Molly doggystyle on Frank's kid's bed on Frank's fortieth Birthday Celebration and I didn't even wear a rubber." She cried, then, and my pain was absent for the first time in a month and a half. I apologized, but what with the way I told her, drunken mess that I was, she saw some kind of writing on the wall and she left four weeks later. Anyway, that's partly why I never challenged myself in school.

Once I got past my gen-ed requirements and was just focused on the major that I had picked out for myself I did alright. It's funny, but now thinking back on it, my gen-eds, and I don't think it'll come back on me and cause me any real trouble, not now that so much time has passed, but I totally cheated in French Class with Madame Adalene. This was like '06-'07, somewhere in there, I think. First thing is, my hand-writing is for shit. And in a class like French or any foreign language probably, you have to take the quizzes and tests by hand. And the second thing is I get terrible test anxiety. I just can't take general com-petency tests. I not only freeze up at the moment, but I also totally psyche myself out and everything gets all sweaty and quick and distracted. It feels like the clock is both stopped and moving way too fast, and then, all of a sudden, I find myself staring at a half blank and half incoherent test sheet and there are only like five minutes left and I have to just fill out the rest really quick and I know most of the answers are going to be half-right at best and completely batshit at worst. I don't know what it is with me and tests, but some-thing's broken there. This is another reason Comms and literature made more sense to me, the tests had many more written components, but there were fewer questions. And I could do that. Anyway, after the first quiz, Madame Adalene pulls me aside and says to me, "You have the dyslexia, no?" And here's the thing, I don't think I do, I have the terrible anxiety, and my handwriting is for shit, and I'm diagnosed ADHD, but my parents were the kind that never wanted me med-icated in any sort of way, so I was never treated, which is something I am just now thinking about in a real way. But I looked her dead in the eyes, and put on a face of shame and regret, and tried to think sad thoughts, and I said "Yes, I do, I don't really like to talk about it." And that was that, she never mentioned it again, but I got the feeling that she would be grading my quizzes and tests and homework differently from then on.

As the semester wore on, Madame Adalene decided we didn't need to be monitored during quizzes and tests, and after she passed out the quiz sheets, she would announce that she was going for a smoke and a café and that she'd be gone for roughly fifteen minutes. Once the door would close behind her, I'd look around and everyone would be focusing on their quizzes, writing furiously, none seeming to register what Madame had just told us, what it meant, I mean. So I decided to just go for it. I pull out my French textbook, open it to the relevant chapter, and just start brazenly cheating in front of the whole class. The thing to remember here is this was a small liberal arts college on the west side of a major university town, and so the class sizes were really small. This French class had like twelve kids in it, and that was probably on the large side. And here's the thing, no one said anything, no one else cheated either, but when Madame Adalene returned no one called me out, it was just never mentioned. So a few weeks later we have one of our big section-ending tests, and again Madame Adalene announces her intention to go for a smoke and a café and that she will be back in fifteen minutes. I barely wait for the door to close behind her before I pull my book from my book bag and just begin no-fucks-given cheating, and this time half the class joins me. Sort of a, well fuck it if he's doing it and no one cares, then I'm going to as well type thing. Those of us that cheated finished super quickly, and we just sat there and waited with hands folded over test sheets knowing what we did, and also knowing that there were so few in the class and so many cheaters that if someone did rat us out, we'd have an okay idea of who it was. Funny thing is, even with the cheating, the blatant copying of answers from the book, I was still only pulling a B+ on every test and quiz. Anyway, and here's the real point I'm driving at, when the midterm, worth however many percentage points of your overall grade, came along and again Madame Adalene says she's going for a smoke and a café, the whole class whips out their textbooks and begin just bald-faced cheating. Every single kid in that class cheated. Even the ones who didn't need to. I think it has something to do with having that insurance policy, knowing your floor is only so far, knowing that you can never really hit bottom, that's just too tempting not to grab onto and hold. It's funny, but my whole life on the sauce, my whole career as a booze-hound and drug-dabbler, no matter how low a bottom I reached, I knew I'd only be allowed to fall so far. I could never be a low-bottom drunk. I'd never have that red flashing stoplight blazing in my eyes and making it apparent that I needed to change. Whenever something terrible happened that should've ended me as a drunk, and seriously derailed my life, there was always something that stopped it from going too far, getting too bad, and so, I was never really confronted with any real consequences for my actions. Other people suffered those. They were the ones who lost homes and jobs and wives and bank accounts. I started off behind, having dropped out at seventeen, and every step forward and away from that was a step up, progress, and even though I was circling a kind of drain, alcohol-wise, I could never tell myself that where I was wasn't better than where I had been. Anyway, I passed both French 1 and 2 with Madame Adalene, and both times I got a B+, overall. And before you ask, no, I can't speak a lick of French.

In the fall of 2008, I was preparing mentally for the fact that I would be graduating from the small liberal arts college and would probably have to find a real job besides cooking at The Antiquated to make it feel like the whole multi-year endeavor was worth it: you know, in the end. I was going to have a Comms degree, I was going to have a literature minor, and no one in the Comms or English Departments had any real advice on what I might do Out There, in the world. Here's the thing, and I think it should be emphasized, you know in the final report or whatever, but kids like me who go to college late and ding-dong it out but have no real connections in the real world, no network, we are probably just as fucked coming out as we were going in. Look, I had to work full-time to keep my apartment and go to school full-time to get out sooner rather than later, when was I *supposed* to start networking, developing relationships, getting out there and mixing it up? Now, I did go out nearly every night after my closing shifts at The Antiquated, but that's only because that was the only time that was free and available to me.

I was thinking a lot about what I wanted to do after graduation. I knew this girl from school, her name escapes me now but she graduated the previous spring and was working as the regional office manager for Obama's Madison Campaign office over on Monroe

Street and she told me I should come down there and volunteer to get some political experience so that maybe I could see if I wanted to pursue politics after graduation, what with the Comms degree and all. If I am being honest, what I wanted to do was go into radio, but I didn't know anyone in radio, and the small Liberal Arts College didn't have any broadcasting classes, so I just never looked into how a person gets into radio and instead convinced myself that I never wanted to be in radio in the first place. But that's how life's kind of gone for me, always not going for the thing I actually want and then kind of falling ass-backwards into another thing that I only kind of want or have convinced myself that I kind of want. It's a real problem. But you know, I can't complain, not now anyway. So there I am, cold-calling senior citizens and asking them if they are supporting Senator Obama or Senator McCain, and if they are supporting Senator Obama asking them if they, too, might like to come down and volunteer some of their time to cold call senior citizens and ask them their presidential preference. Real scut work. But I hung in and made my calls week after week and I would smoke in the back alley with the local campaign staff who were, by a measure of a couple of years, in most cases, younger than myself. That has been another near-constant in my adult life, working and studying with people who were a few years younger than myself. Entry-level, anyway. My point of entry into any given field, or life plateau, was always just slightly delayed, and I know I only have myself to blame for that, but still, it has a way of making a person just kind of feel wrong, on like a very basic level. Like at the center of myself there's always just this wrongness that is both terrible and self-destructive, but also essential to who I am and where I now find myself. The position I am now in. Like if I had it all to do again, from like middle school on, and I changed, then, and did things the right way, I'm quite positive that I'd be somewhere completely else right now, somewhere okay, but not where I am now, you know. Like I need to do things wrong and backward for anything to work. Honestly, the straightening out I have done truly frightens me — butterfly-effect-wise.

Then he wins, Obama that is. It was a crazy night on Monroe Street, I can tell you that much. Many, and I do mean many, a Spotted Cow was drunk that night and I am not ashamed to say that I was responsible for my fair share of them. I'm not ashamed to say it because that was the night I met and impressed Kevin O'Leary. The thing you have to know about Kevin O'Leary is that he was a Pittsburg transplant who'd been working for AFSCME WI for the last ten-plus years, and his union was always neck-deep in Democratic business every election cycle. Anyway, Kevin and I got to drinking together at the party at the Obama offices on Monroe Street, and we were both smokers so we ended up on the same smoke-break schedule, so, like, we really got to know each other that night. And the funny thing was, it wasn't my ability to maintain a conversation with the Union Boss that impressed him, or my ability to drink all night without getting completely sloppy, but rather the way I treated him, and everyone else around me, like they were unimportant: The State Party Chair, a couple sitting State Senators, him, and the Campaign

Staff who all seemed to think they were going to be on the next flight to Washington D.C. Kevin O'Leary said he liked me because I didn't act like any of them were better than me. I told him that's because I didn't think they were. He laughed. He programmed my number into his phone that night and gave me his business card and told me to expect a call from him about a job after I graduate. I said okay, but I figured it was just some of that old tenth beer bullshit, which, was just fine with me.

So a couple of months later I graduate early, after first semester, because I packed it full with what remaining credits I had left and didn't really sleep at all. I walked across the stage and my Mother and my Father were there and looking really, really proud. But just as I had thought, no call from Kevin O'Leary, which as I said, was just fine with me. But now I had to go about finding a job in Comms, whatever that looked like. It's funny, thinking back now, but I only looked at Madison, WI, for jobs; I never looked at another state. I didn't even look at Milwaukee. Maybe I lack imagination. Maybe I'm just afraid of real change. Moving from Dekalb, IL, to Madison WI, when I was eighteen wasn't so bad because my folks were moving to the greater Madison area too, to be closer to my Grandmother in Mauston, WI. Maybe I was hoping I could get Flo back, or that Molly would leave Frank eventually and would want to start something up with me. Maybe I just really wanted to sabotage any career before it got off the ground because if I got a real 9-5 and got myself deadlines and real responsibilities then I'd probably have to take the foot off the gas, booze-wise, and admit to myself that the drinking would hold me back from real success in that kind of environment. So, anyway, there's only a handful of places that can use a Comms guy in Madison, and I was pretty sure they weren't hiring, and I really didn't want to go to work at TDS Metro-Com being an office admin-type person. So, I just applied anywhere that sounded cool and stayed at The Antiquated. I was a line cook making $11 an hour with $40k in student loan debt and a Comms degree. But funny thing is, I wasn't embarrassed or anything, I was enjoying myself and I had shown that I could hack it in school, and I had redeemed myself from my high school dropout days, and I felt I had proved something to myself and everybody else, so I wasn't sweating the whole career vs. job thing, and like I said, staying put allowed me to party and drink and fuck around and not have to worry about disappointing anyone, work output wise. Then Christmas '09 happened, and you know that whole story.

For my part, I don't know what much new I can tell you guys except that I didn't see any of it, didn't witness a damn bit of it, but that it profoundly changed my life and bottomed me right the hell out and got me to finally see my life for what it was and where it was going, which was an early death, a jail cell behind an OWI turned vehicular homicide, or the mental ward for unresolved and numbed-out issues. Nowhere good is what I am saying. The funny thing is, the booze kept me from seeing or witnessing anything graphic in the extreme or too horrifically terrible that night. If you want that kind of firsthand info you guys need to be talking to Michael, he was right there, I think. So, we weren't really low on beer by that time in the night, but I had volunteered to go walk to the liquor store about a half-mile away and get some more before the 9:00 P.M. mandatory liquor store closing time, because I didn't even want the threat of running out of beer, and also, I figured that I could collect some money and get a pint of E&J for myself to drink on the walk back and that that would be a win-win for everyone involved. So that's what I did. And on the way back I stopped to pee and drink my pint and set down the two cases of beer for a minute and I don't really know what happened but I must've lost a couple of hours because by the time I was getting back to Molly's house it was ablaze with emergency vehicles and cops and whatnot, and the place was cleared out completely. It's funny, but no one stopped me from walking in or going down to the basement, and what I saw there changed my life for good and for keeps. It was like I was meant to see what I saw, meant to brownout and lose time, meant to be exactly where I was so I could become something else, something better, something a little less wrong, if that makes any sense. Frank's body had been removed but the scene had not been cleaned and there was blood spraying the walls, which if I am being honest, looked kind of neat, but then there was the place where he had clearly fallen and taken his last breath. There was a large pool of coagulated blood that looked like the beginnings of like a red-velvet pudding, which had pooled around Frank's body. It looked like a lake's edge; the blood pool did. The shoreline of the blood pool was roughly the height and the shape of Frank — including a pretty clear outline of his lips and the slope of his forehead and the curvature of one eye socket. It was surreal. It chilled me to my bones. It sobered me right the fuck up. Not like how seeing a cop makes you alert when drunk, but like actually sober-sober. I ran from that room and down the street and I didn't stop until I was at the apartment I had shared with Flo, and I was on my computer looking up AA meetings so fast that my head likely spun. That was my bottom. But in the cold light of the next morning, I hate to say it, but I didn't follow through on the whole meeting thing. I had seen how out of control my life had become and I drank that whole next day alone in my apartment to the point of sickness, of bone-in sickness, and I puked, and I sweated, and still, after I slept and recovered, I did that same thing off and on for two more months before I finally dragged ass to the Blue Monday Group downtown Madison, WI. The next day I quit The Antiquated without a plan.

By spring of 2010, I was living in my Father and Mother's basement, sober, but aimless. I had maybe seventy-five days in and The Blank that was always there was a little less so. My Mother was truly supportive but also thought that I should maybe start trying to figure out the rest of my life. I told her that I was just barely hanging on to my new-found sanity and that anything that could jeopardize that would be a boneheaded wrong-move kind of deal at this very precarious spot I now found myself in; but still, and she was right, making myself useful and becoming a contributor would help with my self-esteem and bring me a sense of pride to go along with my new sense of clarity. I was just about to start an account at one of those online upload-your-resume sites where they just spit anything tangentially connected to your degree and experience at you for you to apply for. I swear to you right now, I was ready to sell insurance for Farmers or State Farm or even work the TDS Metro-Com gigs that are always around. The difference was that I needed to get one of those ding-dong 9-5 kind of cubicle things because I wanted to show myself that I could sacrifice the debilitating part of the identity that I had scaffolded my ego with that said I was special, God's own rebel, and that I deserved more than the drone-like existence my peers had settled for. I was ready. I wanted ordinary. I wanted drudgery. I wanted a boss who was an ass. I wanted the water cooler and to talk with Bob about The Badgers. That's when Kevin O'Leary called and changed everythi . . .

But then again

He hears the hollow sounds of high heels click-clacking on the cement floor of the empty subterranean hallway which leads to the room he's been in for what he assumes is at least three days, but as there is no clock on the wall or windows (obviously, what with the room being at least — by his own best guess as the elevator had no numbers displayed as They descended? ascended? — fifteen stories underground) he has no way of actually knowing. When he had arrived he was told why he was there, but that was just about it. And They had treated him kind of roughly, Bob Helens and Bill Stevens had, and kind of shoved him into his room in that clichéd way authority figures sometimes shove captives into rooms with doors that only open from the outside. That kind of shoulder shove where the shover has the shovee hooked under the one arm and then kind of shoves them up through their armpit and into a cell, or padded room, leaving the shovee to stumble awkwardly and off-balance into the cell, or padded room, only to catch their balance just in time to hear the sha-lunk of the deadbolt driving home. The sha-link of the deadbolt in the metal door retracting snaps his head away from the wall-length mirror to which he's been speaking. He sees a woman that he does not recognize open the door. She's framed by the doorway and backlit by the hallway's florescent light. He does, however, upon seeing her, get the eeriest of feelings where his blank still lives. Déjà vu. Her skirt-suit is slate gray and she wears a white collared shirt underneath her suit jacket. The suit jacket has one button fastened, but she unbuttoned the one button as she opened the door. He's still sitting on his stool and he faces the highly polished mirror, again. His reflection in the mirror seems to him to be HD. Her reflection is now present over his shoulder. He was talking before he heard her high heels click-clacking but stopped when he heard that noise because it made him lose his train of thought. He did not think the noise was coming toward him, but rather he had perceived it as moving away from him. But here she is. The déjà vu intensifies as he continues to look at her reflection until it crests and breaks and rolls back and leaves him feeling ill at ease. She's holding a clipboard and a pen is attached to a piece of string and the piece of string is attached to the clipboard's metal loop thing that pokes out from the top of almost all clipboards, which he is just now realizing is for the purpose of attaching a pen. This realization produces an a-ha moment but that does not last, either. He does not feel stupid for having not realized this sooner, this thing of pens and strings and metal loops. She places her hand on his shoulder and he nods to her reflection in the mirror in that curt way his Father used to nod to him. She marks something down on her clipboard and says, "Jedidiah Lucas Jr?" with an upturned inflection that tells him she is asking him if that is who he is, though he knows that any woman in this setting, wearing a skirt-suit, and carrying a clipboard, having just unlocked the room he has been locked in for like three days or more, knows exactly who he is. He assumes this is a tactic to gauge his cooperation. He wants to be very cooperative and says, "Yes, that's me."

"They will see you now."

"They aren't back there? Behind the mirror, listening."

"No, They don't operate that way."

"Shame." He'd hoped They had been listening as he'd been speaking, he's more comfortable speaking when he doesn't have to look at the people he is speaking to, the eyes of others kind of confuse him and make him uncomfortable, and it would've saved Them all some time.

"Some questions first."

"Okay."

"Understand, you should save elaboration for in there, with Them, these are yes/no questions in here. Simple. Don't belabor any points or tangentialize."

"Understood."

"Were you an associate of Molly Duch and Frank Novinsky?"

"Yes."

"Did you work at The Antiquated Brewing Company from roughly 2001-2009?"

"Yes."

"Are you now a homosexual?"

"No."

"Were you ever in a homosexual relationship or have any homosexual experiences?"

"No. Well, sexual identity can be a spectrum, maybe, and once I . . ."

"Yes/no Mr. Lucas."

"I'll stick with no."

"Are you an alcoholic/drug addict?"

"Yes. Alcoholic."

"Yes/no Mr. Lucas."

"Shit. Understood. Yes."

"Are you now employed by Wisconsin State Representative Phillip H. Kilroy as a Research Assistant LVL 1?"

"Yes."

"Do you recall the events of December 24th, 2009?"

"Yes."

"Can you recount those events, from your perspective, when asked and with some detail and specificity?"

"Yes."

"Okay Mr. Lucas, They will see you now."

She walks him through the labyrinthine hallways for at least twenty minutes, not speaking to him at all. She gives no type of indication of where they are, exactly. When they arrive at the door where They are Jed is pretty sure it is the door directly adjacent to the one he'd been kept in, but he can't be sure. He's lost track of which cup the bean is under, so to speak. There's a long stainless-steel table with suited and Brylcreem-headed men sitting only on one side. They are facing a mirror much like the one he had faced in his room. They are silent and seem to be studying their reflections. No one invites him to sit. He shifts his weight from one foot to the next. It goes on like this for a while, not quite a full minute because that's a long time to stand and shift in silence, but a while by polite conversation and interpersonal interaction standards. Finally, she says to the older gentleman seated at the table's middle, "Well, let's begin then." And, They do.

Chapter Ten

Explaining herself (Redux)

HER NAME IS MOLLY and she can concentrate, or not. Level of concentration has very little impact, They find out. Some days are good and some aren't. She is lucid and not. Same and not. History, personal and otherwise, has an impact, They discover. You feed on your past your whole life and never really recover. Auburn hair streaked with white. Not gray. White. It began happening sometime in year three. Her room is unadorned because she finds that that helps with giving Them what They want. She has given Them what They want to Their satisfaction exactly three times, but that's about to change. She has almost given Them what They wanted but fallen short a total of 2,127 times. The times she has given Them nothing of what They want is unknowable. The floor of her room is cement. They gave her an area rug six months in. She ate almost a quarter of it starting with the NW corner on the first night and it was removed. They had to do surgery. They tried giving her books under supervision. She does not read. They tried giving her a television. She screamed without cease until They removed it. She sits, mostly. She paces infrequently. The door to her room is made of thick metal of a variety she cannot place but she tries it (the door) regularly. It is locked, she finds. This is new information every time she tries (the door). Her snaggletooth unsnaggled sometime in year four and no one knows why. They suspect she did it but she refuses to confirm or deny. If she would only confirm the unsnaggling of her tooth was her own doing it could be recorded as the most significant application of her anomaly to date. Of it, she said, "I don't know," then refused to ever speak on the subject again. She seems to brighten when allowed to listen to the interviews. Her mirror has a switch she can flip. Her room is not adjacent to Jed's room and neither is the interrogation room, which is a real shame. She's growing bored with questions and answers and is finding diminishing returns w/r/t her anomaly. She hasn't tried in forty-five days. She knows a new year has come because she can feel it happen in her bones but is otherwise uninterested in the concept of time and purposefully forgets where she is in her chronology whenever she inadvertently takes in some information that tells her the time of day or the day of the week or the month of the year or the year. She is unsure if she feels a new year as in the capital N capital Y, New Year, or she feels a new year as in her personal birthday. She has forgotten her exact birthday. She has exceptional hearing and can often hear conversations in the hall she is not meant to hear. She knows exactly who is in the building at all times though she has no way of confirming if she is correct in her knowledge or not. She was insane for a time. Her bed is the lower half of a bunk bed that has had its upper half removed. This happened before her arrival. Sometimes, she can identify with the lower half of the bunk bed on a personal level. Her name is Molly, and she knows that but has forgotten all of her middle name and all but the first letter of her last name. It is D. The word Molly and the letter D are stitched onto the breast of all her scrubs' tops. She is unsure if she remembers this information because it is stitched onto her scrubs' tops, or if she genuinely remembers this information. How well can we internalize the information that we have constant access to? She does not know. Her slippers are thin and she can feel her feet make micro-adjustments as she paces. They place odd objects in her room three times a week and she knows these objects are both electrified to make them painful to the touch and also outfitted with equipment to track their movements. She wants to deliver what They want. She does not want to leave. She wants to leave badly. Since she has been in the room, she has thought about sex twice and never once acted out sexually. She can no longer tell when she is hot or cold. She sleeps in her scrubs and never uses a blanket. Unbeknownst to her, They have discovered the ideal temperature at which human skin, while wearing thin scrubs, is at peak comfort and is neither hot nor cold. She believes she is somehow related to Archduke Ferdinand, Babe Ruth, Sirhan Sirhan, Oliver North, Oliver Stone, Tom Robbins, Russ Feingold, and the guy who played Special Agent Skip Lipari on the hit U.S television series *The Sopranos*. She knows who Babe Ruth and Russ Feingold are. She is unfamiliar with the rest. She is somehow related to all of them. Her toilet flushes counterclockwise. All other toilets in the compound flush clockwise. She is aware that this is strange but has never mentioned the phenomenon to Them. It would raise more questions than it would answer. Her sink drains clockwise which only serves to confuse her further. She has a lot of time to think about the objects she has in her room. Today, there is a toy John Deere tractor, two golden chalices, and a length of cured ring bologna. She hears Her click-clacking down the hall. She knows when Helen is close. Helen hasn't been close in forty-five days. She gets up from her lower bunk and stands before the ring bologna and she both tries and doesn't. As the click-clacking gets closer she puts her back into it. The ring bologna tremors on a molecular level. This she can feel. It is not visible movement. She tries harder and she pops a blood vessel in her left eye. She begins to leak tears from both her eyes. The ring bologna levitates. The click-clacking is about to pass her door. She tries harder. She cries blood. The click-clacking passes right in front of her door. The ring bologna takes off like a bullet and slams against the metal. She hears the prettiest of yelps as Helen jumps. She sees the prettiest eyes she'd ever known flash the door's window's diamond-wire patterned glass. She sits back down on her bunk. The camera in the corner of the ceiling moves and the lens focuses on her. She looks into the lens and wears an expressionless face. She is sane.

Chapter Eleven

This viral moment

BAKER THOMAS SAT ALONE on a couch that moved with him to Madison, WI, from DeKalb, IL, in 2001 — seventeen years ago. His guitar sat next to him but he had not played it in over a year and a half. He moved it around his apartment with the intention to play. His paunch had grown untenable, and what's more, he knew it too. The television was on and he stared at it as he would stare at a tree or a cloud, or a river burbling with a slow current. He couldn't think of anything in particular. He'd owned the complete set of 7th Heaven DVDs since the show completed its run in 2007. The show ran for eleven seasons and Baker Thomas used to watch The Show as it aired on The WB, and then later on The CW. He was watching the DVDs for the fifth time in three weeks and he could complete all eleven seasons in only a couple of days if he tried. When he started watching 7th Heaven in 1996 he used to sexualize and objectify the young Jessica Biel, but not anymore. Now he was in it purely for the wholesome moralizing and the repetitive narrative structure, which was comforting to his real soul. It was the same, the show. It was stasis. Constant. What Baker appreciated about it was it followed a pretty standard arc each episode: child has moral issue/is keeping an important life secret; child tries to hide moral issue/secret from Father and Mother; child is found out; child is given a good and proper talking to; child finds own way to doing the right thing; then all is right with their little world. Its sanitized and simplistic Christian moralizing were things he could stare at idly and take in without any need for conscious thought. He believed that by doing this (this ritualistic viewing of *7th Heaven* off and on for the last ten years) he somehow became a better person by internalizing the lessons the Camden Family had to teach him.

Disc One of Season Two had run its course and skipped back to the main menu. He had to get up to put in Disk Two of Season Two if he wanted to continue watching *7th Heaven*. And he very much wanted to keep watching *7th Heaven*. It was hard for him to get up. He'd been slouched into the couch for several hours at an angle that was both unnatural and extremely comfortable, that and his paunch acted like one of those speed-control tables They placed on roads in suburban subdivisions that just about drove a person nuts. He needed to sort of get some momentum going and kind of roll himself over his paunch. Also, he was completely doped out of his mind on prescription Oxycontin and his ANXIETY meds. He liked to take them at the same time as it produced a kind of Nowheresville buzz that allowed him to be both down and kinda up and just blank and not there. When he was halfway up he could feel gravity trying to sink him back into his couch but he really wanted to keep watching *7th Heaven*, and there was not a single chance that any *7th Heaven* episodes would ever be re-run on the CW ever again — not after the ugliness. Baker still believed in the righteousness of Eric Camden. He successfully put in Disk Two of Season Two and he hit play and the *7th Heaven* theme song began and he then made it back to his couch where he nodded off and passed out for several hours and woke only when the repetitive thirty-second loop of the *7th Heaven* theme song on the disc's main menu began playing over and over. It had become dark outside and he was unsure of the time, but it felt like really late at night so he shut down both the DVD player and the television and tried to fall back asleep but couldn't. So he did what many do in this kind of situation, he scrolled on his phone's various social media apps and that's when he came across the news of the death by suicide of Verne Troyer. Almost reflexively, he went and got his laptop and his webcam and without thinking, an idea came to him. And he called it "Too Soon Radio." The video he recorded was of himself shirtless and with paunch on full display playing his guitar and adlibbing a song about the death of Verne Troyer in a tone so earnest it must be ironic. And it went a little something like this:

You were small (so small)

You drank big (so big)

Now you're tall (so tall)

And you are missed (so missed)

Chorus: Out from Powers' shadow you're no Mini-Me to me. You rock-and-rolled your life away and we were all too blind to see. We laughed at how tiny, but Mr. Troyer I'm here to saaaaaaaaaaay . . . you're as big as a naval-destroyer, to me today.

You came (and went)

Too soon (too soon)

Now we're sad (so sad)

And singing, the blues (so blue)

Chorus: Out from Powers' shadow you're no Mini-Me to me. You rock-and-rolled your life away and we were all too blind to see. We laughed at how tiny, but Mr. Troyer I'm here to saaaaaaaaaaay . . . you're as big as a naval-destroyer, to me today.

They said (they said)

You did this to yourself (yourself)

But I say (I say)

You had our help (our help)

Chorus: Out from Powers' shadow you're no Mini-Me to me. You rock-and-rolled your life away and we were all too blind to see. We laughed at how tiny, but Mr. Troyer I'm here to saaaaaaaaaaay . . . you're as big as a naval-destroyer, to me today.

Talking in a whisper part: Verne, I'm sorry you are gone. You brightened up our days and made us laugh and fawn. You could find no peace, and I'm sorry you were too good for this earth and had to move on away.

You were small (so small)

You drank big (so big)

Now you're tall (so tall)

And you are missed (so missed)

Baker Thomas created the Too Soon Radio YouTube Chanel, and after uploading The Verne Troyer Blues, he found his sleep again. He wouldn't wake until half-way through the next day, and when he did, his world wouldn't be the same.

Jesse is himself, and, of course, not at all himself

He is holding a spiral notebook that has obviously seen much better days in a hand that is still dirty from the morning's work at The Antiquated. The caked-on detritus of over a decade of standing on the same tiles prepping the same food and mopping the same floors. All the faces have changed there, but his remains, and that's just a-ok with him. His hair is a greasy shag mess and he has grown thick with age. It's been so long. His five o'clock shadow just makes his face look dirty, which it is, also. His eyes' blue had dulled to a flat finish. His torso is barely covered as he is wearing only a torn fishnet tanktop. His jeans are more holes than jeans, and his legs are visible to the extent that the interior of his jeans' pockets hang outside his jeans. He looks manic and dangerous. He is manic and dangerous. Has been for some time, though he doesn't believe he is. The only time he can get himself to perform anymore is when he is manic and agitated. He flips a few pages. "That's not a thing," he like growls into the microphone. The crowd laughs a distant nervous laugh and they all kind of in unison shift in their seats and along the standing-room wall. For the most part, they all knew what they were getting themselves into. There is, however, a very confused bachelorette party that seem incongruous to the setting and general feeling of the place, the cold and narrow and forever hollow room, and they seem genuinely disturbed by the man's appearance. Ricky who works the door, and smokes out back in the alley on his break, should have warned them when they came in, but he thought it was funnier this way. Anyway, Jesse, Ricky knew, needs some unsuspecting people in the crowd so he can do his act, not just the ones who were used to him. "Motherfucker," he growls, another smattering of uncomfortable laughter coming his way. "Don't laugh at my pain, man." More laughter. Jesse is about halfway through his notebook when he says, "Here's something," then sets the notebook down and addresses the open space that smells of night air and cigarette smoke in his rapid-fire rat-a-tat-tat style thusly: "What'd'ya get when you mix a Mexican, an Italian, and Jew? No clue but the food's out of fucking sight. How come cars all come with backup cameras now? Because dead kids aren't funny anymore. How many women does it take to screw up a marriage? Just the one, as it so happens (screaming "as it so happens"). What makes a clock tick? Time, I guess. Did you know you can breed a hippo with a zebra? Yeah, what you get is that lady back there wearing stripes. How come no one loves me? Because I'm a depressive with no fixed address. Black people, am I right? No, I'm probably not right. Hey there, you in the back, you from here? No? Where you from then? Chicago, huh. The Windy City. Do you know how it got that name? No, I'm really asking. You don't? I'm saying. Don't interrupt (followed by a guttural yawp). I'm saying I have a genuine curiosity. Okay, fine, fuck you too then Mr. 'I'm too good to tell people about my city.' Actually, I would love for you to come down here, as a matter of fact. That's what I thought buttercup. Anywho, Black people are always like, 'stop killing me,' and white people are always like, 'no.'"

Jesse takes a step back from the microphone and the people are still laughing and he doesn't know why.

It takes a moment, but the laughter fades and he flips through his notebook again, looking for a jumping-off point. He has not done the same show twice in over five years. The Comedy Club on State books him every second and fourth Thursday night as the club's only regular headliner. He has a committed following in the upper Midwest, despite the fact that he refuses to travel further than Milwaukee or Appleton — though, he only books shows in those cities like twice a year when he needs to get away. Once, one of the big-name headliners from NY saw Jesse's act and filmed his (Jesse's) sets throughout his (the NY headliner's) Thursday-Sunday run of shows and stitched them all together into an hour-long special and threw it up on the internet, and not even on YouTube, just on like some seedy video-sharing site that mostly hosted the rankest of pornography, but people found it anyway and it went viral nonetheless; however, Jesse never saw a red-cent from the monetization of his content, but he didn't care because that wasn't the point anyway. The bachelorette party, who've indulged him up to this point as they were curious, look uncomfortable.

"Here's something: New Segment, Stuff I think sometimes — Also, David Foster Wallace, Warren Zevon, and Mitch Hedberg are the same person and he is living on an island with Tupac Shakur, Biggie, and DB Cooper, but that's just my opinion. Also, Television was better before cable, and the internet was better when it was just AOL, and all it was really good for was talking dirty to other dudes pretending to be chicks and also luring children from Iowa to places that aren't Iowa. Also, Cholula is a perfectly acceptable hot sauce. Also, sometimes alcoholism is a perfectly acceptable response to the circumstances of the world, especially if those circumstances are beyond your control, but then, like, you have to commit to the thing for a long while. Also, most people with dogs are bad dog owners and most dogs are mistreated by well-meaning people in some innocuous way because they fundamentally don't understand the nature of dogs. Also, I believe I am a dog that has been mistreated. Also, women want to be right more than they want to be happy and it shows in the way they fight when they think they have been wronged in some small, psychological way. Also, men want to be right more than they want to be happy and it shows in the way they fight when they are challenged at all in any way at all. Also, neither of the sexes are ever happy when confined to a long-term thing with a member of the opposite sex. Also, I'm now, essentially, a-sexual, but I jerk off a lot. Also, you can lose interest in yourself because yourself is boring and not funny, and also who wants to fuck the same boring and unfunny hand for the rest of their lives? Also, when you fuck another person's hand that's called a hand job and costs between $5 and $15, depending. Also, pennies are useless as currency but super useful when you are down on your luck. Also, if I could buy a home with a wife and have a family, I would, but only if I could make that home with the woman in the back wearing the stripes. Also . . ." The Bachelorette party move on, almost in unison, and begin walking out while the bride is saying very loudly that this isn't part of the comedy show, an act, and also kind of really depressing, and her bridesmaids are telling her not to think on it anymore because they will go across the street to The Buck and

Badger and they will do Shot-skis and have the kind of fun that they had been expecting to have when they came down this end of State Street. "Also, it's okay to hate me but not okay to be a dick about it. Also, some people believe that they aren't dicks but they are. Also, I know who I am, what I am, and I am both a dick and strange. Also, toast is not better than bread, it's just crunchier. Also, bagels should have two thick sides because it's always disappointing to eat the thin side of anything. Also, I think I'm done now." Jesse doesn't wait for the applause that always accompanies the end of his act, he just leaves his stage and runs toward the cavernous exit, smacking into two slate-gray-suited and Brylcreem-smelling agents of the Federal Paranormal/Psychological Investigation Bureau, the impact of which causes him to fall on his ass in front of Them.

They look down at him with a curiosity like They are both asking Themselves the same internal question and coming up empty. He looks up at Them with a blank expression that betrays nothing of internality. The bigger one, Bob, who is built like a linebacker, reaches a meaty hand down and Jesse accepts it and is lifted to his feet without much effort on his part. The smaller one, Bill, is slight in a way that would suggest an eating disorder. His suit almost wears him. "She's set herself to contacting you," says Bill.

"I know, it's not as if it's like a big secret to me."

"Knowing and *knowing* are two entirely different things, know what I mean Jelly Bean?"

"I know what I know, you know?"

"Anyway . . ."

"Yeah."

"So, the deal is that The Bear wants you down FP-PIB way no later than July first."

"So, like, what, that's two weeks? Right?"

"Anyway . . ."

"What's she doing?"

"She drew a circle in the middle of her room with the dust of her ground fingernails and she is chanting. The word Ramada seems to come around often."

"So . . ."

"Yeah."

"What can I say, I'm not that way anymore. Nobody is, the world's gone flat to me. Kind of. It was round, but it's flatting out now."

"We told you from the outset this would happen, and when it did, you'd have to do your bit. We need her to try. We need her to make good. We need her to un-block herself and harness herself and control what happens. We need her well."

"How am I going to explain this to Flo? She's been a real sweetheart, you know? Accommodating."

"She can be compensated if that's what you are worried about if worse comes to worst."

"That's not at all reassuring to me. I don't know what to do with that. Why did you even have to tack that on? It could've just gone unsaid."

"It is what it is. You knew what you did when you did what you did and you did it anyway, Messy-Jesse."

"Did it ever occur to you that she's just playing with you?"

"Every god damn day."

Sitting on a park bench

Reagan was a good man and The Bear loved him. Slow towards the end, but good. The Bear met with him exactly fifty-seven times, and he met Oliver North exactly four times, and he met George Herbert Walker Bush exactly three times when he was VP but met with him all the god damned time when he was President. He also met LBJ, but that's a whole other thing. Before he was The Director of the FPPIB, he was a Company Man through and through. Hell, he made his bones under Kennedy. No one could say he was a partisan. Back when Nancy urged Ronny to create the FPPIB, the general wisdom was that spinning off the psychological/paranormal divisions to create a wholly new and secretive investigative agency would create the need for more defense allocations and spending, which everyone from the tippy-top on down just absolutely loved. In Reagan, there was something innocent, childlike, and it was that exact quality that allowed the man to do what he did and not just come across like some sort of corporatist, which of course he was. Some would have you believe that that quality was a put-on, an affectation, a façade designed to disarm and persuade, and it was useful in that pursuit, and Reagan was smart enough to know that, but it also happened to be, as The Bear knew, quite genuine; and that was why The Bear loved Ronald Reagan. It had nothing to do with being named The Director of The FPPIB — though, he was grateful for that. Also, Reagan allowed him to pick the location for the FPPIB headquarters and he didn't balk when The Bear chose

Madison, Wisconsin. The Bear appreciated that as well. Reagan never even asked why. If he had, The Bear wouldn't have lied. He'd have said it was because that's where his wife was from and wanted to return to, and after a career out east, he owed her that; and he knew Ronald well enough to know that that would've carried some weight with him and he would've been granted permission even with only a personal reason for wanting the location. Yeah, The Bear loved Ronald Reagan; those that came after, besides H.W. (whom he also had a deep affection for and still considers it to this very day to be one of our nation's most tragic miscarriages of will that he was not afforded a muchly deserved second term) he merely tolerated.

There is a small park across the street from the nondescript entrance to the subterranean headquarters of the FPPIB. The park has a lone bench on its far-west corner where Agents routinely leave dead drops for various covert types. The Bear eats his lunch on that bench every day, which can mess up the drop schedule some days, but what are the Agents going to do, tell The Bear where he can and can't eat his lunch? The bench is dedicated to John and Bethany Ellison who both died on December 26th, 1999, and who, according to the small plaque on the bench's back, loved to watch their grandchildren play in the park and would often pack a picnic lunch for them. The way they died is not disclosed on the plaque nor is their age. Just their names, the date they died, and the reason for the park bench being a fitting memorial to their memory. The Bear spends his lunches on the bench and watches children at play and eats the sandwiches (always two sandwiches the variety of which rotates between roast beef, ham, and egg salad) his doting wife packs for him every day. His thoughts often wander to the Ellisons. He supposes that they died in some sort of accident — car, boating, got lost hiking, something like that. Often that is the case when people die on the same day, especially people who are old enough to have grandchildren but still young enough to watch said grandchildren at the park and have picnic lunches. He hopes they went in an accident, prays they went that way, and prays it was fast. He reads the paper, too, at lunch on the bench, and every so often there will be a story about an elderly couple both succumbing to some illness on the exact same day, within hours of each other, or sometimes within like one day of each other, and he thinks to himself, privately, how terribly awful that would be. It is The Bear's opinion that being terminally ill, all on its own, is bad enough, but it is cruel and unusual for God to inflict the suffering of terminal illness on a person and then heap on top of that the suffering of watching the one person that that person loves the most, also suffering terminal illness and degenerating right in front of them. Of course, this cruelty is compounded and multiplied by the fact that the person that the first person loves the most in this world, and is now having to watch suffer and become more and more weak and feeble, is also having to watch the first person suffer and become more and more weak and feeble. And also compounding all of this suffering, thinks The Bear, is the fact that because both individuals both love each other more than life itself, their mutual decline into feebleness almost guarantees that they will both die with the knowledge that in their final moments on God's Green, they were not only absolutely powerless to do anything to stop or alleviate the suffering of the person they loved most, but were, in all actuality, an additional source of pain and suffering for the one that they love most. They die knowing they caused a hurt so deep that only death would cure the guilt of it. The Bear likes the Ellison Bench very much.

There is a boy whose hair is so blond it's almost a pale blue when the sun hits it just right swinging not twenty feet from The Bear as he eats his egg salad. The boy looks to be eleven years of age and fatherless on this crisp fall day. The Bear puts his paper down and watches the boy. He swings not high. He has no power in his legs, which The Bear is now noticing are smaller than they ought to be, smaller than the proportions of the rest of his body would suggest, somehow atrophied. The Bear sits and he supposes that the boy broke one or both of his legs sometime over the summer, possibly playing soccer, or riding his bike, or his friends dared him to jump off his garage. He sits and contemplates the boy's skinny and de-muscled legs and he believes that he can stimulate the boy's legs and help them grow strong again by concentrating on the boy's calf muscles really hard. He (The Bear) believes that he can perform a kind of mental EMS (Electrical Muscle Stimulation) on the boy's struggling legs. He focuses. He lines his eyes on the boy's pumping left leg and he begins to chant (internally) Power, Growth, Power, Growth, and he believes he sees the height of the boy's swing increase, albeit, unevenly. He focuses on the boy's right leg and chants the same and he believes he sees the altitude of the right side and left side of the boy's swing even out and the boy rise even higher on his next swing. The Bear is satisfied with his efforts and their results, and he stops chanting (internally) and he picks up his paper and his sandwich and he resolves to finish his lunch without any further thought about the boy, an effort in which he only somewhat succeeds. He continues to think about the attempt to mentally alleviate the boy's suffering through what he assumes is months of rehab for the two broken legs, and he comes to the conclusion that it does not matter if a) the boy does have atrophied legs or b) the boy did actually break his legs or c) that he helped the boy in any way while sitting on that bench, because all that matters, as far as The Bear's own personal mental wellbeing was concerned, was that he (The Bear) believed a, b, and c were all true. Because he believed they were true and believed it so completely, then as a matter of fact, in his mind, they were true, regardless of their actual basis in real-world-type-fact. His mind was a universe unto itself and could make up the laws that govern that universe all on its own, and given that fact and the fact that he believes that he can manipulate the electrical field that is naturally occurring around everything in such a way that it has real-world effects, then it stands to follow that he (The Bear), indeed, can, if only in his own mind, which is exactly where The Bear chooses to live. The boy flings himself from the swing at the apex of a particularly forceful swing and clears at least fifteen feet before planting both feet in the sand and running toward his bike, which he then pedals with all the force he can muster away from the park and toward a home that The Bear assumes is a happy one, and therefore, it surely is.

The door across the street that leads to the hallway that leads to the elevator bank with the elevators that only go down, opens, and the six agents that make up The Bear's inner circle file out and are heading for The Bear as he tries now to finish the last three bites of his second sandwich before they arrive, and he is unsuccessful, but just. He is chewing in that way that people chew when their mouths are too full of food, when they've literally bitten off more than they can chew, but he feels no embarrassment at this and he has no issue with holding up one hand and extending one of that hand's fingers in a gesture of "just a sec" to Bill and Steve and Rodger and Bob and Helen and Abel. He continues to chew for more than just the additional sec as indicated by the hand's extended finger and he thinks about this while he chews, thinks about how it is more or less the social norm that the raised hand and extended finger gesture is always taken to mean "just a sec" but it is also understood that the actual time taken is always going to be longer than just a sec because just a sec is a supremely short amount of time when considering the average human's capacity for expediency in doing something like wrapping up a phone call, which is almost always when the just a sec gesture is employed, or in The Bear's case, finishing the chewing of the egg salad sandwich that his loving wife had so lovingly prepared. He deliberately slows his chewing, wondering how long he can hold his hand aloft with extended finger in this gesture before Bill and Steve and Rodger and Bob and Helen and Abel start to shuffle their feet and shift their weight from side to side in subconscious gestures of impatience. He knows that the subordinates would never outwardly display impatience, like checking their watches in an overly dramatic fashion, but still, he wonders how long he can keep Them standing there. His chewing slows even further. He is now chewing so noticeably slow that the Agents have to know what's up. He knows that the Agents have to know what is up. He ponders this knowing, and the knowing of the knowing, and he considers how this will alter the experiment in patience that he is running. He considers that the mere fact that They now have to know and that he now knows that They have to know has irreparably altered the base experiment of how long before their subconscious leaks though and They display the odd bit of impatient gesturing. He concludes that that experiment is shot and now further concludes that to continue with the so-obvious-it's-painful slow chewing and hand-alofting and finger-extending would only serve to see how long before one of the Agents, or himself, cracks and makes some sort of wise-ass remark acknowledging what is, in fact, happening, and he realizes that though extending this painful slow-chew until its breaking point may be considered fun and funny in some circles, his is not one of those circles and these days it is hard enough getting anyone in the greater D.C. area to take his various memos and psychological assessment papers seriously without adding purposeful tomfoolery to the mix. He swallows. No one mentions the chewing. He de-extends his finger and lowers his hand. No one speaks yet. He considers not speaking himself and seeing how long until someone does speak, but ultimately decides this too would only be an exercise in frivolity and decides against it. "And so?" he finally says.

Chapter Twelve

A kid has almost six bucks

IN LATE WINTER 1973, Frank Novinsky was conceived to a teenage Mother and a Father whose age was never disclosed to the Mother but suffice it to say the man, Frank's biological Father, was much, much older than Frank's Mother. It was a one-time deal, the affair. It was just some acting out in order to gain some kind of sense of control in response to the parents who raised her overly strict and no one was ever supposed to know, but, of course, she would always know, and that was the whole point because that knowledge was supposed to sustain her for the four remaining years that she was to have to live with her parents. She was fourteen but it was different back then. Things didn't feel so loose, or free, and there were fewer ways for independent-minded young girls to escape into themselves.

She met the man, Frank's biological Father, at a gas station in Antigo, WI. She was there by herself, as was her custom, as her parent's strict nature didn't lend itself to her having many friends, and the friends she did have weren't really her friends, but rather acquaintances from the twice-weekly Bible Study she attended alone on Wednesdays and Sundays. The upshot to the Bible Study was that she was allowed to walk (actually required, as her parents thought the walking provided time necessary for quiet reflection upon the material that was studied that day) the six miles to and from the Bible Study, which just so happened to take her past the Krist Food Mart Gas Station and Truck Stop. Most Wednesdays and Sundays she didn't stop as she never had any money as her parents didn't believe in children, even fourteen-year-old children, being allowed to possess any money of their own. But sometimes the Youth Pastor (a younger gentleman) would give Frank's Mother twenty-five or fifty cents to help put away the folding chairs and sweep the floors. Sometimes he gave her a dollar if she hung around and made the coffee for the weekly meeting of drunks who came an hour after Bible Study broke up and met in the basement. She didn't always have time for that, however. Frank's Mother would save her money in a coffee tin that she kept hidden in the back of the storage shed her Father had built out back on their property. On the day she met Frank's Father, she had five dollars and seventy-five cents.

A happy home is found

Frank grew up in Greendale, WI, a suburb of Milwaukee, and he was raised by a nice Jewish family and attended Lake Park Synagogue where he had his Bar Mitzvah in 1986. His Mother was a slight woman named Mitzi Novinsky and his Father was a giant of a man named Howard, and they loved Frank with all that they had.

Frank Novinsky had come to them without a name before he was even four months old. The nurses and caretakers at the place where he was staying called him Blue Boy, for his eyes. Howard Novinsky had lost his testicles to a rather extreme case of testicular cancer and was thus rendered sterile. He was thirty-five when this happened, and Mitzi was only twenty-five. They both had wanted children and were only married six months when Howard was diagnosed, and for a long time, they accepted their fate. Ten years later, Mitzi brought up adoption to Howard and he surprised even himself when he found that he was quite open to the idea. They filled out the paperwork and they waited.

It took an additional three years before Frank was brought into their lives, and by that time, they had expended so much time and effort and resources in the endeavor of becoming parents that they considered Frank to be theirs in everything including blood. He was a Novinsky, and he was going to be raised a Novinsky. He was never supposed to know. It was easier back then to hide things.

Yeah, but it was still predatory, regardless

The man, Frank's Father, was sitting in an idling truck, its bed full of lumber and his left hand dangling from the driver's side window as he puffed on an unfiltered cigarette and listened to the radio. She, Frank's Mother, didn't see him when she went into the Krist Food Mart Gas Station and Truck Stop, but she smelled his Lucky Strikes. He, however, saw her and he waited and he tuned his radio to the country station and he lit another Lucky after he'd finished the first and he rubbed at his 5'oclock-shadowed chin as he waited for her to come out again. She, Frank's Mother, was wearing tomboy jeans and a baggy gray sweatshirt, and a pair of off-brand tennis shoes that some of the other girls at school teased her for. She looked plain to him, simple. Something told him she might be slow. (Though he would come to understand she was anything but.) His presumption could be forgiven, however, on account of the fact that unless a person actually spoke to her, she did come off as extremely aloof and off somewhere completely else.

She came out of the Krist Food Mart sipping at a bottle of Coke with a striped straw sticking from its top — an indulgence her Father would have beat her for. He watched her cut through the parking lot and fired his engine and the lumber in the bed of his truck rattled and thunked together and made that particular clapping sound that wood makes when it strikes other wood. This wood was destined to become custom chairs and bedframes. He put his truck in reverse and he backed out, then he sort of let it idle in drive and roll forward while applying no pressure from his foot to the gas pedal. The foot hovered just above the gas pedal very deliberately and with great concentration, not making contact. It would've been easier if he'd just set his foot on the floorboards in front of the pedal, but that would require less focus and thus he'd be forced to think about what he was about to say instead of just saying it. What he was about to say needed to sound as casual as possible. It needed to not come across as dangerous. He needed to not think about this part.

She walked slowly, he saw, the man, Frank's Father. And he couldn't help himself but think that she was *actually* waiting for him to say what he had decided he was going to say. That she wanted him to say what he was going to say. He'd seen her kind before. Slow and innocent, but only up to the point where he says what he says and they trust and they go with him, and then the whole other side of *them* comes out and he gets to do what he likes to do and everyone gets a happy afternoon indeed. Slow girls scare as easy as they convince, though, he knew, this man, Frank's Father. Care must be taken. He rolled alongside her and hung his Lucky'd hand from the window and said, "Where you heading?" just as casually and smooth and innocuous as if he was saying "hot one today, huh," like he didn't care if she responded or not. He applied some pressure on the brakes and his truck stopped rolling.

"Home," she said, Frank's Mother.

"Where's home?"

"Does that really matter, Mister?"

"If you want a ride, I suppose it might."

"Now why would a reputable man of distinction in town, and business owner, concern yourself with giving girls rides home in the middle of the week? Don't you have other business that needs your attention?"

"Sorry, I didn't mean to offend you, I'll just be on my way."

"You took the time to wait, and you obviously wanted to give me a ride for a reason, and you've already opened yourself up here, so now why would you be cutting bait that quickly if all you want is to offer a poor girl a ride?"

"Listen . . ."

"Leanne."

"Listen, Leanne, I don't want you getting this mixed up here and spreading any rumors that something happened here that didn't happen, this is a small community."

"I'm not mixed up, Mister."

"Well, you seem to be inferring something about my character, and I don't think you fully understand the potential ramifications if you went and spread it around that I tried something here that I most certainly did not try."

"What am I inferring, Mister, about your character, that is."

"Well, I'm sorry to say, I think you are inferring that I am attempting something untoward here, when the reality is, I've seen you walking all over this town, for years now, since you were just a little girl, and it just seemed like the Christian thing would be to offer you a lift. Like it would be the charitable thing to do. Give unto others and all."

"So you're just being a good and morally upright citizen. Nothing untoward will happen if I get in that truck with you?"

"Well Leanne, now I'm not so sure I should give you a ride. You seem to be the kind who makes mountains where there are but molehills, and I just don't think I can risk you telling tales on me. My family goes back a way here and people love to gossip."

"Your family and my family go back the same way, Mister, and now that you are rescinding your offer of a ride because I showed some reservation at getting in a truck with a man I know of, but do not know, makes you seem more than just a little suspect. More than just a little dangerous."

"Suspect?"

"Yeah, a little, but also dangerous."

"Look, kid . . ."

"So now you acknowledge that I am a kid? That's a start."

"What?"

"It's a start, your acknowledgment of the situation."

"Wait, I haven't acknowledged anything."

"That's a shame, we were just making progress."

"Look, kid, I got a family, a wife and child of my own, and I don't think I like all that you are implying here."

"You think if your wife and your son knew that we were having this conversation they'd think something less than reputable was going on, something untoward."

"I think by the way this conversation has unfolded that you are trying to turn my good deed for the day on its head and imply that I am trying to do something that I am not with you."

"With a kid?"

"No, not a kid, a teenager."

"So, it's teenagers that do it for you. Good, we are getting closer to the thing then."

"What thing?"

"The thing where you tell me what it is that you are doing here, right now, and you admit it to me, and we go from there."

"Go where?"

"Anywhere you'd like, Mister."

A very lovely day was had by almost all

On the occasion of Frank's Bar Mitzvah, he was nervous and anxious and he thought that he may just vomit as he read his Torah portion, but he didn't. His parents were very proud of him. Howard, in particular, was the kind of proud Frank assumed people made up feeling. The kind of proud that a person bursts with. He was the kind of proud that compelled him to say to everyone with which he shook hands that day, "Did you see my boy up there? Huh? I don't think another boy has done so well up there!" and the people he shook hands with were compelled to agree whether they believed it or not because Howard was so emphatic and effusive in his pride for his son, Frank. Frank, on the other hand, felt no pride whatsoever in the performance of his Torah portion, believing that he'd done a poor job and that he'd flubbed at least three of the words and that Howard and Mitzi must be so embarrassed, and that they were both only being so emphatic and effusive because they were covering for their embarrassment. It was a real shitshow, and everyone was just being transparent and false in a way Frank always thought he could spot a mile away, and he couldn't be convinced otherwise by any of the compliments he received after his reading. He told no one that he was feeling like a failure. He just accepted the fact that he knew that they thought he was a failure and that everyone was too polite to shove his failure directly in his face, but that they would all be talking behind his back about his horrendous reading at their homes, later, when they were alone with their wives or husbands, and probably in earshot of their children, Frank's friends, and could speak freely.

Frank watched his Father shake hands and smile and throw his head back and laugh and generally be very convincing that he was not mortified, and as Frank approached his Father, he could feel the fraud and the falseness radiating his way. His Father clapped him on the shoulder and pulled him in for a tight embrace, and his Father said to him, in his ear, real close so no one else could even have the remote possibility of hearing and thus there was to Frank's way of thinking no performative aspect to this moment, "I am so proud of you, son. You made us so proud and we love you very much." Frank thought it was a nice touch designed to reassure him *because* he'd done such a terrible job and not a true statement of fact, nothing more. "Thanks, Pop," Frank whispered back.

The party that followed was like the party that follows all of these things. There was family, and drinking, and food, and dancing and Frank was surprised to find that he could, if he tried really hard, enjoy himself and relax. Part of what helped him enjoy and relax was that he had a cousin named Bernard Cohen who was twenty and attended UWM and snuck Frank his first proper drink. The reception hall was a one-story affair with tables arranged throughout its middle and a carved-out space for a 15x15 dance floor and bars on both sides of the large room, and a DJ booth where a guy played records somewhere in the far left of the space. Bernard didn't dress up for the occasion, and he was absent at Temple, and he showed up late to the reception. Frank wanted what Bernard had, a seemingly nonchalant way of just being. What Frank was unaware of was the great effort it took Bernard to appear nonchalant, so, to Frank, it just seemed like his cousin was really, really comfortable with himself. Which, of course, no one is. No one can be if we are all being honest.

Frank left the dance floor when he saw his cousin arrive and he tried to walk toward Bernard without seeming like he was walking toward Bernard, and he allowed himself to be stopped several times by Aunts and Uncles and friends of Aunts and Uncles to be congratulated, and in some cases, to have $18 pressed into the palm of his hand with a knowing wink. By the time he made it to the bar from where Bernard hadn't moved, his pockets were full and bulging. Bernard said, "Hey, congrats," and Frank said, "Thanks, man." And then Bernard said, "Follow me a second" and Frank totally did. Bernard was holding two Jack Daniels and Cokes and led Frank to a side door that led out back to a small alleyway where the deliveries were made on Mondays and Thursdays for the regular dinners the hall hosted for the near South Side Polish Super Club Set. He handed Frank one of the drinks and he said, "Finish it quick before anyone sees," and Frank totally did. He felt warm and he felt comfortable and he felt relaxed after that, but surprisingly, even with all that, and the fact that it felt like a psychic weight had been lifted off his brain's chest, he was not compelled to ask Bernard to procure him another drink; he did, however, bum a smoke off his cousin and that did trigger in him an obsessive desire for another.

"Everyone in there's telling you about how you're a man now, huh?"

"Yeah, pretty much."

"You know that's all bullshit, right?"

"I mean, I dig the tradition of it, but like, yeah, I know it's all horseshit."

"You're not a man, you know. Hell, I'm not a man."

"What's that even mean? Being a man?"

"I'm not talking some philosophical what's a man anyway? B.S., I'm talking about the expectation and trust thing. We aren't men in *their* eyes, you follow?"

"Not really."

"Like they don't trust us with anything. They don't believe we are capable of taking on the tough stuff without freaking out and breaking down. They say they love us, say we are family, but they keep us out of the important shit, you know?"

"I guess."

"No man, you really don't know."

"Well then, Bernie, why don't you just tell me what I don't know?"

"Can't."

"You can't?"

"Right."

"Then what the fuck was the point of this talk?"

"Look, like my Dad, your Uncle, he's like a prick, right? Everyone knows that. But, he's also like a rich prick so people let the being a prick thing slide on account of the being a rich prick thing. Follow? Anyway, and he wants me to do this college thing and then come to work for him and I'll like be a rich prick too. But the thing is, and he knows that I feel this way so I'm not like talking completely out of line here, but the thing is, he won't tell me certain things about his business. Import/Export and Textiles is all he'll say.

Like, okay Dad, you Import/Export and are in textiles. Like, okay. But what's with the late-night meetings? What's with the weekends when you go back East, or to Florida? Like, we all see this. We all kind of know. But, like, he won't shoot straight. And I'm supposed to like come in with him on his Import/Export whatever after I get my Law Degree. Yeah, I said it Frank, my *Law Degree*. He said that was like a prerequisite for me coming into the business. Said I'd be a rich prick just like him and that he'd have a lawyer in The Family that he knows and can trust and yadda, yadda, yadda. Anyway, I'm what, now just supposed to like go on faith? Make this huge commitment and go to UWM and major in something that will look good to UW Law and then what, like eschew working in some like fancy-fuck firm in Madison to go do legal work for my rich prick Dad's Import/Export/Textile business without any of the particulars that everyone just knows has to be there? Like, Frank, would you go into a situation like that, without being fully trusted with the particulars?"

"I don't know Bernie. I've felt like I don't know any particulars either. But that's just life, I think."

"Buddy, you really don't know any of the particulars."

"What's that mean?"

"I can't man, my rich prick Dad would kill me."

"What?"

"Look, this doesn't change anything, okay."

"What?"

"Say that you understand that this doesn't change anything."

"I understand."

"What do you understand?"

"That this doesn't change anything."

"Okay. So here it is man. And like don't fuck me on this, okay. Just like internalize what I am about to tell you and like store it away for later and like confront Howard and Mitzi in your own time with it and like tell them you found out some like other way, okay?"

"What?!"

"Frank, like, you're adopted, and your Mother was some shiksa slut from like the North Woods. That's all I'm gonna say."

Birth and death and exile in Minnesota

Leanne didn't begin to show until somewhere around the five-month mark because she was slight and wore loose-fitting clothes but then it all became so apparent and obvious, and her Father beat her with a belt until she curled up into a ball on their family's home's living room's floor, and then he beat her some more. After that, he took her to a religious home in Minnesota that dealt with girls like her, shames to their families, and left her there. She mostly stayed in bed for the remainder of her pregnancy with Frank, only leaving it to eat in the communal dining hall with the nuns and the handful of other girls who'd gotten themselves in trouble. Her Father told her when he dropped her off that she was to have the baby at the home for sluts, and that if he found out she managed to escape the home for sluts and terminated the pregnancy, or decided to not give up the bastard-child after it was born, that he'd leave her to fend for herself and never speak to her again. Leanne Rachel Schultz gave birth to Baby Boy Blue on November the 2nd 1973, in a home for unwed Mothers in Minneapolis, MN, and immediately turned him over to the care of the nuns there, and then phoned her Father who told her that he would be coming around to collect her in three days. When the day came, Leanne packed her small suitcase and waited in the foyer of the home for unwed Mothers, and was left standing there for six and a half hours for a Father who never came. She walked out the door into a cold Minneapolis afternoon and was never seen in Antigo, WI, ever again. Leanne's Father came to the house for unwed Mothers a week later and asked if the product of his daughter's shame had been placed in a good Christian home; the nuns informed him that he'd been placed but that the specifics were, unfortunately, sealed. His daughter had requested it be that way — to protect all parties involved.

Late on Christmas Eve, 2009, Leanne Rachel Schultz felt a shudder so intense and so deep that it stopped her dead in her tracks as she carried eggnog and cookies to her family who were awaiting them as they sat huddled on a couch in front of a fire in a home in suburban Minneapolis. The shudder was not temporary and it grew in intensity as the moments stretched on before her. She felt her brain hemorrhage, actually felt it when it happened, and she dropped the tray of cookies and eggnog, and her family, whom she loved so much, rushed to her, and her husband of thirty years held her as she died. Her last word was Blue.

Excerpted from Interpersonal Interrogation and Statement Aggregation of one Molly Abigail Duch: ??/??/????

TB: "We're going to talk about Frank, Molly."

MAD: ".........."

TB: "It's time to confront what you did that day; how it has affected the rest of the world. It's unhealthy to sit here, internalizing, forever, never letting go, never finding your own deeper meaning and truth. It's not only unhelpful but also quite counterproductive. You can't just keep it all tucked away in your mind, thinking on it, ruminating on Jed, and Baker, and Jesse. And especially not on Helen. None of it is healthy for you, and, in the end, all we want is for you to be happy and healthy. We feel it's in that state that we can unlock all that is going on, up there. You have a gift, a true and provable and observable gift, and that is a rare thing. The rarest of things. Everything else pulls you away from your purpose, your true calling, it pulls you away from you and what your mind can do, what it can accomplish and achieve, it pulls you away from our work. Our most important work."

MAD: ".........."

TB: "I know. Look, I, more than most, and I would wager my whole buffalo head nickel collection on this next statement, know what you are saying, and can empathize and feel your struggle as you feel it, I know what this is like for you, in there, that head of yours, but I know that you know that it's not as simple as bringing him here, you know that I know that you can feel that as truth. There is a point where you are just tilting at windmills and putting off the inevitable and faffing about with the things and people who, truly, no longer matter to the universe. Plus, and also, I know you know that you can't just expect him to come in from the cold and be the same guy that you knew and connected with all those years ago, too much time has passed. He hasn't exactly changed, you are right there, but he is not the same, either. He's fragile. More so now. And we, well I, am concerned at what it might do to you to be in the presence of a mind such as his, at this most crucial moment for our work together."

MAD: "..........."

TB: "That may be so, and I am really tempted to let you make the attempt, to try, but I can't also help but think that it is my indulging you your flights of fancy that have led us to this place we are at, this impasse. We are so close, and you have done so much, already, but that last hurdle, no, that last bridge across that last and great yawning chasm, it is long, and it still stands before us, waiting, toes on the precipice of greatness, and what's more, we are ready, you are ready. You can show Them all what's possible, what the mind can endure and do, what being made stronger by what does not kill actually looks like. And also, I'm afraid bringing Jesse to you just makes no sense, for him, I mean. Truth be told, and I haven't sent anyone to confirm this, but he probably doesn't even remember you, those moments you shared, and how it made you feel, how special it was, that sort of thing is just not in his nature, and I think you know that. We can't risk it, besides."

MAD: "..........."

TB: "Rage is good, I think, this is a good emotion for you to be expressing right now. So you can throw all the fits you want, Molly, and you can lose your shit at me and the FPPIB all you like, but that all doesn't change the fact that what you've done, what you've unleashed on this world, that bell can't be unrung and we need to talk about Frank . . . where he is, where you sent him . . . And how. We need to talk about how. The how is almost more important than the why, the how will tell us the why, I think. We need to know what Frank's purpose is, to you, internally, in your mind, and, we need to know what Frank will do, eventually. How all that emotion will manifest when the time comes and all the string is played out. We know he's out there for a reason, and I know that you know that reason. And I also know that you probably couldn't stop any of it, even if you wanted to, that's not the nature of your thing, but I do know that you know that we can aim it, guide it, minimize the fallout. And I know that you know that, to me, it would be a great favor if we could harness, and show, and prove."

MAD: "..........."

TB: "Don't give me that existential 'there is no how and there is no why and there is no provable reality,'

159

Molly. We both know that nature, even your nature, behaves on a set of laws and principles. You can color within those lines, and I know that you know that you can even warp those lines, bend them and color just beyond them, and then snap them back, the color remaining where you placed it, but the line returning, but, the lines themselves, still exist. You exist. I exist. We are time. We are space. We are proof of the universe's functionality. There are still rules, and where there are rules, there is order and sense, and you need to start helping me make sense of Christmas Eve 2009."

MAD: "..........."

TB: "I know the story. I know what they all say. I know what even Helen says. That's not the truth and we both know it. The truth never lies in the aggregate of memories collected, that's not how any of it works, the truth can't be gleaned, not ever, it's not that objective, it's not about finding the mean in a story, a circumstance, a remembrance, it's about feeling your way to the bone of the matter and intuiting where the center lies, where true north is, and, in this case, only you can know. Only you can tell. And I know that you know that I know and understand that whatever it was you did to all of them, not just Frank, is still being done to them, actively, as we speak. It's an ongoing process and one that I don't even think you know the end of, where it goes, or how it all plays out. Whatever you've done to Frank, it's obvious that it's a permanent state, still being done, but it also rippled out, that poor woman in Minneapolis. We need to talk about the how, Molly. You need to tell me how, and you need to learn how to control the severity of it."

MAD: "..........."

TB: "Of course she was your fault. Intentionally or not, your reach had consequences. That woman was a consequence, Molly, of your actions that night. That's real. And, I'm not here to say how you should feel about that or pass judgment on what happened. It's neither good nor bad. It just is, just a result of your thing that we record and catalog, but you must acknowledge your culpability in order to grasp what you have done."

MAD: "..........."

TB: "I'm not laying a mind trip at your feet. I'm talking about work, my work, our work, this place, and your role in defining what we are and how we move forward with our shared knowledge of what you are capable of, what you can do that no one else can do. You are anomalous, truly. A one of a kind. You are special in this arena. The one true and provable psychological/paranormal entity walking this earth. And I need you to do the work, Molly."

MAD: "..........."

TB: "That's absurd, there aren't any more, they aren't everywhere, people like you, and you have nothing to feel guilty about. It's just nature, your nature, like any other creature on God's Green. The skunk feels no shame at his stink nor does the rat at what it must do to survive. And that's just it, isn't it, in my entire tenure as The Director here, we've never come across someone like you, someone with your nature. Millions, no billions, spent and you are the only provable psychological/paranormal phenomena we've ever successfully documented. You are the reason we are not still just a big joke back in DC, openly mocked as a defense spending grift for corporations and contractors to fatten their pockets and remain fat and happy so when the time comes, we can shovel even more money their way to really defend us, providing the necessary tools, if the shit ever truly hits the fan, WW-wise. This guilt, I think it's in your head and I think it prevents you from replicating, and we need you to, eventually, replicate the phenomena. Moving things around is a parlor trick. We need you to remember what you did to Frank."

MAD: ".........."

TB: "Don't you threaten me, little miss."

Molly Duch's room swims at its edges and the floor is as waves are and The Bear can feel the soles of his shoes start to rock with the tide of it, and Molly's face warps and bends and she smiles, but only slightly, which unnerves The Bear, but he doesn't let this show on his face and he places both of his oversized hands on his thighs and he closes his eyes tight against the malformations and he breathes deeply and rides the whole experience out while Molly finishes her little trick while leaning against the gray, concrete wall of her room which no one refers to as a cell, but everyone knows that's exactly what it is and everyone also knows that as far as cells go this one would be particularly ineffective if Molly Duch ever decided to make good her escape. The Bear feels the room re-normalize and he opens his eyes and he knows that that was only a fraction of what she can do, since the pencil moved again on Christmas Eve Eve, 2009.

MAD: "..........."

TB: "I get it, I do. And I empathize greatly, more than anyone else could ever hope to empathize with a person such as yourself. We are not so different. I can feel around your edges, but I need you to fill in the rest. I need you to explain the whole, not just the sum of your parts."

MAD: "..........."

TB: "Yes, of course, I'll bring him. But Molly, I need you to understand that you may be extremely disappointed. He is himself, but more so, now. I need to warn you that certain things will not be tolerated."

MAD: "..........."

TB: "Calm down, obviously no one is threatening you, that would be ridiculous."

MAD: "..........."

TB: "I know."

MAD: "..........."

TB: "I know!"

MAD: "..........."

TB: "She'll come when she is ready. She walks by, you know."

MAD: "..........."

TB: "Now that's interesting, but don't tease, you are not willing to go there, not with her."

MAD: "..........."

TB: "I know."

MAD: "..........."

TB: "Well, if that's true, then Frank is an even bigger liability than we had initially thought. A threat still looms."

MAD: "..........."

TB: "Molly, c'mon. You can't know that he's dormant. You can't know that he won't activate, spaz out, and fuck the whole McGilla."

MAD: "..........."

TB: "I know."

MAD: "..........."

TB: "Tell me how."

MAD: "..........."

TB: "That's now, officially, an unacceptable answer."

MAD: "..........."

TB: "I honestly no longer believe you. And what's more, I can feel that you don't care what I believe, anymore."

MAD: "............"

TB: "This conversation is not over Molly."

MAD: "..........."

TB: "After you see him, then."

Chapter Thirteen

The world reacts to Baker Thomas

Verne Troyer Blues
Too Soon radio
478,935 views – 04/21/2018   SUBSCRIBE

Sean Harter   2 months ago
This is fucked up
ImortaljesusH 2 months ago
Lighten up Nancy! This is hilarious.
Logan f-bake   1 month ago
This guy should be fucking ashamed of himself, his Mother must
be proud
Killian red   2 days ago
In porr taste or no, the fucked up thing is that the guy can't fuck-
ing sing to save his life
Lumplumplump   2 days ago
The fucked up thing is your retarded ass cant spell
Killian red   2 days ago
*can't
Lumplumplump   2 days ago
Thanks Mom. True sign of someone with no argument, the gram-
mer correction
Killian red   2 days ago
*grammar

Lumplumplump   2 days ago

Fuck you

K-2   5 months ago

Whatever, he;s hot

Gordon L.J   2 months ago

Let the poor guy rest this is obscene

Lumplumplump   2 months ago

Your obscene, this is hilarious

Gordon L.J   2 months ago

*you're

Lumplumplump 2 months ago

Fuck you

Bo-diddlysquat   4 months ago

Can we talk about the actual song?

Rema-rem   4 months ago

Sure, it's not that great

Bo-diddlysquat   4 months ago

Agreed, but can't stop thinking about it, who comes up with this shit

Magahat2   5 months ago

Watching the snowflakes melt in the comment section, priceless, get a life assholes

HanYOLO   1 month ago

I can't wait to see who dies next

Lumplumplump   1 month ago

Me either

Bearbear   today

A can of MTN Dew raises all the stakes

Ronny123   today

Gotcha Big Guy

Bearbear   today

Holistic medicine is ineffective

Ronny123   today

Totally

Jack Friendly   1 month ago

Who the fuck is this guy?

So-so-so   1 month ago

There are ads running before this now! He monetized the channel! I hope another celebrity dies soon and this kid becomes like a billionaire! This world is the worst! I love it! All hail the suck!

Helen234   today

I hear ya

Killian red   6 months ago

God, I hate us

Homo-genius   6 months ago

It's like pomo performance art ---- how soon is too soon, hours after death is perfect!

Killian red   6 months ago

This is sick! You can't hide behind art to explain away trash----- sling your BS somewhere else

Homo-genius   6 months ago

You just don't get it

Hotnudehotnudehotnude   6 months ago

I can't believe what they let me do on my IG story ---- hit me up @squirtthot4you

Redpillredpillredpill   today

PIZZAGATE!!!!!!!!!!!   SAVE   THEKIDS!!!!!!!!!!   OPEN   YOUR EYES!!!!!!!!!!!!!!

Bearbear   today

Loud and clear. Doom. Retread the tires

Redpillredpillredpill   today

Done

Derek François   4 months ago

Musically, this isn't half bad. I like how you can tell that the artist put minimal thought into what he was producing and just sort of let the concept guide the work. It's not something that is easy to pull off, but when done well it can certainly be effective in making a salient point. I believe what this particular musician is trying to say is that the very nature of celebrity is the commodification of the individual as product to be sold and consumed and that that covenant that the celebrity makes with the public does not necessarily end upon the death of the celebrity and that even after death, we the public are still entitled to actively consume the product i.e. the celebrity. R.I.P Verne Troyer, may your spirit find a rest that you never knew in life. As for the song, the art, I think it is valid, but I have to wonder, if the artist keeps it up beyond this one celebrity death, will he then just be cashing in on the popularity of the concept and thus diluting his original intent with this piece? Honestly, I hope when the next celebrity death happens, we get silence from this channel, especially if it's a big name, think Depp or Pitt, however, say a real d-lister goes next, like a Troyer, I hope we do get another song. That, to me at least, would be a very interesting concept. Memorializing the bit-players and sad cases that Hollywood just throws away when they are no longer useful. Even Gary Coleman deserves his Candle in the Wind. Brava to the artist I say, a real intellectual conversation was started with this piece. Until next time, ciao, François.

Killian red   4 months ago

Fuck you, you French Fuck.

Dereck François   4 months ago

Real nice, asshole

John   2 weeks ago

They should really pull this channel or at least not allow advertising, this is ghoulish

Outer-limit   2 weeks ago

Agreed, but it's freedom of speech

John   2 weeks ago

Freedom of speech but that doesn't mean YouTube has to allow it

Outer-limit   2 weeks ago

That's slippery thinking toward fascism

John 2 weeks ago

Always with the Nazis

Outer-limit 2 weeks ago

Who said anything about fucking Nazis all I said was the censoring of speech we don't like should be considered carefully

John 2 weeks ago

You called me a fascist!

Outer-limit 2 weeks ago

I'm out

Lumplumplump 1 month ago

MAC MILLER!!!!!!!!!! New Jam Soon???????????

Killian red 1 month ago

Why no song?

Lumplumplump 1 month ago

Like you care

Magahat2 1 month ago

Three days and still no song, where is BakeBake

Lumplumplump 1 month ago

Hope he hasn't turned pussy, gave in to the cancel crowd

Magahat2 1 month ago

A week and nothing, fuck BakeBake

Lumplumplump 1 month ago

I'm worried.

Chapter Fourteen

Biggest deal of his career

THE SMELL OF FRESHLY LAID BLACKTOP in the new morning's hot summer sun offended his nose and upset his stomach. And his day hadn't even started yet — not really. They (whoever does this sort of work) had not painted the lines for the parking spaces yet, so it was going to be a free-for-all first-come-first-served kind of thing. At least it was going to be that way for those who are not like Michael A. Greene, who preferred to show up to work early and get his day organized and prepped before any real business could start (legally speaking). The blacktop went down overnight when the strip-mall parking lot was vacant. There had been a notice put up at the beginning of the week. It read:

NOTICE!
Blacktop Resurfacing – WED (8/11/10) – THURS (8/12/10)
Crews Work at Night
All Cars Must be Moved by 9:00 P.M. (Latest)
Cars May Return 6:30 A.M. (Earliest)
THANK YOU FOR YOUR COOPERATION!

It was a reasonable assumption that similar notices went to all the businesses that occupied The Morning Sun Strip Mall and that the resurfacing of the blacktop was some sort of forced maintenance thing that was now being required after some sort of city inspection, possibly triggered by a complaint about the sorry state the parking lot had been in going on five or six years because ownership fixed or maintained nothing without first receiving an official-type complaint and threat of fine or other sanction. Ownership is motivated most efficiently when threatened monetarily. Most people are motivated most efficiently when threatened monetarily. Michael knows this in his bones.

The occupants of The Morning Sun Strip Mall included: A8 China Buffet and Carry Out, Family Dollar, Roy's Old Gold, TGI Fridays, Table Top Game Shop, and Capitol Capital (Michael's place of business). None of the proprietors/managers of these businesses ever lodged a formal complaint with the city over the state of the Morning Sun Strip Mall parking lot, but they did complain to each other about it when they would cross paths at A8. But that was just so they'd have something to talk to each other about.

Michael was given a key to Capitol Capital by his supervisor and boss, Betty Von Trier. Betty had hired Michael three years ago and had let him do his own thing from the jump. For instance, Michael was supposed to arrive at work at 9:00 A.M to start organizing his call sheets, but this caused Michael anxiety and he would feel rushed and become flustered, and cranky, and his face would become red, and he'd feel embarrassed at his face becoming red, which would make him sweat, and then he'd yell at the monitor of his computer for flickering, as it was old and to quote Betty "on its last legs." Michael had asked her, after only working at Capitol Capital for a couple of weeks, if he could have a key so he could come into work an hour (or so) early in order to organize his call sheets, thoroughly research his marks, tidy up his space for the day, and as a tradeoff for this consideration, he'd also get the coffee going and make sure the bathrooms were fully stocked with TP. She consented to the arrangement.

At 8:00 A.M. on 8/12/10, Michael opened the Capitol Capital office and he turned on the fluorescent tube lighting that lit the large bullpen which served as the call center. On the glass door of the Capitol Capital storefront (the space used to be a comic/trading card/coin store called Anything's Collectable) was stenciled the Capitol Capital logo, which was a rudimentary line drawing of the dome of the Wisconsin State Capitol with two dollar-signs (like these $$) laid over it in sun-faded green. It was an ugly logo. Just barely visible to the left of and in the middle of the Capitol Capital logo were the A and the C from the old Anything's Collectable sign. The lights flickered some, Michael swore under his breath, and then rushed to the men's room where he vomited up the breakfast he'd made at home. Afterward, he felt better which confirmed his suspicion that the nausea was due to the smell in the parking lot and not the potato and egg scramble he had made himself in the only pan he had left to his name (Lodge twelve-inch black cast iron), or the horrendous hangover with which he awoke. He started the coffee in the large communal percolator and he went to his desk. He forgot to check the TP situation. The lady's room was, as a point of fact, out. His desk was organized from the night before, and the list of marks and relevant case files were laid out in the order in which Michael thought it best to make the phone calls; i.e., calling older men and women (aged 30-65) earlier in the morning and calling the young and irresponsible (18-30) sometime after 11:00 A.M. As far as systems go, his worked about as well as any—meaning, about average. His was a numbers game.

At 9:00 A.M., his day started (legally speaking). Yesterday he called a woman (aged twenty-four) at 2:30 P.M. at her place of employment, which was one of those twenty-four-hour gyms where she worked as a personal trainer earning a commission on every lesson given, and that was on top of her hourly pay of $15. She lived in an apartment that Michael knew to cost $1,250 a month, and like most everyone else in her cohort, she spent between $250 and $400 a month on going out to eat, drinking, marijuana/other recreational substances (cocaine and the like), coffee, and misc. entertainment. She had never once made a payment on the loan that her Father had cosigned with her when she began college. Student loan debtors are Michael's easiest marks. They are young, malleable, talk-to-able, and convincible. They don't think twice about putting a bunch of late payments on a credit card, and they are eager. Eager to keep their heads just above water and make the incessant calls stop. That and there is no bankruptcy for them to view as a potential way out. Michael, as a specialty, targeted outstanding student loan debts held by young women, most not yet twenty-five, but delinquent nonetheless.

This was especially true of young women who had had a parental co-signer. And if that cosigner was a Father, then according to Michael, "Just watch the fuck out because we're talking cake now, easy money, gold in the street money." When he called the young woman her employer answered, and it was explained (to the employer) that he was looking for the young woman in order to talk about "a personal matter," and that the faster this "personal matter" was settled the less need there would be for continued disruption during everyone's workday. Michael was put on hold, but not really on hold. The employer (male mid-forties by the sound of his voice) just covered the receiver with the palm of his hand, which was a thing males of a certain age did, believing that the person on the other end of the line could not hear what was being said and that a certain amount of privacy was afforded; however, this was rarely the case and the person on the other end can, more often than not, hear exactly what is being said, as was the case with Michael because he could hear the employer paging the young woman over the gym's intercom, which meant she was being pulled from a client, and then he could hear the employer say to the young woman, "Another one of these fucking calls comes through to this line and you're out on your tight little ass" which Michael thought was exceptionally rude, but advantageous to his own personal self. He had opened that conversation with the young woman in the following way: "So far, you're just over $11,000 behind and you need to settle this debt or you will not only be jeopardizing your financial future but your whole future in general, really." She did not respond, just breathing on the other end to let Michael know she was still there. He continued, "Don't you want to own a home? A car? Maybe even start your own fitness business?" Still no response, and it was becoming clear that the fiscal responsibility tact was not going to work here, so he switched it up and he asked her to imagine her future family life, to really picture it, to really visualize it, to imagine the conversations she would have to have. "Think about meeting someone, or think about marrying someone," he started in again. "How much are you planning on telling them about the debt you're carrying? Wouldn't it just be easier to start paying it down now, start rebuilding your credit score now, before those conversations have to happen, before you have to make excuses and try to convince a potential partner that you are worth it?" The young woman made a noise like the message was starting to get to her, starting to sink in, so he finished with the children, the ones he figured she was certainly planning on having. "And what about kids? How do you plan to save for their education, for their future, if you're still paying for your own? That's called the circle of poverty, and in the circle of poverty whole generations are lost, doomed, and damned to struggle. Plus, you don't want me calling this line again, do you?" Sometimes, that would work (most of the time it didn't, but as was discussed above, this game is mostly a numbers game, and the more lines you cast the more mouths you feed) and the young woman would give Michael her credit card number and he'd run it for $1,000, or if he was lucky, $2,000. It was never the whole late balance, only a bite at the edges. Since the day Michael was hired, he'd been praying (literally bent knee-type praying at night just before he laid head to pillow) that he would, eventually, call to collect unpaid credit card debt from someone he'd convinced to make a student loan payment on their American Express/Visa/Discover/Diner's Club/Capital One card. Yesterday, it didn't work and the young woman called him a motherfucker, and a sonofabitch, and a leech, and a real cock, and a sucker of cocks, and a parasitic capitalist zombie, and etc. and so on, and etc., and so on, and etc., and then she had hung the phone up with such ferocity and strength that it left his right ear ringing for some time.

Today, Michael would call the cosigner — The Father.

There is a rule, a law, and usually, it prohibits Michael from speaking to anyone (with any specificity) about the personal debt of anyone else, which is the reason for the whole thinly-veiled business about the "personal matter" when speaking to the young woman's employer. However, in the case of a young woman with a patriarchal co-signer, Michael could contact The Father. Speak with The Father. Reason with The Father. Guilt-trip The Father. The Father was responsible too. The Father who only wanted what was best. The Father who could wield disappointment and guilt and his own pocketbook (depths of aforementioned pocketbook still yet to be determined). In this game, it was Michael's experience that it was Fathers of daughters who were the easiest of easy marks — especially the ones who themselves have struggled and scraped.

Joe Callaghan worked as the foreman of a factory printing press that printed business forms for businesses which made far more money than Joe Callaghan's printing press business made. His daughter had studied English Literature at a good school. She'd planned to continue her studies to get her Master's and then her Ph.D., and then she had planned to become a professor, while at the same time continuing to write, publish, and work the creative angle, and she also had planned to work very hard in academia, getting tenure eventually, and then use the stability to take the pressure off of her artistic dreams. Both angles working to prop up the other to create stability for her passion. She'd planned to have three cats, zero boyfriends, and a nice apartment in which the second bedroom would be used as a study and personal library. Michael called Joe Callaghan at 9:35 A.M. at Genoa Business Forms in the town of Sycamore, Illinois, on the date of Thursday, August 12, 2010; their conversation was recorded as per company policy and went thusly:

"Yello," said Joe Callaghan as a way of greeting Michael Greene when Michael called the direct line he knew to be the office of Joe Callaghan. He was planning on leaving Joe a message, it being early in the day and Michael suspecting Joe would be about the morning business of making sure that the printing presses that printed business forms were up and running and the printing press operators that were running them were not too hungover to perform the task with some efficiency.

"Hello, sir, this is Michael A. Greene with Capitol Capital and I am very sorry to be bothering you at work, but I am afraid there is no other way. You see, we have been in contact with your daughter regarding her having missed all of her monthly payments on her student loan since leaving school, resulting in a net late balance of $11,579.98. With the interest accruing, I can assure you that this situation is not only very bad but is also quite untenable. She's doing real damage to her future, sir."

"Doreen's behind?" The question is asked rhetorically and with concern, "Every time I call, she says everything's fine, that she's fine, and not to worry."

"It's my experience that children, especially the older ones, tend to downplay the struggle and trouble they find themselves in, they tend to play-act at adulthood long before they actually achieve it, at least, that's the case with my eldest." Michael A. Greene had no children, he has no wife (at least, that's how it was beginning to look), and he certainly wasn't old enough to have a child the age of Doreen Callaghan.

"That they do."

"The question now is culpability, responsibility, and getting this thing back on track . . . once and for good."

"I know what you're saying, mister. I know what my signature on those pages means."

"Sir, I don't want to involve you more than I have to. I can tell you're the responsible sort. I can see your credit score and it can weather a hit, but sir, and I can't stress this enough, Doreen is looking at starting out way behind the eight-ball with falling this far back this early on."

"It was some man, some asshole, I think." He said it with an even kind of practiced anger. Not rage. But like resigned hate.

"Be that as it may, sir, we still need to figure this issue out. Get this put behind Doreen and yourself."

"Call back tomorrow, it'll take some doing, but I can take the cash from deferred comp, maybe a loan out against my pension and my IRA."

"Tomorrow? I have your word?"

"Tomorrow," said Joe Callaghan and hung up the phone.

These were middle-class people, Joe and his daughter, and he made a good living, nothing to write home about, but enough, and after the death of his wife, it was just him and Doreen (at home, when she wasn't among her friends, and no one else was around to hear, he called her Nory). He provided a good life for Nory but not as good as what could've been provided had a dual income home not been so cruelly and suddenly taken off the table when she was twelve. None of this was in Michael's file, just a notation that there was currently no Mrs. Callaghan.

Michael went to lunch at the A8 China Buffet and Carry Out at 12:00 P.M. Betty Von Trier sat alone at a table near the rear of the mostly full restaurant, and Michael thought she looked content and happy. He saw her seeing him as he walked in. He planned to order the Mongolian Beef Combo Special with Pork Fried Rice and two Crab Rangoon and then walk back to Capitol Capital and eat at his desk while he waited out the hour and possibly made some phone calls regarding his own ongoing personal matter. She, however, had other plans and waved him over to her table with a smile and a look that said 'Come, sit.' He came and he sat. "There," she said, "now, I don't look so alone."

"Never thought that was a big concern of yours."

"Moods you know, they shift and they turn. Sometimes I'm lonely and it doesn't bother me, sometimes I'm lonely and it does. Anyway, you look like you could use some interpersonal interaction, some honest-to-god exchanges with someone in the real, not over the phone."

"That bad, huh?"

"Not really."

They walked together to the buffet station and filled their plates with heaping mounds of rice and meats coagulating in various sauces — fried egg rolls and fried wontons, too, which were kind of limp. Michael placed his plate on their shared table and then went back and poured two cups of hot green tea from a communal carafe into small earthenware cups and brought them back and handed one to Betty. She took a small sip and her red matte lipstick smeared against the greens and browns of the cup. He wondered what her home life was like. He wondered if she had a boyfriend and if that boyfriend liked her shaved head or if he liked *her* enough so that the shaved head, and the tattoos, and the neo-goth clothing didn't much matter to him. Michael wondered if she had a girl-friend, maybe. She gave off the impression that she could have whatever she wanted because she knew what she was and she didn't particularly care what was said or thought about her. Michael was envious. She hadn't collected a single debt in her life, she just *was* the boss, and everyone seemed to think that that was just about as natural as the wind blowing hard in the fall or people getting sick and fucking tired of winter by late February. They ate.

"You ever heard the one about the bar with the jar of fifties?"

"Yeah, I think so, the old lady with the rotten tooth?"

"The dog has the rotten tooth! That's the whole joke!"

"Yeah, I remember, the punchline is 'now, where's this old lady with the rotten tooth,' and the dog got it in the end."

"Yeah."

"Yeah."

"I always liked that joke — it's about the importance of listening, I think."

"I suppose when you make a mistake that bad because of a simple miscommunication, the lesson *would be* to listen more."

"Something we should all remember, from time to time."

"Fair point."

"How are things?"

"Things?"

"Life, Michael, life, how's life?"

"One day, then another day, and another, you know how life is, we all *know* how life is."

"I suppose."

"I suppose too."

They finished their first plates and Betty said, "We should get our money's worth," and they loaded up another and another after that — Michael bringing them refills on their green tea each time until they both felt full and jittery in their guts. They walked back to Capitol Capital together, and Betty held the door for Michael and he made sure to thank her for holding the door and also for the company, and he admitted that he was indeed in need of some true-blue human interaction and that it had done him a world of good and that they should maybe do it again, maybe next week, if she was so inclined to repeat spending time in his company, and then without waiting for her answer he went back to his work-space and made twenty-seven additional fruitless calls before the day was through and he could go home.

The next day at 8:00 A.M. the lines, as promised, had gone down in the parking lot — all bright yellow and standing in stark contrast against the deep black of the surface of the lot. And the smell that had bothered Michael for most of the previous day was gone. The lot looked clean, organized, purposeful, and was, in fact, now, the best-looking thing about the Morning Sun Strip Mall. The rest of the strip mall now somehow looked worse, more depressing, more like a place people didn't *want* to visit but a place people *had* to visit because of their socio-economic status.

There were unofficial spots in the parking lot. Meaning, that the ones in front of any given business went to either those who worked in that business or the customers who patronized that business. This unofficial rule was more or less followed by the owners and employees of the businesses, but the customers really couldn't be controlled, and it is not only a matter of fact but also some kind of common knowledge, that unless there is a city regulatory code at the bottom of a sign in a parking lot (i.e., a handicap parking sign) the reality is that that sign holds no authority. So, the signs that said A8 Customer Parking Only were, as a matter of routine, ignored by customers of, say, Table Top Game Shop when the spots for Table Top Game Shop were taken and the spots for A8 China Buffet and Carry Out were the next closest alternative. The same went for the Capitol Capital spots when customers were in a pinch. This was another reason why Michael showed up when he did. At 8:00 A.M. the issue of not getting one of the four Capitol Capital spots right in front of the Capitol Capital door was not an issue that he regularly had to deal with. Of course, there were the times that patrons of the TGI Fridays got too drunk and called themselves cabs, and as a result, their cars were still in the lot come the A.M., and sometimes those cars were in the Capitol Capital spots, which irked Michael in a way that he could not really explain. That, however, was not the case the morning after the lines went down. The morning after the lines went down there was no one else in the Morning Sun Strip Mall parking lot. Everything was clean and everything was right and the payment he'd slipped the line painters at roughly 1:00 A.M. when sleep wouldn't take him and he'd gone for a city drive had, in fact, bought him exactly what he'd paid for. The spot next to where he always parked his car was now marked quite clearly with the abbreviation RSVD and the initials BVT. It was the spot directly in front of the Capitol Capital door.

At 9:05 A.M., Joe Callaghan was true to his word and Michael was genuinely surprised to be answering the phone this early in the day and hearing the voice of the raspy and tired-sounding middle-class Father on the line. The total amount from the missed payments and associated late fees and accrued interest on those missed payments was exactly $11,579.98. That number got things back to square one. The sum total of the outstanding balance of the student loan which Nory owed, and would still be responsible for after things were made square, was $62,579.98. That number was freedom. "We're going the full-boat," said Joe Callaghan without much preamble.

"Sir, of course, we can process that payment for you. And you should know, you've done a great thing for your daughter's future," Michael told Joe. "You should be proud of yourself." Joe had spent the rest of the previous day gathering paperwork and calling his financial institutions and, in the end, he pulled $57,000 out of his IRA. He wasn't allowed to touch his deferred comp, so he took the rest as a loan against his pension and property.

"I thought Nory had been doing good for a couple of years after college," said Joe after Michael gave him his payment confirmation number. "She was on her way, but she just couldn't keep up, I suppose."

"So few can."

That day nothing else mattered. The story of The Biggest Single Collection was all anyone wanted to talk about, and Michael told the story over and over. The setup, the rhetoric, the play-out, the finishing touches, and the pay-out. It was a little like when a golfer gets a hole-in-one and has to buy a round of drinks for everyone in the clubhouse, except Michael bought everyone's lunch at the A8 China Buffet and Carry Out and they all felt a little like *his* win was *their* win, too, like they had something worth celebrating, like when it came down to it, people like them were good, and good at what they did, and were worthy of being made to feel special.

After work at 5:00 P.M., Betty and Michael and Stu and Larry and Kent and Mary and Bob went to the TGI Fridays and Michael bought everyone a drink, and then another, and then another, and afterward, as they walked to their cars, Michael made to approach Betty but she spoke first. "You didn't have to treat all night," she said.

"Anyway, I was wondering, if, you know . . ."

"I'll see you tomorrow, Dylan's (ambiguous) waiting at the apartment. I should have never given them a key."

The radio remained off as he weaved home, and he did not replay how he'd played the "old man" in his head again. He just sat and thought the same thought until he arrived at his apartment, alone — she never mentioned the parking spot.

Two Weeks Later, Joe Callaghan called. It wasn't the first time. He'd ask to speak to Michael, but Michael wouldn't accept the call, and let the transfer go to his voicemail, and later he'd delete the messages without listening. Eventually, the receptionist was forced to say, "I am sorry, sir, but Michael A. Greene will not be accepting any calls from past debtors at this time. Our collectors are very busy and it is company policy to refer any grievances to corporate. If you have an issue with the way that Michael handled your daughter's account, you may wish to go to our website and print out our complimentary complaint form and mail it to our home office in Lexington, Kentucky, where it will be addressed in the order it is received. We do take these matters very seriously, so, I am sure you will receive a written response in no more than three business weeks."

"I just needed advice and he seemed so nice," said Joe. The IRS had sent him a letter informing him of their receipt of a 1099-R, addressing the amount of money withdrawn from his IRA before he'd reached the age of 59 ½ and informing him of the importance of adjusting his next year's tax filing. The letter contained words like adjusted gross income, penalty, and late fees for non-timely payment. "I just wanted to ask if he knew a way to navigate all this with the IRS . . . they're talking about money owed on my filing next year now. He seemed to know what he was talking about . . . you know . . . money-wise." The receptionist relayed the message to Michael. She noticed that thumbtacked above his desk was a Xeroxed copy of the $3,100 commission check he'd earned on what had come to be known in the office as The Callaghan Collection. "We've all got problems." He didn't look up from the papers on his desk when he said it, he just kept scanning, shuffling.

Ghostly wanderings

Walking the shoulder of an interstate is dangerous business under the right circumstances but it is almost suicidal during the rush. His thumb is not out to the rush, that is not what this is, he's both hurrying and not, he feels the steady stream of 70-90 MPH traffic, the wind generated by the autos breaking against his torso and his sun-cracked face. He can feel his age in his bones. He'd been walking since winter, and the going was slow for him, but not for lack of effort — he is ever forward. But he lost time occasionally, made to start over and double back without realizing it was happening. He could remember four times that he had to begin again, but he was absolutely certain that there were more, and each time he remembered a little more, but not enough . . . never enough. Fucking infuriating. He doesn't know exactly who he is, which is also maddening and frustrating. He feels like the traffic can't see him, and he wonders if he stepped out in front of a truck if it would end it all for him, or if the truck would drive straight through him. He would just begin again. God fucking damn it. Nothing is clear and every thought he has makes him angry. I-90 transitions to I-39 somewhere around Portage, WI, near Cascade Mountain Ski Resort. It's the furthest he's made it, and he can feel the tug backward, again. She is with him, always, lingering in his anger and hatred, but he has no idea who she is or what she wants. He feels like she won't let him get too far away from home base, not just yet, not while she's just a sense-memory to him, just an influence, but he also feels her compelling him onward. At this rate, he won't make Antigo, WI, for another eight years, though he has no way of knowing that. Time not only feels irrelevant to him, he no longer recognizes it as a valid concept. There is only the moving of his feet and the not moving of his feet. There is only traveling to Antigo, WI, and beginning to travel to Antigo, WI. One of his rough and calloused hands rubs at the left side of his throat and it feels smoother than it did the last time. Like nothing much ever happened there, to that spot of flesh, and he doesn't know how that could be, how whatever happened to him happened to him, and the thought of it makes him angry, so shakingly and viscerally angry. He walks the I-39 exit backward, facing the traffic, glowering at the visible faces of drivers and passengers there through the windshields of the slower-moving vehicles, but this is more like a merging exit so the traffic doesn't slow that much, and horns blare, and he thought he could feel he was about to be called in to begin again, and again, this made him very angry. He's not made to begin again. 156 miles he is yet to walk. Eight years' time, if he still considered time.

On the shoulder of I-39, he does not think about raising his thumb because he does not wish to feel anger. Without wanting to, he begins considering whether or not he has felt any other feelings besides anger since he can recall beginning feeling feelings again, and he concludes that he has not, and then he feels anger, again, and considers whether or not it was the thought involved in the considering that made him feel the anger, or if it was the conclusion that he's felt nothing but anger since he could feel again, and then subsequently concluded that he actually can feel nothing but anger, all of which makes him very angry, indeed. He stares blankly at the road and the thoughts and anger fade. Left foot then right foot then left foot then right.

While the skin on his face has gone through hell in the months (how many is completely unclear to him) he has been at it, showing the wear of both being chapped by cold in the winter and burned by the sun in the summer, the clothes and shoes he wears remain unchanged from the day that he put them on. He is not aware of this fact. He is also unaware that he, himself, even dressed himself in the clothes that he is wearing.

He no longer conceives of himself as a being who has ever done anything but walk to unknown ends and purposes. And a being who has another being inside, talking only sometimes. He knows only the road on which he walks, and starting over on the screened-in porch in Madison, WI, and anger. Anger. He now hears the word being spoken inside his head as if it were being spoken outside of his head, which means it technically isn't a thought, so the word being spoken inside of his head, ironically, doesn't make him feel the feeling of anger. It's just a word repeating in his midbrain, in a mind's voice that isn't his mind's voice, as if placed there on a recorded loop. The repeating of the word is not bothersome to him, but soothing, calming somehow, and he can left foot right foot for some miles without a single thought entering his brain — just anger, anger, anger, anger, anger.

Somewhere near Portage, WI, he thinks his own thoughts again. He thinks about how the road's material crumbles so easily, once broken apart from the whole. It seemingly so wants to become gravel again. How it is strong only as long as it remains connected to the rest of its body, and so weak when it fragments and chips. He thinks of how if he picks up even a large chunk of road, one that he'd have no business being able to lift, and he hurls it at oncoming traffic, both the large chunk of road and the windshield of the car it strikes, will shatter. How even if he picks up an even larger chunk of road, one so large that it could just be considered the road itself, and he drops it from just over hip height, it will break into thousands and thousands of smaller chunks of road. He thinks about this. About how the infrastructure meant to sustain community and civilization is tenuous at best, and of course, this angers him a great deal. This angers him to the point of blind rage and red-faced mumbling to himself. Crazy half words out of his mouth's corner, inaudible to all but only the closest to him, which of course there are none. He backtracks, but only thirteen or so steps. His feet stomp as he walks at the very edge of the road, where the construct is most vulnerable, attempting to break chunks off the side of the rural highway for him to hurl into oncoming traffic. He's activated. The primary objective becoming clear on the path to Antigo, WI. His mind runs away with him, and the pervasive mid-brain repetition is there but drowned almost completely out by his own mind's voice's violence, and his anger intensifies past all left foot right foot functionality, and he wants to now not only hurl the larger and larger chunks of the road into traffic, but also himself, and then he's doing it, too, picking up the road, just the little pieces that are already fragmented from the whole, and he is throwing them wildly, shouting becoming louder, but no more intelligible. Then he finds a traffic cone and he throws that too. Anger, spiraling. Uncontrolled. He picks up a large chunk of road and it is heavy but it does not feel that way to him. Then he is running, full-bore, against traffic, legs moving faster and faster, torso having so much trouble keeping pace, and he feels he will fall on his face, flat, and that pisses him off. Then a car is coming and he is not stopping. He is lifting the road and he is throwing the road. Then he feels her. Really feels her.

He is on the back porch of an apartment on Madison's west side and he is stepping through the porch's screen door and he is walking down a driveway, and then he is turning left onto the road in front of the apartment, which is a house that has been converted into two flats, and he begins walking, and he thinks nothing and so he feels nothing. Frank Novinsky is going to Antigo, WI.

A hack is born

Kevin O'Leary rang his phone just as he was about to leave his Mother's home and head in for the first of what was supposed to be a series of interviews at EPIC Systems' hodge-podge headquarters in Verona, WI. He was looking forward to the interview because it was the first real lead he had had on a job in three months, but also because the EPIC campus was legendary for its absurdity. There were buildings resembling magic castles and others resembling barns. There were treehouses for lounging and buildings with slides between floors. There were recreations of famous city streets and a sculpture of a wizard in a courtyard. It was a silly place, but he'd heard also a very serious place as well. "Judy's crazy," a friend had warned him, referring to the company's founder and CEO. "She's built herself a playground where she can pay people extremely well but also likes to work them to death." His phone rang as his car idled in the driveway and he thought about not answering it. It had been over a year.

"Hello?"

"Kid, we got something for you. You interested?"

"What is it?"

"Look, kid, I'm not gonna blow smoke up your backside, one of our incumbents is a real lazy piece of shit and we need to hold his seat if we are going to have a shot at holding the State Assembly. He's demanding staff up there, and we got no one to send him. So, I says to the ADCC (Assembly Democratic Campaign Committee) director, I says, I got a guy who'd be perfect, so don't make an asshole out of me, okay."

"Where?"

"Baraboo, Portage, a little south of The Dells, and the other little dinky towns around there. Not Reedsburg though, that's some other asshole."

"Kevin, look, I got this interview today. It's a good job, money-wise."

"Where?"

"EPIC."

"Kid, look, and like I'm not gonna tell you how to live your life, but Judy is fucking nuts, and in three years, tops, you'll be burnt out and on the verge of a nervous breakdown. Do what you want, but at least working a State Assembly race you'll only have to work hundred-hour weeks for four months, not four years. And I can't promise anything, but you bring this home for them and there is literally no way that anyone in Madison forgets it. Your ass will be warming a seat in The Capitol before you know it. And, as a bonus, you won't have to spend your whole life traveling for fucking EPIC. And look, and I don't want to have to push the hard sell on you, but you'd be doing me a huge favor, and you'd have an ask coming your way kid. Plus, and, don't forget, you'd be doing your state a huge service, like for its future. If we lose this seat, we're fucked on redistricting next year, which means we're fucked for a decade. But, like I said, I'm not here to tell you how to live your life or what kind of person to be."

"How much does it pay?"

"Kid, not nearly enough."

Baraboo, WI's downtown is a large square with the County Courthouse taking up its most northern edge and mostly bars and restaurants lining the other streets which make up the square's other lines. Jed was told that he should not rent the cheap month-to-month he found right on the downtown square, and should instead allow Kevin and The ADCC to set him up in free supporter housing. Free is always better, they had said. The house he ended up staying at was an old farmhouse somewhere out in the deep country between Baraboo and Portage, and The Man he stayed with was without a wife because his Bride had left for the summer to go watch her Mother die somewhere in Kansas. On his first night at the farmhouse, The Man offered Jed some whiskey and Jed declined and explained that he was newly sober; to which The Man remarked, "You either picked the wrong time to start working in politics or the wrong time to quit drinking, not sure which." Jed liked The Man very, very much. The Man was in his sixties, with gray hair worn as most former hippies who never quite gave up the old counter-culture do, and a long gray beard, and he exclusively wore jeans and white T-shirts, and he would spend his days using an ancient backhoe to move giant rocks with which he was trying to construct a sort of natural back porch before his Bride returned after the Bride's Mother did, eventually, die. He'd already constructed two rocking chairs out of salvaged wood for them to sit in on the porch and watch the evening's sunsets over the bluff which their large yard had a particularly good view of. For now, though, The Man settled for sitting in those chairs with Jed and smoking Kool cigarettes instead of drinking. And Jed couldn't help but think that Kevin O'Leary and Jed's employers at The ADCC were right, free is always better.

He worked his days in a chicken coop that had been converted into a home office on the edge of the property owned by State Representative Glen Clarkson. Jed wasn't allowed inside the home of Rep. Clarkson, and the chicken coop's only facilities were a composting toilet in which Jed had to throw handfuls of sawdust after he shat, and then spin a lever that activated the toilet's tumbler. It was awful. There was other staff working other races who worked out of the Democratic Party Regional Office in Portage, WI, but Jed wasn't allowed any space to work in that office because Rep. Glen Clarkson refused to pay the dues required for that, so Jed worked out of the chicken coop, because, it was, after all, free.

She volunteered on the weekends at the party office that Jed was not allowed to work out of, and that ended up being a good thing because most of the other campaign staff working out of that storefront spent the majority of their off-time drinking, and by late-October Jed had still somehow remained sober. She wasn't sober. He'd found a home group over the summer, and a local sponsor, and he worked his steps and he did exactly what they told him to do, which included avoiding starting any kind of romantic relationship with anyone. Her name was Sophia Ahrens. Every couple of weeks Jed would drop off Glen Clarkson yard signs at the party office in Portage, WI, for them to give to anyone who wanted one; he came on Mondays; she worked every Saturday and Sunday; they didn't meet until October 27th, 2010. When they did meet, Jed had been sober for ten months and three days. She was married but the relationship was ugly, and she had had an incident of a domestic nature recently, which had involved law enforcement. When she arrived home Wednesday last, she found her husband in a kind of super-charged and energetic stupor that she believed to be induced by a whole lot of cocaine and rye whiskey. The two children they had together cried in a locked bedroom upstairs. "Brian, what the actual fuck?" she had asked knowing what the fuck actually was as this was not the first time she'd walked in on him like this. It was, however, the first time that she'd walked in on him like that with their children still awake and having been attempted to be made to fall asleep early so that Brian Ahrens could indulge in his only two loves. When he attempted to explain himself, he said, "What, they just woke up when they heard you come in all loud like that," and she grabbed the little cross that dangled from his left earlobe and she tore it out of his head, and she felt the warm blood drip down her clenched knuckles, and she felt good and happy, and then she took that balled fist of hers, the one clenching the earring, and she punched Brian Ahrens as hard as she could right in his right eye. Unfortunately, she had forgotten about the cross that her fist clenched, the cross-beam of which poked through between the knuckles of her index and middle fingers, so when she punched Brian Ahrens in his eye as hard as she could, the cross, on which hung Jesus, punctured his right eyeball, shooting blood and eyeball juice all over their living room floor. The cops came and took Brian Ahrens to the hospital and told the couple they'd have to be separated for the night and that charges would likely follow for both of them, though now, she was unsure of when she'd be charged or what she could get them to plead her down to. She told Jed all of this on the first day they met. She was open like that. Jed didn't tell her he was sober, or that his sponsor advised against romantic relationships, or that there was a man who recently copped to a relapse, stumbling into his local AA group with both a bandaged ear and an eye-patched right eye. He handed her the yard signs on Wednesday, October 27th, 2010. Neither of them was adhering to their normal routines. She greeted him thusly: "Well, look at you," and he looked her up and down without thinking about how he appeared to her. She stood up and crossed in front of the little folding table that the Regional Democratic Party Office used as a reception desk and she walked over to him and she gave him a long and thoughtful hug that lasted a tad too long, but he felt, for the first time in a very long time, something. That was how they met and fell in love.

"Jed," said Jed and set down his Glen Clarkson signs.

"My shift ends at 1:00, pick me up then."

"Okay."

Over dinner, at her place, she told him the story of how Brian used to be and how they came to have two kids together before they married. She told him how she married him only after he had two years of sober time, and how he relapsed on the honeymoon. "That was four years ago," she'd said, "things have been escalating since." He told her about high school and his DUI and the lake of blood with a man's face-shaped shoreline. He also broke Tradition and told her Brian was back in AA, and that he seemed sincere and he had shared that he thought he had everything that he'd gotten from her coming to him, and that he didn't press charges but the DA seemed like he was going to anyway, and that Brian had been calling the DA and imploring the DA not to, telling the DA that, "She's a great Mother and woman who's put up with a lot and she deserves to be free of this and me." Sophia Ahrens listened to Jed talk up her husband's efforts on her behalf, and of his attempt at once again improving himself, and she listened as he told her that, "In all actuality, I'm probably no different than he is." When Jed was done, she rounded the table and she kissed him deeply on his mouth and she told him her children were at the in-laws and that he could spend the night if he wanted, and he did, want, but he then told her he had two months left to make his year and that he was going to do whatever his sponsors told him to do, and that what they told him to do was not get involved for at least a year. She kissed him again and told him he could come back to Baraboo and spend Christmas with her and her kids. He said he would.

In his car that night he drove the lonely and darkened two-lane rural highway between Portage and Baraboo, heading toward the farmhouse and Kools on the now-finished salvaged-rock porch with The Man.

About five miles away from the Farmhouse Jed saw him running on the shoulder of the road and seemingly shouting obscenities to himself and angrily holding a Moses-stone-tablet-sized rock. He was running at Jed as he drove. His eyes bright and crazy. Jed watched as he cocked back his arms holding the large rock that was actually a piece of the road itself, and raised it above his head, and in that moment, the realization that Jed was looking into the anger-distorted face of Frank Novinsky felt like it crept slowly over him, but had, in reality, occurred to him in a flash of recognition, and just at that moment, Frank made to hurl the large piece of road at Jed's car. As the piece of road somersaulted through the air, Jed watched in disbelief as Frank dematerialized like he was being summoned somewhere beyond our solar system. The piece of road crashed Jed's windshield, and both the road and the windshield shattered into a galaxy of black pebbles of road and clear glass shining under the light of a cloudless moon, and he swerved then, a bit too late, and went off the road into a very steep and deep ditch. His airbags deployed and he was knocked unconscious and was not found for five hours, not until The Man came around.

Chapter Fifteen

Lunch is had

THEY ARE SERVING HOTDOGS in The Mess, that much she knows, the rest she'd have to piece together from accounts later. Lunch at the FPPIB is a family affair. Everyone is made to attend, even if They aren't hungry. Unless an agent has a good reason to be absent (meeting with a source, dead drop, chasing a lead, etc.), The Agency, in toto, eats at the same time. It's loud in the way that group eating is always loud — clamorous — with hundreds of conversations all going at once, the din of flatware scraping plates (although on this day the noise is not present as They are, as previously mentioned, having hotdogs which comes with a pickle spear and Utz potato chips, and is thus being eaten with just so many pairs of hands), and the noise of an industrial kitchen cranking out enough food to feed the over 200 Agents and their support staff. Because of the insistence of The Bear that all Agents and support staff — sans himself, of course, as he eats his lunch of lovingly and dotingly made sandwiches across the street at a small park in order to maintain a healthy separation from the Agents below him, and also to ensure that the Agents all felt free to chat amongst Themselves without fear of being overheard by the

Head Tuna (a name he wished someone would adopt for him, replacing his current moniker of The Bear which he'd grown tired of back in '55 but had told no one to quit calling him) — eat together, The Mess is the largest room in the subterranean complex of The FPPIB Headquarters. From a design standpoint, it is simple. Just a large rectangular concrete room with large service windows, the kind with metal shudders that pull down from the top, on its north wall that opened to the large industrial kitchen on its north end. Agents typically line up on the western wall in single file to be served whatever is on the menu for the day. Except, of course, on Tuesdays, when Agents line up outside The Mess a full hour before lunch is to be served, believing that this could guarantee They receive their portion of fried chicken so good you'd slap your mama for some, regardless of how many times the poor ladies who work the kitchens explain that the one time They ran out was anomalous, and would never be repeated, They swear. Still, the habit persists. No one wants to be left without fried chicken on fried chicken day.

Trays and flatware are available to the Agents once They get within like five people-lengths of the service windows, which They are to grab and to ready Themselves for lunch distribution before They reach the service windows. If there is no flatware available, say like on a day like this day, the Agents can assume They are having either hotdogs or hamburgers. There is only one day of the week where the menu is fixed, Tuesdays, otherwise, who knew? There are never any vegetarian or vegan options, and The Bear makes no concessions for either Kosher or Halal requests. It isn't a discrimination thing, he doesn't abhor religious custom in non-Christian dining options, he also refuses fish on Fridays during the Lenten season, it's just his way of instilling a core principle and belief that he has held for most of his adult life into his agents in a so-not-subtle-it's-really-not-aggressive way: that principles, beliefs, don't matter, not really, and that customs, real customs, once broken, cease to hold any real authority and power over the lives of the observant. Nothing bad ever comes from breaking the pattern, only an innovation of the inner self, or so The Bear believes. The only exception to this belief that no custom should be upheld or recognized and observed as sacred and unbreakable, is the eating of fried chicken on Tuesdays. Not even The Bear himself would fuck with that, though, as noted, he also does not participate in that little ritual either. So, every agent is made to eat the same thing, and bowel movements are tracked by all Agents of The FPPIB. Nothing is ever done with this data, but The Bear collects the logs on the first Wednesday of every month, the same day on which FPPIB Headquarters has its monthly tornado drill despite it being underground.

She sits down with her tray at the table where Bill Stevens, and Steve Rodgers, and Rodger Roberts, and Bob Helens, and Able Wojciechowski are already sitting. Today is the day, she already somehow feels.

The men at the table are all uniformly slate-gray-suited and Brylcreemed, except for Rodger Roberts who began going bald ten months ago, and made the dangerously atypical decision for an Agent of the FPPIB to shave the rest off last week. The jury is still out on whether or not he'd mysteriously stop showing up one of these days. She picks up her hotdog and she takes a bite, and while she's chewing, she sets it down again and then picks up her bag of plain Utz to open, but while she pinches the two sides of the chip bag, Bill begins to say something truly off-color about her and the hotdog. Except he doesn't call it the hotdog, he calls it the weiner, and he doesn't call her mouth her mouth, but rather her "face's hole." She stops chewing and swallows the only half-masticated meat and bread and ketchup and mustard. She looks around The Mess and it dawns on her, again, as it dawns on her about once a month even though it *was* explicitly pointed out to her when she was hired, that she is the only female Agent of The FPPIB. She picks up the hotdog with her teeth marks on its end and she says to Bill and the rest, she says, "Looks like Bill's after his wife got through with it, amiright?" and the whole table laughs, and Rodger pats her back then squeezes her shoulder for a moment that is just too long a moment, and all the ranking Agents at the table go back to eating their bephallused food and discussing the business of the day.

"We're sending in Michael today," says Bill.

"The Ex, going first . . . why?"

"Fuck it, right? Someone's gotta be first," says Bob, sitting next to Bill, cutting him off because from Bob's vantage he cannot see Bill's mouth move to open and begin speaking again, "everyone gets their turn in the barrel."

"Like I was saying . . ." Bob doesn't notice the slight annoyance in Bill's voice because, let's face it, Bob's not the sharpest on the uptake, and Rodger, for one, is glad of this because it's little instances like this that have been taking the pressure off his decision to shave the old noggin bald rather than attempt the old Brylcreem combover thing that other Agents who are similarly afflicted tend to favor. "She's been asking for Baker or Jesse, and sometimes Jed. She seems to think that having someone from that night around will help her recreate whatever it was she did to Frank."

"Where is Frank, by the way?"

"Somewhere near Sun Prairie, last we checked," Rodger answers. "The doubling back and starting over has gotten less frequent of late, he's making more progress each time. She hasn't said, but we're like 100% sure he's going home."

"Frank's not the point anymore, and you know that, Helen." Bill's hotdog pauses in the air, awaiting entry into his mouth and a bite to be taken after he's done speaking, a bite that will never come. "I'm trying to think of a dick joke, Helen. Just so you know."

"I guess, but like, and I was just wondering this this morning, you know when I walked by and she threw the ring bologna at the door and it dented the metal? So, if she can make lunch meat dent six-inch thick steel, why do we want to figure out so bad what she did to Frank? Or the how of it? Why is replicating that freak occurrence more important than harnessing and capitalizing on the powers we already know that she *can* control? The powers that we helped her develop and strengthen. Doesn't make any sense."

"My bologna can dent metal."

"Low-hanging fruit."

"My low hang . . ."

"Look," begins Bob, but he's shut up with a forceful hand on his left shoulder. No massaging forthcoming from the hand, just a firm squeeze and release.

"Look," begins Bill, "she's obsessed with her past, the stories she's told herself about herself over and over, the stories that have come to define, in a very real way, just who she believes that she is. She holds tight to that definition, despite all the evidence pointing to the fact that she is no longer the person she was, and can never be that person again. She's fundamentally unwilling to see that she's not that person, not anymore. She believes that by recreating the circumstances of her past, she can regain some of what she was, what she lost to time, and mistakes made. She wants to feel control like she thought she felt in her youth. She wants to relive the parts of her past that she feels were better for a while; *before* it got worse. There was one glowing and shining year when she'd outrun the trauma of her past, but before the disappointment of realizing the future she had always pictured for herself would never materialize. There were these few and fleeting bright months before she noticed those two walls not only closing in but having already closed in completely at some previously unnoticed moment. There was a time, which she reveres and makes sacred above all other times, when she knows she was happy and content with her choices, and had sufficiently suffocated her deep past, and had nothing but open skies stretching for miles out in front of her. It was golden to her. Precious. And she appreciated it, in the moment, she really did. She was able to notice when it was happening and focus on the times that were good, as they were happening, and as a result, she was able to hold them in her hands longer than most do, but, that she noticed and appreciated the good times before they were the good old times could do nothing to stop the inevitable, and time passed, like it does, and the walls went unnoticed until it was too late, and she was snuffed out in that moment of recognition, along with all her happy and contented feelings. She believes if she can get you all back together, she can live in that moment, recreate it in her mind, and keep you all there, forever. Before cuckoldry robbed Frank of his balls, before Jed started becoming pathetic, before Michael realized he wasn't ever going to be somebody special, before Baker bottomed out, and before you completely left her in your dust. She thinks she can use her gift to hold you all in stasis when *she* was happiest. It's bullshit. Believe that. But what she did to Frank, how he is now, that's real power. There have been unproven whispers of others who could move objects, dematerialize, control weather for short bursts, or control the minds of men, but none could do what she did to Frank that night, none could make a wraith of their own past. Manifest their own ghost and set him on a mission. No one's even suggested such a power. She can break the bonds of this dimension and has found a potential next. We honestly have no idea what she's done. Don't think she does either. This is why we need to indulge her, monitor her, and get her to do it again. We need to see it happen in person. We need you."

"You want to send me in with Michael, don't you?" Helen drops her dog with a wet schewlap on the table's metal top.

"Helen, you'll be fine. We've told her she will get Jesse and the others too; we just want to test the waters . . . see how she reacts. We believe that there is a less likely chance of it going haywire if you are there too.

"Okay, Bill, okay. It's time for me to do what it was you guys hired me to do. It's what you brought me in for, anyway."

"The only reason you are here is because she is here." Bill drops his dog on the table, unbitten, looking dismissively in her general direction. "Believe that."

Rodger rubs his smooth head. Bob straightens his tie. Helen smooths her skirt over her thighs. Steve runs his palms over his jet-black hair, flattening it. Bill stands first and tightens his belt as he hasn't touched his food and his pants have actually loosened throughout the meal. Abel speaks for the first time in 689 days, he says, "The Bear needs to hear about this, STAT," and also stands. Helen is no longer hungry and grabs her tray with both hands and stands and allows herself to be escorted by the others to the place where trays are deposited, then to the hall, and then to the bank of elevators. Bob grabs her left hand and squeezes it which no one else notices, or if They did, ignore. Bill pushes the button with the arrow pointing up and it illuminates in green light which splashes Helen's right hand and turns that hand's ring finger's ring's small diamond a shade of kryptonite. They ride in silence. When They are topside, They escort her to the door and out into a bright day that hurts all of their eyes. They cross the street and come to the bench where The Bear sits and They are made to wait while

The Bear does The Bear things in his mind, chewing slowly as he does them. Then They wait a while longer, and, finally, he says, "And, so?"

A star isn't born

Baker walks in circles in the middle of the room he is kept in and he fumes and he rages and he can't quite figure out what it is, exactly, that he did in his life to deserve to be in a place like this for so long without any indication of when he'll be free to leave. That and he has really gone through full-on detox for the first time, and that without intervention in the way of either opioids or cocaine he'll be in an even worse way, shortly. It can always get worse, the cravings, he's sure. Plus They'd taken his cigarettes when They took him. He sweats freely as he paces and rages. "Motherfuckers!" he yells at no one in particular and in random intervals when the mood strikes him. It isn't like a yell per se, but more like a guttural exclamation of the word motherfucker. Like an animal growling it. Also, he periodically starts screaming for a laptop with a highspeed connection and demanding that the non-ranking Agents who bring him his lunch tell him if any celebrities have died while he's in this weird-ass place. No one at the FPPIB is aware of Too Soon Radio, or that Too Soon Radio is actually on the precipice of generating actual really-real money for Baker Thomas. About a week ago, an Agent of the FPPIB opened the slot in Baker's door and pushed through a tray on which sat two pieces of cold fried chicken and a bag of plain Utz-brand chips, no drink. The Agent said, "Mac Miller has passed away. Apparent over-dose." Baker Thomas threw himself at his room's door for hours until he finally hurt his shoulder so badly that he required actual medical attention. The Agent in charge of Baker had tranquilized him upon entering the room and when Baker woke up, his arm was in a sling and his shoulder hurt like nobody's business. Now he just paces and screams mother-fucker and demands his laptop near constantly. He screams like a junkie needing his fix, "I don't even need my guitar, I can go a capella! I can go a capella!"

Sometimes, when pacing, he smells Winston smoke and he wonders who it is that smokes out there, and if They are doing it to tease him with the aroma, knowing he hasn't had a smoke in God knows how long. He's pretty sure it's just one of the slick-haired men taking a regular-type break, but still, he considers it rude. He waits.

The next time he hears the shuffling outside his door and the schlink of a Zippo top flipping open and smells the smoke of that unique and so smooth American cigarette, he stops pacing and walks with intent. He stands by the door to the room he's been kept in for an undetermined amount of time. He knows that he's been there so long that his detox sweating is all but non-existent and his cravings have faded to a man-ageable, dull longing. He stands by his door and he raises his hand and balls his fist and just as he is about to pound wildly, he stops short and his breath catches in his throat and he thinks this is just what They want me to do, what They hope I will do. He can't help him-self and he knocks on his door anyway, and he hears the person on the other side of the door drop his Winston and scrape it out with his shoe. He hears the person start to move and Baker Thomas backs up a step. The slot's deadbolt schalunks open and the slot's flap falls creakily. A set of blue-gray eyes appear, and Baker can smell egg salad mixed in the man's smokey breath. "Baker Thomas," says The Bear, bending at Baker's slot. Outside Baker's door, The Bear bends at an almost perfect ninety-degree angle, and his buttocks point leftward down the hall. This means that his head is turned almost completely sideways on his neck and his torso is parallel to the gray cement of the holding wing's wall. When standing, The Bear measures seven feet tall and weighs just over 350 pounds. He carries his weight well, evenly, and it is often joked that he looks like a bear after a long and restful hibernation. Which, honestly, isn't too far from the truth. He believes that rest is the key to longevity, and, so far, he'd been proven right. No one exactly knows how old The Bear is, or when he started in intelligence work. All anyone knows, including Presidents Reagan, Bush, Clinton, Bush Jr, Obama, and Trump, is that one of The Bear's favorite stories to tell is the time he participated in The Bay of Pigs debacle. The way The Bear tells it, it went off without a hitch, and a fully entrenched communist Cuba and Castro as hero-figure, and the resultant missile crisis, were all in the strategic interest of the United States, and lead directly, "point A to B style," in The Bear's words, to forty-plus years of unprecedented boom-type economic growth for the good old U.S of A. The Bear himself landed with the Cubans, as he told it, and made sure to really bungle the thing and scuttle the whole McGilla in a way that, while making America *look* foolish, actually set up an end game that would, ultimately, end in the dissolution of the U.S.S.R in toto. Every President who heard this (except Trump) questioned it, but the way The Bear told the story with such nonchalant deadpan, every President, eventually, had to concede that The Bear was probably a man of his word. President Obama put The Bear's age at 102. And the general consensus was that Mr. Obama was not too far off.

"Listen, man, you gotta get me outta here."

"Why?"

"What d'you mean why? I'm being, like, held without whatever, like, cause, man. This is not legal, man."

"Even still . . . the question is valid. Why should I let you out of here? What purpose would that serve? What would you do, out there, that's more important than what you are doing at present, in here, with us?"

"Look, man, I need to get outta here. Mac Miller's dead. People are expecting me to . . . to . . . like, react."

"Who's Mac Miller?"

"Mac Miller is like, a rapper, he's Mac Miller!"

"I don't understand. You need to get out of here, where important work is done, and you could be a vital part of that work, because a rapper named Mac Miller has died, and people are expecting you to have a reaction to that death. Is it that the death has long-ranging consequences for those intimately involved with Mr. Miller's career, and you need to help sort through what is sure to be a lengthy settling of his estate? Are you a probate lawyer of some kind?"

"I need to get to my computer; I need to record a song for Mac Miller. I need everyone to know that I know, that I am aware and on top of it, and that I'm still here. That I can keep it going. That I won't disappoint. I can't let this thing die."

"What thing is that?"

"I've done nothing, like my entire life, I've done nothing good, and then the one thing I do that anyone pays any attention to comes along, and you assholes snatch me up the next week. I was on my way to one million views, dude. This is such bullshit!"

"This thing you did, it defines you then? It has the power to make you feel certain ways because you've been given some validation by this thing you've done, correct?"

"What?"

"You say you've never done anything your whole life, nothing. That you've been trying your whole life to do something, but all the things you've done have gone unnoticed, unvalidated, and as a consequence of that, you don't consider these things that you have done as worthy of being counted as things you have done. Esteem-building accomplishments. Gone to work, paid rent, had relationships, became addicted to prescription opiates and cocaine, alienated a friend or two, you don't consider these things to be things . . . a life. You consider the thing that got noticed, viewed one million times, stirred up a reaction, to be a real thing . . . a valuable thing. The thing that will make your efforts and the events of your life mean something. This is what you are saying to me?" The Bear lights a Winston and passes it to Baker, then lights another for himself, knowing that when he leaves the smoke will linger, with its scent of smoke turning stale and also lingering, and that that scent will be pleasant for Baker, at first, but as there will be no more Winstons forthcoming, that scent will slowly turn sour and only serve to trigger cravings in Baker over and over again, until such time as the smoke and the scent of the smoke fades for good, which could take hours, maybe even a full day.

"Yes. Nothing else has ever made me feel like what I felt watching the number on that video go up and up and up, and the rude comments, and the people defending my work against the rude comments, made it so much sweeter. And knowing that each time that number increased another living person was hearing something I made, it's indescribable. No one has ever cared about me, my art, and now they do, and you guys got me locked up, and now everyone probably thinks I pussied-out and quit making Too Soon Radio because there was some backlash; but I didn't, I wouldn't."

"How did you feel, Baker, watching the number?"

"I don't know, like I said, really good."

"That doesn't seem sufficient enough of a feeling to jeopardize what we need you here for, not nearly good enough to allow you to go back home and record your Mac Miller song."

"No, I mean, really, really good . . . euphoric. Better than anything, better than drugs or that three-way with Molly and Helen back in the day when Michael and Frank were working and we had some blow and the day off. I can't describe it."

"You better do better than that, it would seem your legacy depends on it."

"C'mon, man . . . just let me go. I need to get back. I need to record and get it up. I need my fans to know I'm not gone, that I didn't stop, I need to feel it again."

"Feel what?"

"Like a God. Okay. Like a fucking God, like I can do whatever the fuck I want because no one can touch me because I've finally shown everyone that when they doubted me, sneered at my playing guitar at parties, or politely asked me when I'm going to do something more stable, job-wise, that I'm talented, that I'm smarter than they are, that I am a fucking God and they are just peons who will never, ever achieve the feelings I've felt watching that number rocket toward one-million. They are below me and I am above them. They are temporary and I am forever. I don't just feel like a God, I am a God and they are not. They will all have to reconcile themselves to the fact that I will be respected and famous and they will not, and that they all laughed at my dreams and I did it without any of them, anyway. Because I am a fucking God and they are fucking not. That's how it made me feel. That's why I need to get home. That's why I must record again. So let me go, or you guys can just give me my bedsheets back and let me hang myself right now, because if you keep me here, I will die without that feeling anyway."

"Thank you, Baker. That's honest of you."

"Please, let me go, or just bring me my computer."

"Sorry, no."

A man both crazy and not

He sits with his left hand handcuffed to a metal loop on the table's top that is designed for just that purpose. At first, They'd just placed him in the room like the rest and were planning on letting him stew for a bit before They started in on the questions. But the second he was alone he'd rammed his head so hard into the door that he'd concussed himself and required six stitches. Thus, handcuff. When he came to and was asked why he'd rammed his head into the door he'd told Them, "So you couldn't access what I know." They'd asked him to elaborate and he explained, "It's like a hard reset, man, all memory erased, no more access to the datum." It makes a sort of sense. Jesse Robinson seems to respect the cuff, though, and now he sits calmly and waits for the Agents to return. He looks at his fingernails as he sits and waits, and they are as dirty as one would expect the average nails of a homeless person to be. He checks his pockets and there he finds that he is still with his pouch of Top Brand Rolling Tobacco and Top Brand Rolling Papers, and his book of matches. Nothing in Jesse's history suggests to The Agents that he's a firebug. Anyway, as Bill had said to Bob, "It's not like he can burn down a concrete room." Which is true enough. Jesse notices that the ashtray in front of him is the flimsy tin kind that's made of a kind of thicker than usual tin foil and can be bent and shaped easily. He assumes that They assume that he will shape the ashtray into a kind of crude shank, and attempt to puncture necks the first chance he gets, and he assumes that They are wanting him to do this so They can have the pretext that They need to torture the ever-living shit out of him, which he also assumes that They will do either way, but still, he doesn't want to play so easily into Their hands. He rolls a smoke, lights it, and ashes it demurely into the provided tray.

Model detainee, he thinks, no room for error now m'boy. He has no idea why these Agents, his colleagues, have turned so hostile toward him and locked him in this room, wanting to extract his datum in such a cruel fashion when he'd give it freely given the proper opportunity. If They just behaved like Themselves, and not like the Skinwalkers he now knows Them to be, then he'd happily download all relevant sets of info for Them; no problem-o, Jackie-Boy. He had told Them so when They came to get him. "Flo is going to be pissed!" he shouts to the room. He ashes his smoke again. His fingers are brown-orange from the roll-your-owns and are cracking and flaking apart. He peels some skin from his right index finger and sets it in the tray. When he hears the shuffling of nice shoes on the concrete floor outside his room's door, he shouts, "Flo is going to kill you bastards for what you're planning to do!"

Outside, Bill Stevens and Bob Helens come to a stop in front of the door of the room in which Jesse Robinson is screaming. They do not hear words, but rather yawps of anger and frustration. Bill peeks through the window with the diamond-patterned wire on his door and sees Jesse there straining against his cuff with his head thrown back in a full-panic scream. Also, Jesse appears to be holding a crude shank-like object fashioned from his tin ashtray, and he has four smokes going at once, all dangling from his mouth. "Fuck," says Bill.

"I know man. I really don't want to have to go in there again. Once was, like, enough."

"He's on her list. The Bear says we need to do his intake interview, just like the rest of them."

"You heard him last time, talking that nonsense, complete schizo-shit. Can't make sense of anything."

"Yeah, he was the same when Rodger and I picked him up. You know he was loitering behind the Comedy Club on State when we found him, back by those dumpsters in the alley there, and he was like performing into the handle of an old wooden cooking spoon that had like the ovoid head broken off. Telling what I suppose he thought were jokes, I mean. People gathered at the mouth of the alley and would listen for a bit, I think believing it was somehow a legit performance, like a comedy in the alley type thing or something, but then it would become obvious what was going on and they'd get disturbed, or saddened by how pathetic it was, and move on."

"No?!" Bob asks in that astonished way that indicates a sort of morbid curiosity about the experience and encourages the continuation of the story.

"Yeah, no, for real. It was crazy stuff too. None of it made any real sense, just like a word soup. But what was really surreal and disturbing, is he'd say something like 'Hitch the giddyup with Black people, amiright?' and then this awestruck expression would come across his face, and he'd smile broadly and look off in the not-too-distant distance, and he'd like bask as if he was being showered with the most applause and laughter and adulation a person could imagine. Then he'd launch back into some nonsense and do it again. Really creepy."

"What happened when you guys approached?" Bob, again, astonished.

"Dude, he fucking freaked out! What the fuck do you think happened? You see him in there. He's off his nut."

"Still," says Bob. "The Bear wants to see the interview notes when we're done.

"Yeah, my plan is we just hit record and ask the questions straight like any other intake and check all the boxes. We'll give him all the time he needs to ramble and freak out before moving on to the next question. Get through our list and be done and send him back to his room." Bill adjusts his tie as it's come loose throughout the day. He shuffles his feet some more and Jesse's screaming begins anew, and Bill sighs a deep and resigned sigh.

"We can't give him to her."

"Probably the best thing for him. Who knows, maybe she'll fix his brain, or best case, she puts him out of his misery."

"Question. Have we tracked down just who Flo is?" Bob asks, running his hands through his jacket pockets, looking for who knows what, probably nothing, probably just doing it so as to have something to do while the two Agents stall going in the room.

"Far as we can tell, she was connected to one of the others. Jed, I think, but there are no substantive connections between Jesse and this Flo. Also, she's like somewhere up in Minnesota now, married as I understand it, two kids, real nice life she's got going up there too."

"Alright then."

"Alright." Bill schalunks the deadbolt and pulls on the handle and the two Agents walk into the room to the blood-curdling sounds of Jesse Robinson's screams. Screams that won't cease until his vocal cords are raw and useless. And even then, Jesse's mouth will hang agape in a silent mask of anguished miming. There will be no coherent answers to any questions provided today, and when The Bear is given the tape later, he is very pleased indeed.

Michael goes in

She's outside the door with Him. Molly had heard them approach. Both of them. Together. He is not pleased, she (Molly) knows. Helen has her own worries, she (Molly) feels. There are no objects in her room for her to attempt to manipulate. Since everyone became present at the facility, her rate of success in giving Them what They want w/r/t the moving of the electrified objects has risen to 100%. She is neither happy nor unhappy about this. She feels no pride of accomplishment. They are waiting to come in and she hears them whispering, hears Helen telling Michael that she (Helen) is sure that she (Molly) can hear them whisper. Michael doesn't believe her (Helen) and says that she (Molly) is just some nut-job whack-a-doo, like any other drug casualty. Helen tries explaining the deal to Michael, but is unsuccessful, Molly hears. From where she sits on her bunk, she can either dangle her feet if she scoots back or place them firmly on the ground if she sits with her ass on the edge. Her feet dangle and her ankles are rotating, each in the opposite direction of the other. She is concentrating very hard on Michael's head beyond her door. Helen is saying that Molly must be treated very gingerly and that she (Helen) recommends that he try and reminisce with her (Molly) about their shared past and that she (Helen) will largely just observe Molly's reaction.

They don't sound too friendly with each other; Molly hears it in their tone. She changes the rotation of each of her feet so that the left is now circling to the right and the right is now circling to the left. She visualizes what Michael's head looks like very accurately, despite not having seen him in person in just under ten years. It is still yet a couple of weeks from Christmas. She now knows that the passage of time she *does* feel when a new year has come is not marked by the occasion of her birth or the actual holiday of New Year, but when a certain time comes and goes on Christmas Eve. Her left hand raises to her forehead and she brushes away some loose strands of hair that had fallen into her left eye. She hears Michael say, "You were a cunt then and you are a cunt now, Helen. I don't believe a word of any of this bullshit and when I get out of here, I swear to God, I'm suing you and whatever the fuck kind of Agency this is for violating my goddamn rights."

"Listen, you don't underst . . ." Helen tries to respond but Molly's room's door's deadbolt schalunks of its own accord and the door opens itself very slow and methodically until it comes to rest against the wall, which is totally creepier than if the door would've flown open crazily. "Shit, well, I guess we should go in then."

"You fucking go in; I'm not going in there." Michael feels the hand of The Bear on his lower back shoving him forward wordlessly, she (Molly) can feel it. Neither he nor Helen heard The Bear's approach. She (Helen) nods to her superior and takes her place a half-step behind Michael. The Bear's hand recedes as Michael's feet begin to move under their own power.

She (Molly) can feel that Michael feels a cold all over his body as the tip of his nose precedes him across the threshold. His face emerges first, then chest, then one knee, then the other. When his ass is through, she (Molly) sees the extent of her mind's eye's accuracy in visualizing his ugly face. Then she sees her (Helen) — her raven ringlet curls bouncing and swaying with her stride, framing her thin and slightly ovoid face. Her high forehead. Her thin lips. Her green and almost too round eyes. Her 5'3" frame. Her figure both hidden and not by the boxy skirt suit. She wears flats for comfort. Confident in her stature without need for extra inches. Michael becomes invisible to her (Molly). There is the ashen white ring of skin on her (Helen's) left hand's ring finger of someone who recently no longer wears a ring after having worn one for quite some time, some relationship she (Molly) was unaware of, but no longer matters. Molly feels something *she*, herself, is feeling for the first time in a very long time and she concentrates very hard on holding on to the moment. Feeling the time and willing it to slow. She feels . . . happy.

"Ummm, hey there . . . Molly," Michael says as if speaking to a slow child, "it's me, Michael, do you remember me . . . Michael."

Molly's expression never changes and her concentration never leaves Helen, who is beginning to feel the effects of Molly's unalloyed attention. Which feels very pleasant and then very unsettling. She (Helen) looks deeply into Molly's eyes and is made to feel like the only person on earth. Molly's expression never changes. But her eyes' pupils narrow in unison and time in the room slows and seems to stretch. The back of Michael's head is about six inches in front of and one foot above Helen's face. She (Helen) sees the skin on his neck pucker and stretch. Molly's expression never changes. Helen's expression does change, she wears a confused look now. The skin on Michael's neck begins breaking along an almost perfectly straight perforated line. And the skin that is not broken by the evenly spaced punctures begins to stretch as Michael's head begins to slowly rise. Eventually, after what feels like a few agonizing minutes, but is in actuality probably seconds, the connecting skin and tissue begin to pop and Michael's head raises steadily into free air, off his shoulders. It then begins to rotate. When Michael's face faces Helen's face, she can see that his lips are moving but no sound is made. His eyes are blinking in a slo-mo render of a rapid blink and his head's hair catches fire now. Then very slowly, like footage captured at 1/1000th speed, his head explodes. Bits of flesh and skull and brain dance beautifully away from center mass, showering the immediate area. Helen's mouth closes tight. Time, then, catches up with itself and the splatter hits Helen hard with a sound like Schh-plot, and Michael's body falls limply to the ground. "He was never necessary," says Molly, speaking out loud for the first time since Christmas 2009.

Chapter Sixteen

Winston Hargrove comes alive

HE SAT IN THE CORNER of the room trying to take up as little space as possible and failing. The man at the Resolute Desk was also a towering figure and spoke in a kind of plain but vulgar way — Winston Hargrove understood him but did not like or admire him. The rumors of the large man preceded him through any door he walked. "Jesus on the fucking cross, Helms!" was something that Hargrove noticed he was fond of saying to the Director. That day, they concerned themselves with Israel. Hargrove sat in his corner, willing himself to be as invisible as possible, and listening. He did not will himself small or invisible because he didn't wish to be that kid called upon in class who was unprepared, quite the opposite: he was very prepared and should the legendarily large President have called on him to answer for the OCI's assessment of Israel's ability to fend off multiple simultaneous Arab attacks and defend herself adequately, he could've done so easily. As they (Israel) could've (defended themselves that is) too. He was well versed in the material, having been part of the taskforce assigned to assess the situation months ago, when tensions in the region began to pick up steam over there. No, Winston Hargrove was willing himself small, blending into his corner, and making himself as invisible as possible because Winston Hargrove wanted to see if he could. And the fact that Lyndon had not seen fit to turn his vulgarity toward the by-then rising star analyst was all the proof (to Winston) that he, indeed, could. From his vantage, being nigh on undetectable in the corner, he put himself in the advantageous position of having both Helms and The President forget his presence entirely, and as a consequence, the two men spoke freely and without reservation. Not that Lyndon ever had much in the way of reservation when speaking his mind in the Oval Office, regardless of who happened to be around, but Helms did, and so it was nearly impossible for Winston Hargrove to ever truly get a sense of what his boss was thinking. He'd tried telepathy, of course, but that proved impossible because Helms had apparently been practicing and employing some sort of psychic blocking technique that Hargrove had yet to crack. So practiced un-visibility was the solution he came up with. It is important to note that Hargrove's practice of making himself small and invisible was not the true gift of being both completely there but also completely vanished, but was more like being completely opaque and non-descript. More like being so completely easily ignored that he was forgotten about, and as a consequence was both in the room and not, in the minds of the room's other occupants. He couldn't, for example, sit in a lady's locker room and get a free show. His presence would be so incongruous as to make his attempts at making himself small and gone ineffective in the extreme. But here, among these men, in these kinds of rooms, he belonged, he was a natural fit, and so he could blend and be gone, and The President and Helms spoke as freely as if they were alone in his presence. And in a very real way, anyone in Winston Hargrove's presence was alone, even if he wasn't making himself as small as he possibly could, even if he wasn't going opaque. With Winston, even when he gave a person his full attention, that person still felt eerily like they were talking to a ghost. Even Lyndon; especially Lyndon.

"Jesus on the fucking cross, Helms!" The President banged his fist on his desk's manila folder for emphasis. "I'm sitting here with an intelligence assessment from the Jews that says you're full of shit. Says here that if they come under attack we might as well kiss their collective asses goodbye, as well as our allied foothold in the A-rab world. Says here the whole place is a damn powder-keg and we need to step up or they'll all be flipping latkes in hell. You say not true, why?"

"I don't think the Jews go to hell, sir," deadpanned Helms, picking lazily at the grit under an index finger and barely looking up as he did so. A particularly irksome habit of Helms which Lyndon suspected Helms employed when trying to aggravate him.

"God damn it, Helms! A: they most certainly do, at least some of them. All bad people on God's Green will eventually find themselves rotting away in the pit-fires of Hades should they not repent their wicked ways and live a life of God damn peace and love for their fellow man. And B: that's not the fucking point I'm driving at here, Helms. The point I'm trying to get across to you is that I asked you for an assessment of

Israel's ability to defend herself should that whole kettle of brown-fish boil over over there. And you come back, only five hours later mind you, with a fully articulated report that says that I should not even fret one iota about the possibility of Israel losing any kind of war with the A-rab. Not even a full-out cooperative assault from multiple A-rab nations. And then like I just knew was fucking coming, the Jews send me this here assessment of their very own saying that you, yourself, are full of shit Helms, and that should an A-rab so much as sneeze in their general direction they'd be good and fucked. So, not to put too fine a point on the thing Helms, but could you please find your way to explain to me why you are right and they are wrong."

"Ugh, sure. Well, sir, and Hargrove over there could attest to this, as tensions began to build over there months ago, I tasked some of my best agents at OCI to form an Israel-Arab taskforce to give me the exact answers that you are now asking for. It only took five hours because we'd already had all the data, we just needed to compile the report. When Egypt closed the Straits of Tiran, we kicked the compiling into high gear, sir." Helms placed some fingernail grit on the arm of the taupe couch on which he was sitting. The grit being black grit, almost asphalt in color, cut a striking contrast to the taupe of the couch which Lyndon couldn't help but notice and had to ignore, lest he let Helms know that he was getting to him, so, Lyndon adverted his eyes from the couch's grit and kept them on Helms so all that was communicated, but not said, was I know you are fucking with me and I don't care to respond in my particular Lyndon Johnsonian fashion, on this occasion.

"Jesus on the fucking cross, Helms! You're still dicking around and teasing the old girl. Just go ahead and slide her on in and tell me just why you are right and they are wrong."

"Well, sir, for one, the Rooskis," invoking a slight, almost imperceptible Stonewall drawl and Lyndon's own peculiar mannerisms, "are going to stay Swiss and not involve themselves in a Jew/A-rab conflict, if they can avoid it. For a whole 'nother, this idea of A-rab cooperation and unification in the face of a shared enemy in the Israeli . . . er, Jews, is pure fantasy. We are talking about primitive and backward cultures that just got the idea to rub sticks together to make flames. They are tribal. They are territorial. And the only thing they hate more than Israel's presence in the region is the tribe from the next shit-hole over. And third, and you know this to be true, Israel is armed to the god damned teeth with weapons supplied by allied countries bent on seeing them hold on to that country of theirs. That and I don't know an Israeli that won't fight like a kicked dog to defend their holy ground. If it's to be war, they will win and win easily. As to why they are saying they won't and that their situation is dire, well, sir, you know how they are when it comes to securing aid."

"God damn it, Helms!" Lyndon used his palm to sweep the manila folder from The Resolute Desk to the floor in front of Helms. "Works for me." He pressed the intercom button on his desk's phone and a buzzing issued therefrom. "Geraldine!" he screamed loud enough to not need the intercom. "Get me the head honcho over there on the horn now!" Lyndon leaned back in his chair and surveyed the room, and his eyes then passed right over Winston Hargrove and did not stop, as if he were not there. "Jesus on the fucking cross Helms, I hope you're right, 'cause those bastards'll have to do it themselves, should it come to it now."

"They are more than up to the task, right, Hargrove?"

"That's, ugh, yes, that's right, sir," said Winston Hargrove.

"Jesus on the fucking cross, Hargrove! When the hell'd you get here, boy?" No one in the room answered Lyndon as Winston Hargrove faded back into his corner.

The following month Israel did fight a war with its Arab neighbors and defended itself easily. The June war of 1967 lasted six days. Winston Hargrove didn't follow the particulars of the conflict, preferring only to be given the broad strokes. It was, as it so happened, that his analysis was pretty much dead-on-balls fucking accurate, and as a result, he was awarded the CIA Distinguished Intelligence Medal in a ceremony held privately and never acknowledged by Winston Hargrove or his bosses at the time. He was never asked to attend a meeting with Lyndon again.

The day after the cease-fire was declared and The June War ended and Israel was victorious, Winston sat on a bench looking at the Lincoln Memorial's reflecting pool and eating one of two roast beef sandwiches prepared by the most doting and loving wife that man or beast has ever known, and he was, well, reflecting. He thought about the tools the mind possesses to achieve its ends (pretty much how the mind goes about tricking itself into making itself happy). There were pathways carved in its surface that defined the routes pleasure would take and also paths carved that would predetermine the repetition of self-destructive behaviors that felt happy but ultimately led to serious unhappiness. He thought about thinking and the habits formed by repetitious thinking and how thoughts could become hardwired into the mind's definition of happiness. How even the darkest and rankest and vilest of thoughts could become a source of pleasure for the mind when thought about often enough, and hard enough. How the mind developed a taste for degeneracy like the body developed a taste for sugar or nicotine or booze or reefers. The thoughts in his mind were of severed limbs impaled on spiked poles in a desert somewhere on the outskirts of Jerusalem. Heads on pikes never bothered him, though. His thoughts become even more grotesque and swimmy and referred back to some of the source materials of modern violence, and he thought about the bashing of newborns' heads against rocks in Sparta when the council of strength judged the infants defective somehow. He thought about the wailing of the innocent babes of the time as they were carried to the foothills and left there to die, how that is a crueler fate than the aforementioned brain-bashing. How, left there, in the elements, next to a cart path (if the babes had any luck whatsoever), they would cry and wail, and the sun would beat down and the rains would surely come, eventually, as would animals, eventually. He thought about the ones whom strangers rescued but quickly drove this thought from his mind. He thought about the ancient story of the wolves and Rome with its excesses of violence. He thought about the babe's wails slowly going silent as the lungs of the babes tired out and the babes' little throats grew raw and weak, and he thought about how in the worst of cases the babes died of exposure over some days, with only tiny hollowed-out rib-bones left to stand in centurion testament to the babes having ever existed at all. The thoughts sickened and repulsed him as they were antithetical and incongruous to the very nature of being. Ran counterclockwise to the pre-programmed software of human existence, so, he thought about them (the babes) even more. He thought about the thinking of these thoughts like acquiring a taste for something that his tongue rebelled against. He thought about thinking about these killings of the innocent babies of Sparta as the eating of tomatoes, which he used to, dating back to his youth, find repellent and which used to make him sick. He thought about how his Mother had made him eat tomatoes over and over and over again until his tongue's palate changed, and he found he liked tomatoes after all, and how his Mother had then rewarded him with a Hershey's Chocolate Bar. He would carve the pathways of his mind to not only find the killings and the murder of the weakest not only not repellent but a source of nourishment, of happiness, not because he was sick, but because he wanted desperately to be among those who chased and caught this world's most heinous monsters. He wanted out of the data basement he only most recently found himself in and into the fight against evil. He sat and he closed his eyes to the reflecting pool and he thought and he thought and he thought.

Eyes closed yet he still saw, and she was out there, ankle-deep in the pool's water, and she more swept his way than walked. She was dressed not like an apparition should be dressed at all. She wore blue jeans and a white shirt with a collar that was unbuttoned down to her navel, framing her torso just so. Her hair was auburn and not yet streaked with white. She smiled as she swept herself toward him sitting there with eyes closed and hands slack at his side, one still clutching his lovely wife's dotingly prepared roast beef sandwich. As she neared, Winston Hargrove believed he could feel the heat of her body radiating from her and breaking against his face, chest, and arms, and his hand lost its grip, and the sandwich, so lovingly constructed, fell to the ground beside the bench. She smiled a snaggle-toothed smile and made to speak, but no words came, yet he heard. She nodded and her smile went huge and discordant and became itself an anti-smile of some kind; somehow sickening. He felt no nourishment or joy in the paths his mind was carving too rapidly now. Whatever she was doing to his brain's software she was not doing it through the process of slow repetition over some weeks and years, but was carving harshly in the moment, and creating a permanent scar on the first psychic slice of her own mind's scalpel. He did not want this at all. She was on top of him now, straddling his lap, her shirt open and flowing behind her, and her hair alight. The jaws of her mouth distended and she screamed her banshee's shriek in his ears, and he felt himself slipping from himself, but also felt her and that losing himself completely to her, just then, wouldn't serve. She backed off a bit but her hair's fire grew large, and ashes and sparks rained from the sky above her onto him and left black marks on his body's own white collared shirt, which his wife had so lovingly and gingerly pressed for him at the home they shared in Virginia. She bent down to him, head still aflame, and touched her lips to his chest and punched his heart with her tongue, and then all was gone. He thought of Sparta. He was unaffected. He had the taste.

Baker and Jed and Jesse leave DeKalb, IL

Baker Thomas graduated from DeKalb H.S., but just barely. There was night school for those for whom behavioral issues were, well, an issue. It ended up being a pretty sweet deal. The School District got the problem kids out of their hair for at least a year (usually just Senior year as the problem kids tended to get extra problemie during Senior Year), and the problem kids got a real jerk-off Jane of an educational experience, which was kind of what they'd always been after anyway. Jed didn't go to night school as his parents considered it the easy way out and instead his Mother enrolled him in some kind of homeschool-by-mail thing, which he was supposed to complete so as to still technically graduate on time. However, there was no accountability, so he never did any of the course work and his Mother never really asked him about it, and by the time he was turning eighteen (the January of his Senior Year), he decided none of it was worth the effort anymore. Nothing, to him, seemed to be worth it at all anymore. So, he dropped out. Which at the time seemed like both the right thing to do for himself, personally, and the completely wrong thing to do, life prospects-wise.

Dekalb High School was a cramped and claustrophobic place in 2001. A population boom coupled with a fairly regressive and conservative voting base within the community had led to the putting off of allocating city funds to the construction of a new and larger high school, with most town residents asking at every town board meeting, where the subject was discussed ad nauseum, "What's wrong with the high school? I went to that high school and I turned out just fine." What was wrong with the high school was that, for the most part, high schoolers are assholes. They are moody and they are sullen and everything, to a high schooler, is so immediate and consequential that they are prone to flights of emoting so annoying that anyone older or younger than them tends to treat them and their concerns as supremely unserious. Kids, on the other hand, are a different story, the ones who are still young enough to be moldable and cute. Every parent is head over heels in love with their grade schooler, but every parent is in a war of attrition with their high schooler. The point being that when the school-age population of Dekalb, IL, had begun its boom in the preceding decades, the town kept up with expanding and constructing the educational infrastructure on both the grade and middle school levels. In the year 2001, when Jed and Baker and Jesse were all seniors, a total of three elementary schools dumped into two middle schools, which then dumped into one two-grade Jr. High (which was crowded, but being only two grades not crushingly so), and then finally into the one four-grade high school, which was just awash in sullen and moody and assholie teenagers. Adding to the overall chaos of the place, DeKalb High School only employed one lonely security guard, so it was really easy for the problem types to get lost in the system and for consequences, true consequences, to never really find them. You basically had to set the gym teacher on fire to even rate notice; neither Jed nor Baker ever set the gym teacher on fire. What they did do, at least Baker Thomas did, was sell a lot of drugs.

DeKalb, IL, is situated roughly sixty miles west of Chicago and forty miles south of Rockford and is a college town. What this meant for Baker and Jed and countless other lost-boy types stretching back decades was that, with the right connections, literally any mind-altering substance could be had. Mostly, they stuck to dealing weed as it was by far the most popular and regularly indulged in substance for the D.H.S set. It was an innocuous drug that was considered largely harmless by the general student population, and one that could be indulged in regularly with fairly limited debilitating effects to future-type prospects. It was safe, so it sold like it was completely harmless. Baker would get quarter-pounds of some really good shit from this guy he knew in The City and he'd set his cruise control and shepherd the shit from the guy's place on S. Halsted and 33rd. He'd make these runs during the middle of the day in the middle of the week. His thinking was that nobody thinks anyone is running dope at 1:30 in the afternoon on like a Wednesday. And he was right for the most part. He had a few close brushes, once getting pulled over for a taillight violation which resulted in a citation and being let go without further incident, but that was it, just close calls, never any real trouble, never consequences. The two boys also dabbled in Acid for a bit.

There was a select clientele for LSD at D.H.S and Jed and Baker served their needs as well. Baker had this guy he knew who had graduated four years before, and he had a brother who was twenty years older than himself and was still living out his sixties-era, free-love happy-hippy lifestyle and working the counter at the Marathon Station on Lincoln Hwy across the street from the Tom and Jerry's, which was a N. Illinois specific take on the Greek has-everything counter restaurant that's found mostly back east, and no further west or north than IL. The hippy older brother of the guy that Baker knew would load up his old VW bug with water and freeze-dried fruits and like nuts and granola bars, enough so that he wouldn't have to stop besides to fill up, and he'd drive to Arkansas where he knew another flower-power refugee who was still fighting the good fight and living the dream and brewing bathtub Acid that was of some of the highest (get it) quality shit in the whole damn nation. The flower-power guy the hippy brother of the guy Baker knew knew, used this really fluffy and high-quality white blotter paper to dose out his acid. He'd use an eyedropper to measure out precise dosages and would, himself, usually end up just like tripping balls after every batch was finished, just from the residual LSD his skin came in contact with. The flower-power guy that the hippy brother of the guy Baker knew was still relatively all there, mentally, considering. Anyway, the guy Baker knew's hippy brother would take ten sheets (100 hits each), which he called a bible, and he'd make an all-night Smokey and The Bandit run back to N. Illinois and he'd crash for like three days after having partied with the similarly inclined flower

235

child in Arkansas. But after that, he'd give at least a sheet to his brother, and that guy would sell Baker like twenty hits at $2.50 a hit which Baker could then turn around and sell for $10.00 a hit to kids at DeKalb H.S without much fear from the cops or the security guard because, for the most part, everyone was just really content in letting D.H.S become the overcrowded mess that it was because, for the most part, high school kids are no longer cute. The crowding was so bad that, by January of 2001, Baker was attending night school and Jed had dropped out (one day after he turned eighteen), but the pair regularly showed up at the high school in the morning to sell drugs to the kids who congregated out back of the school in the A.M. to smoke cigarettes before first period, and they went completely unnoticed. And this was months after Columbine.

Jesse smoked before first period out back but other than that broke no rules whatsoever.

By February of that year, Jed had moved out of his Mother and Father's house and had taken up residence in a shitty apartment that was meant for college kids. He'd paid the rent for the place by trading the current occupant his 1988 Lincoln Town Car for six months' rent. The current occupant was a classmate of Jed and Baker's named Scott Ratfield. Scott Ratfield had too dropped out when he turned eighteen. The reason that Scott had a two-bedroom apartment all to himself was that on the occasion of his eighteenth birthday his trust was availed to him. He wasn't rich. It wasn't a gigantic trust. His Father was serving a hard six years for fraud and embezzlement. The trust was for $250,000 and had come from a settlement with a particular car manufacturer and a particular driver's insurance company. The horror had begun early on a Thursday morning in April of 1992 when, after having just completed a bus tour of O'Hare Airport's runways, and after just disembarking said busses to go tour the terminals and eat a lunch, a car jumped a curb and seemingly floored it, plowing through dozens of children and their adult chaperones. Scott Ratfield was dragged some twenty yards underneath the car which resulted in the losing of his left ear and the complete and total disfigurement of the left side of his face. He also broke his left arm, right leg, and hip, and just a whole bunch of ribs. The damage to his face was the hardest thing for the young elementary student's parents to accept, and he underwent multiple surgeries between the ages of seven and nine. His face more or less looked normal by the time he made the acquaintance of Jed Lucas, but the ear, which had to be constructed from spare skin and cartilage from various parts of his body (including the backs of his upper thighs (he insisted it was upper thigh skin and meat) which caused his classmates to call him ass-ear from 4th-9th grades when then he finally transferred to D.H.S from S.H.S (Sycamore) and never told anyone about the ear thing again) and then attached, never really took and hung kind of lopsided off the left side of his head. All told, after the surgeries and the money his parents got, and the money put aside for young Scott's education and future in the trust, the total was north of $1,500,000. Neither Jed nor Scott worked and Baker was allowed to peddle his wares out of the apartment's living room on the weekends, so long as he provided Scott with a few grams of free marijuana a week and the occasional hit of high-power blotter acid on the fluffy cloud blotter paper which made Scott feel a euphoria that his young life had been forever missing since that fateful day and the '88 O____'s seemingly faulty accelerator. The party never stopped, and one day rolled into another, and the whole scene was taking on a life of its own and everyone involved was burning out and escalating their own personal use and bad things were beginning to happen. There were fights and the walls were tagged up, and one girl was assaulted in the bathroom but told no one for years, and only then did she confide her trauma to her therapist who helped her work through her lingering issues w/r/t the trauma, but she never did fully recover, and Jed and Baker and Scott all knew that they were heading for something truly serious (consequence-wise) if the plug wasn't pulled and they didn't bail. Scott was dosing daily by June and was pretty much out of his $250,000, anyway. That and the lease was up in August.

Jesse Robinson was a frequent attendee at the parties, but no one noticed him or knew how he knew Jed and Baker and Scott.

Also, a number of unmarked vehicles were seen by all three of them to be lurking in the parking lot at all odd hours; and they all knew that they were both being paranoid but also that they were, in fact, being closely watched at that point, so, it wasn't really paranoia. So Scott opted to not renew the lease. Jed was never on the lease anyway so fuck it.

Baker's decision to skip town was made for him when the dude he knew with the hippy brother who worked the counter of the Marathon Station over by

Nae-Nae's apartment never came back from his first trip to Arkansas with his brother to meet the flower child who brewed the acid that everyone who took acid on a regular basis just loved. Everything had gone off without a hitch on the ride down and they made really good time and they then spent the requisite three days on the flower-power dude's compound while he prepared the batch for them, and they partied, and dropped acid, and made free-love-style love with the men and the women who were there and were kept in a near-constant state of flying-highness, and when the time came, they took their bible of high-power blotter acid on the fluffy cloud blotter paper and they stashed it under the black part of a CD's Jewel Case that both holds the actual CD but also pops out easily for the concealment of small sheets of perforated blotter paper. On the drive back, the VW quit on them. It wasn't that big of a deal at first, and the hippy brother of the guy that Baker knew called AAA, and they waited. AAA, however, must've been having a really busy night and it was taking forever, and the guy that Baker knew's hippy brother lit a joint he'd copped from some half-naked hippy chick during the previous evening's love-sesh and he toked it twice before passing it over. At that very moment a do-gooder highway patrolman who was, by all accounts, a very reasonable man when treated with respect, spotted them there on the side of the road in the middle of the night and did his duty to them as citizens of these United State and pulled his cruiser over to ascertain the severity of the breakdown and to offer them assistance and a ride if they'd only put out their cigarettes and didn't mind riding in the back. Only, when he hit

them with the old high beams and the siren-less red
and blues to alert them to his presence and willing-
ness to help, they got all cagey, and the older threw
what the patrolman now recognized as a kind of communal cigarette that they both were smoking on into
the ditch, and that raised the patrolman's suspicions,
and he decided that the pair needed a good questioning as to what brought them to this deserted stretch of
Arkansas highway in the dead of the night smoking
communal cigarettes and getting all cagey at the presence of law enforcement. The pair did not stand up to
questioning. They didn't confess or anything, they
just couldn't provide any kind of reasonable answers
to the patrolman that would assuage his suspicion so
he could see clear to letting them just keep on waiting
for AAA. That and their whole demeanor and way of
being was a sign of disrespect toward the usually
completely reasonable patrolman. He took them in after finding the communal cigarette near the edge of
the ditch on the side of the road and ascertained that
it was highly powerful organic marijuana. The car was
thoroughly searched upon arrival (by tow truck) at the
highway patrolman's highway patrol station. The LSD
was found within an hour of the car being in police
possession and was only found because a junior patrolman was interested in seeing what kind of music
the gutter-punk and the hippy were into, and then
when he opened the Jewel Case for an album called
Butchered at Birth by the band Cannibal Corpse, the
bible just sort of fell out and lay there all incriminat-
ing and obvious. The junior patrolman could only
stand and stare and blink for a moment before it sank
in what had just fallen out of Butchered at Birth, but,

eventually, he regained himself, and the gutter punk whom Baker knew and his hippy brother were proper fucked, and but good.

Baker knew the guy he knew wouldn't rat him out or anything, and even if he did, it wasn't like Baker was in possession of any of the fluffy cloud blotter acid, which would carry real-time, prison-wise, and the marijuana he did possess was the dregs of the last run and thus fairly inconsequential, but he didn't want to take any chances and presented to Jed the idea of moving to Madison, WI, for both a change of scenery and a chance at a new beginning for the both of them. For him (Jed) he wasn't necessarily keen on the idea of moving to Madison, WI, with Baker, but a number of mitigating factors had presented themselves and deeply affected his decision-making process w/r/t the whole skipping town thing and fucking off to figure the rest of his life out. For one, he was (by that point) fully succumbing to problem binge-drinking and substance abuse, and he could feel the hard-partying lifestyle's toll and thought that maybe a geographical change would help alleviate some of the underlying issues which caused him to turn to substances in the first place. But also, for two, his Mother and Father who had always provided him with a stable, if not particularly loving, home were moving from DeKalb, IL, to the greater Madison area to be closer to the Father's Mother who was in failing health after taking a particularly nasty fall down some painted basement stairs that were painted with that slick kind of paint with the high-gloss sheen that seemed to be a popular choice for painting basement stairs sometime in the mid-sixties, which makes no damn sense when thought about for more than a minute or so. And also, as a third reason, but not one he realized was a reason, just a notion that hung around in the subconsciousness of the people who were particularly in tune with the frequency, was that DeKalb, IL, is a place that eats its own, especially its young, especially the ones who are afflicted with the gene. So a week after the LSD bust two things of note happened. The first was Jed's Mother both found and secured a two-bedroom apartment at 408 N. Henry Street in Madison, WI, setting the boys up to make the big move on the 15th of August. The second thing of note that happened was a package from Arkansas arrived at a PO box Baker had had a freshman open up in her (Kathy Bauman of the Bauman's Books — local independent bookstore done in by the opening of the B&N sometime in the mid-nineties — Baumans) own name. In the package were three jars of homemade apricot jelly, five jars of pickled asparagus, two vacuum-sealed two-pound packages of buffalo jerky, two large bottles of homebrewed dandelion wine, and one pound of dried figs. The small vile of unblottered LSD had been carefully inserted into one of the jelly jars. Also, Nae-Nae planned a going away party for both Jed and Baker (the latter of whom she had had an affair with the summer last which involved a threesome with Dickless Jones that turned into a foursome when Anatoli had caught them after they had all lost track of time and he'd come home mid-Eifel Tower) for August 14th.

The plan was that on August 14th, in the hours leading up to the party, Baker and Jed would go to Nae Nae's apartment and she would begin the process of turning the raw ketamine she had procured from a sneak-thief who specialized in breaking and entering veterinary clinics, into its snortable version, Special K, and Baker and Jed would put on their gloves and begin eyedroppering hits of the LSD onto blotter paper to be sold at $15 a hit as it would be the last of that stuff the town would probably ever see. The process of cooking Special K is fairly straightforward. Nae-Nae started with a pot of low-boiling water, and when she had a good steam going, she put a plate on top of the pot and poured the liquid Ketamine on top of the plate as evenly as possible, then she waited for the water that the Ketamine was diluted in to evaporate, leaving behind the pure powder. The only real trick was having the patience to wait for the Ketamine to cool before scraping it and snorting it and going to that beautiful hole where you can barely feel anything and can't move and are happy.

Jesse lurked awkwardly around the park by Nae-Nae's apartment, waiting for 7:00 P.M. to come and go so he could wait another half an hour so it didn't seem like he was just waiting for the appointed hour to come and go so he could excitedly be the first one to the party, like some sort of goober.

The eyedroppering of LSD is so straightforward it doesn't need any real description, just knowing that being really careful is really important, is enough. The thing Baker liked to do when he was blottering acid (having gotten a raw unblotterd vial on two other occasions) was transfer the contents of the small vial, which can't really be set down owing to its rounded bottom, into a wide and flat-bottomed shot glass. The whole process took about forty-five minutes of careful hand/eye work and was just wrapping up when there was a tentative knock on the door, which Nae-Nae answered as all she had to do, Special K-wise, was wait for the substance to cool enough to be scraped. When Baker looked he didn't recognize the boy who'd entered and he said to Jed, "Watch this," and poured vodka into the shot glass which had been used as a receptacle for the 1000 hits of LSD not five minutes prior, the remnants of which still gave the inside of the glass a wet-looking sheen, with some still puddled at the glass's bottom. He carefully lifted the glass so as to not spill, and walked it to the living room where the boy he did not know was seated on one of Nae-Nae's Goodwill couches, and he handed the boy the shot and he said, "Thanks for coming, man . . . it means the world to me," and he lit a cigarette and watched that boy take that shot and then smiled a smile so big and happy that it kind of broke Jed's (who was watching this whole thing from the kitchen) heart. The kid who neither of them knew then proceeded to tell Baker how much that one time in middle school when Baker had stood up for him in the cafeteria when some dickheads were picking on him meant to him, and how he never would forget that, and how maybe he, too, would move to Madison, WI, and that they could all hang out there too. Baker just said "Yeah man, that would be awesome, you should totally do that," then walked away back to the kitchen where he was barely through the kitchen's threshold before he was doubled over laughing at the kid who he did not know, and saying, "That dude's in for some sort of time tonight."

The next morning Baker and Jed both had pounding headaches and were puking up bile as they haphazardly packed the U-Haul Jed's Mother had gotten for them with the boxes containing everything they collectively owned.

Jesse had not been seen after 10:00 P.M. the previous night and would not be seen again for another three months, when he was only able to mutely fill out his application for employment, under the supervision of his court-mandated caretaker, as a morning clean-up guy and pizza dough prepper at The Antiquated Brewing Company. During his interview he presented Frank Novinsky with a note on an index card that had been laminated that read: *I have mental issues that prevent me from speaking in a way that is easily understood by those to whom I speak, but rest assured, I am a more than capable individual and would excel in this position. For further information about my situation and rehabilitation, please contact Dr. Friedman at the Mendota Mental Health Institute. I would also advise you that it is illegal to discriminate based on mental issues or a prior criminal record which would have no bearing on employment. Thank you for your time, and I truly look forward to being a part of this wonderful team. Sincerely, Jesse Robinson.* The court-mandated caretaker did not speak. The note had been typed and on the back was the contact information for Dr. Friedman at the Mendota Mental Health Institute, and Frank had the distinct impression that should he not hire this silent Jesse Robinson, for this most menial of work, there'd be issues with this Dr. That, and hiring special cases with some kind of disability always came with a write-off, tax-wise.

A Relapse and a reckoning

Nine years after all the charges against her were dropped and Sophia and her ex moved to Madison, WI, and Jed had gone to work for Representative Kilroy, and everything seemed like it was on the trajectory to be just A-ok, it happened, and it was bad. It was splashy too. Everyone knew and it was all out in the open and there would be no taking it back, and Jed would have to do the one thing that he'd always swore he'd never do after he got clean. He'd have to turn his back and walk away from a person who just needed a hand extended in friendship. He wouldn't give it away. He would not be of service. Sophia Ahrens was devastated too after it all happened, and there was no one around left to explain. As was Brian, her ex, but mostly at how upset the cataclysmic event had made the woman he still loved and cared for. The family had come together and really gelled once it was decided that Brian would follow Sophia as Sophia followed Jed. The years since the meeting and falling in love were good ones, sober ones, and the kids that the three of them were co-raising were the light of everyone's lives. They were in their teens now, and getting into the teenage trouble that typical teenagers get into, and that was a real load off of both Jed's and Brian's minds. Sophia got it too. That the trouble was mild in comparison to the two men's. But she still worried. For example, Brian and Sophia's son, Abner, stole a bunch of glassware from his chemistry class and he along with some friends were caught smashing it out back of West H.S. on a Friday afternoon in late fall of last year, and all Brian and Jed could say was, "That's a hell of a lot better than what else they could've been doing with it," and all Sophia could say was, "You guys are morons; he could've been expelled," to which all the men could think to respond was, "But, he wasn't." Theirs was a fundamental difference in thinking about how trouble worked.

Brian didn't live under the same roof as Sophia and Jed and the kids. He lived in a small basement apartment on Madison's immigrant south side. The place was cheap and allowed Brian to be only minimally employed. He used the mountains of free time that this minimal working afforded him to work his program, which he'd not faltered from since the child-locking and eyeball-rupturing incident of 2010, and to be of service to his homegroup's needs. He sponsored about a half dozen guys (never women . . . Brian was a lot of things, but he also knew himself and did not trust himself to not go the way of the thirteenth step, and that made him behave in a way that came across as cold and sexist in how he interacted with his homegroup's women), driving them to doctor's or probation appointments, and he attended multiple meetings every day and made the rounds around S. Wisconsin and N. Illinois doing speaking engagements at meetings that were not his own. He had not slipped even once. It also allowed him to spend just like a fuck-ton of time with his kids. In lieu of any kind of child support, Sophia accepted Brian taking on the role of den-Mother of the clan. He'd pick the kids up every morning and take them to school. He'd shuttle them to their various practices. He'd be the one to go to the school when there was trouble. And, he even chaperoned all the kids' field trips over the last nine years. Jed only attended one meeting a week, and it was the meeting across the street from the Wisconsin State Capitol where he was working for Representative Phillip H. Kilroy, and even then, sometimes the demands of the job would require him to skip his once-weekly meeting and go without his fellowship. Which was hard at first, but got easier and easier as the years went on and he neglected his program. The neglecting of his program was something that Brian worried about for Jed's sake, but not something that Sophia even really thought about. She'd met him when he was sober, never knew his before times. That and from what she'd heard, and what he'd told her, he was never the kind of drunk who did damage to others, only himself, and then only incrementally, never a whole big shebang in one go. Never a life-ruining moment of drunken regret to look back on and say that's where it all went cockeyed. Jed, himself, never thought about relapse as a possibility for himself. He never thought about booze anymore at all. That was part of what made it so easy for him to become too busy to go to meetings and not worry about the consequences of largely giving up the support system of AA. It's not like he kept it all for himself, didn't give it away, he still had a couple of sponsees, but it wasn't like he was going balls-to-the-wall, like Brian. He wasn't checking in on them, wasn't following up, letting weeks go by without hearing from them, and, honestly, and though he would never say it out loud, especially not to Brian, he was kind of relieved when a sponsee stopped calling for a while. Happy to have the reprieve from having to do the constant emotional heavy lifting that it takes to see someone through the early years of sobriety. When a sponsee stopped calling, he felt like he was on vacation somewhere where no one knew him or his issues, and he could feel free of himself and from his past. But a person can only take a vacation from their past, never really leave it truly behind.

The Argus Bar and Grill was where Kevin O'Leary wanted to meet for lunch and he was running extremely late, and Jed was left waiting, which normally would've made him anxious and frustrated, but because this lunch had been the reason for him to skip his weekly meeting, he was perfectly content to sit, sip at his lime and seltzer, stare at the muted televisions mounted in the corners which required neck craning, and simply let his mind go numb and blank with the boredom of it all. He'd assumed that the blankness he'd felt most of the time was caused by the drinking and the drugging, but it turned out that the drinking and the drugging only made the blankness tolerable and turned it into a happy feeling. Now, over the last nine years, he'd learned to take that blankness and work through it, to make it feel less so, to make it feel less nothing. In order to power through the blankness he'd think of Sophia and the kids and how proud his Mother and Father seemed to be of him now, and the pride he'd felt walking across the stage and accepting his diploma, and that worked, for a bit. The thing about sitting and willing yourself to feel, thought Jed, was that the things you use to chase away the nothing feelings, the happy memories, start to feel really lame and stupid the more you think about them. Focusing on the things that made him feel good in the moment that they happened to him turned those moments lame for Jed. Like, for example, when Sophia told him that she had got a job at the DAIS Shelter for Victims of Domestic Violence in Madison and that she'd be moving herself and the kids down to where Jed was, and that "no pressure, but we'd love to spend more time with you too," he'd felt so positively elated that he was able to recall and hold that memory for months, years even, and use it to chase away the all-encompassing blank, but now, sitting on a stool, bellied up to the bar at The Argus, that memory just seemed so saccharine to him, so embarrassing, so lame. It felt to him now like the kind of memory a total dweeb would recall as the best feeling he'd ever had. Though it certainly was a good memory, it felt corrupted and used up. Like he was just making this life with this woman and her kids and her ex-husband for selfish reasons. Just going through the rote motions of normalcy so that he wouldn't kill himself with booze, and maybe, not just kill himself in general. It felt Hallmark to him now.

The bell rang atop The Argus's door and it was not Kevin O'Leary. Jed texted Phillip H. Kilroy informing him of Kevin's lateness and asking if he was needed back at the office or if he should continue to wait and was told to just sit tight; Kevin would be there. He was becoming agitated and anxious. He un-craned his neck and rolled his head on his shoulders to alleviate the stiffness from watching the silent T.V., and it occurred to him, all the sudden, that he'd not been reading the closed captions and had no idea if the man Maury was talking to on the couch was, in fact, the Father. The bell rang again, also not Kevin O'Leary.

The blankness was gone and he was not bored. He was feeling a lot. This was a thing that happened to Jed, sometimes. His blankness and complete inability to feel himself gave way to bursts of feeling all of himself, and it was almost always anger and frustration and malice toward everyone and everything. He did not consider taking a drink in that moment. He was too far removed to think of that as a solution to all of this, now. He remembered what she'd said to him once. "Feel through it and it will be fine." He banged his fist on the bar before he realized what he was doing and everyone turned. He said, "Sorry," and felt his face flush. The bell rang and it was still not Kevin O'Leary, and Jed looked at his phone again to see if he'd somehow missed an email or a text, but he had not. He remembered another thing she'd said. "You don't have to express everything . . . it's okay to just feel it and process and let it float from the top of your head as light as a cloud, instead of firing everything from your mouth like a bullet." The door's bell rang and it was not Kevin O'Leary. "Motherfucking cocksucker," said Jed and the bartender turned on her heels and shot him a filthy look. "Can I get you anything," she said. "No," he responded, but that was only because he still had some seltzer and lime. She turned back around and began wiping the rich wood of the bar with a rag and not paying attention to Jed Lucas. The bell rang again, and again it was not Kevin O'Leary.

The last time that Jed saw Kevin O'Leary was at this very bar and was about three weeks ago, and he was late then too. About forty-five minutes. He was distracted, then, but that was not something that was unusual; Kevin had recently left AFSCME and had taken up the job of Executive Director of The Democratic Party of The State of Wisconsin, and was often busy and distracted. But he did seem particularly out of it and somewhere else, then. This time it had already been an hour and the lunch rush had passed and the bell stopped its ringing at regular intervals. When Kevin O'Leary had shown that last time, Jed had told him about his plan to finally ask Sophia Ahrens to marry him, and also that he'd like to ask Brian if he could adopt the two children, not because he wanted to strip Brian of custody rights, or because he thought Brian was not doing all that Brian should be doing, but rather because he wanted all-in on the family, and he wanted the children to know that he was all-in on them as well. He was happy, then, for him (Jed) that is, and he (Kevin) clapped him on the back and pulled him in for a bear-hug and told him how proud he was of him (Jed) and that he was glad that he had gotten to be there for the beginning of this whole journey in politics thing. Kevin had had a double whisky rocks, then, and Jed had had his seltzer with lime, and they'd both ordered burgers and ate with no discussion of the state of state politics. At the end of that meal, Kevin had mentioned that he was unsatisfied with the current Communications Director for the Democratic Party of the State of Wisconsin and wondered if Jed would ever consider making the leap over and joining him, knowing that the job would come with more responsibility and only matching pay, but he'd be moving up the ladder, as it were, and proving to people, out there, that he could do this kind of work at a higher level and not just for one back-bench State

Representative, and that this was how people moved all the way up and made it to D.C., and this was a great opportunity being presented, but that it too would also come with insane hours for which he could also expect no additional compensation. Some folks ruptured ulcers in jobs like these. Jed had said at the time that he'd think about it, and he had, and now this lunch was the lunch where he was going to tell Kevin O'Leary that he'd spoken with Sophia Ahrens about it and that she knew what this would mean for the life they had made together, and that he'd be gone more and working more, and that her routine would not change — work-wise — but domestically she'd naturally have to pick up the slack with the home and the kids, but she also reassured him that they did have Brian, with all his dedication to service of his fellows, and that she was reasonably sure that she could redirect some of that energy, not all of it mind you, she wouldn't ask that of him, but some of it away from AA and toward the family's home. She told him to go for it. To take it. To show everyone there (at The Democratic Party of The State of Wisconsin) just who she knew him to be, and that he would kill it, and before you knew it, he'd be on MSNBC talking about the state of things, nationally.

The bell had not rung in some time and appeared to have no plans on ringing again in the near future and Kevin O'Leary had still not shown and Jed now knew that something had gone wrong (work-wise) for Kevin and that he'd text him and say that, yes, he'd take the job and that he understood he was busy, and was sorry to have missed out on their monthly lunch, but was excited to be working much, much more closely with him moving forward. He sent his text and then he left The Argus Bar and Grill and the bartender did not seem sad to see the back of him, but was later, about thirty seconds later, surprised to find a twenty with a note saying sorry and to keep the change as payment for Jed's three seltzers with lime.

The office of Phillip H. Kilroy was absolutely abuzz with it when he returned from his aborted lunch plans with a rudely absent and non-communicating Kevin O'Leary. The story was on every screen and being read aloud by an intern named Binyamin Abraham to the Representative, who was standing over the shoulder of the intern with his left arm raising his left hand to his face so his left hand's fingers could cup his chin while his right arm cut across his mid-section so his right hand's fingers could cup his elbow. The Representative's junior assistant sat reclined fully in his desk's rolling chair with his feet planted flatly on the ground, and he was using his legs to swivel quarter-moons as he too listened to the intern reading the breaking and vague news of the tragedy at the condo of Kevin O'Leary. The intern must've only started reading aloud around the same moment Jed Lucas Jr. entered and was just finishing what was clearly the first line of the article. "–eary, who until recently was the Regional Director for Political Advocacy for the Wisconsin branch of the American Federation of State County and Municipal Employees, and is now the current Executive Director for the Democratic Party of the State of Wisconsin, brought the unconscious woman to the emergency room at Meriter Hospital in Madison around 4:45 in the morning, where she was pronounced dead upon arrival," the intern read.

"Holy fucking shit," said the junior assistant.

"................." Representative Kilroy just stood there, hand cupping both chin and elbow.

"What the fuck?" asked Jed.

"Kevin's fucking fucked," said Kilroy. "The party is fucking fucked."

"It was determined that the woman, some sort of associate of O'Leary, had taken heroin laced with fentanyl at some point in the evening and succumbed to an accidental overdose. The Madison Police Department has confirmed to The Capitol Times that Mr. O'Leary has been interviewed and that a search of his personal truck uncovered a postal scale and a cache of small baggies typical of drug distribution. No charges have yet to be filed against Mr. O'Leary and the investigation is ongoing at this hour," read the intern, Binyamin.

"Holy fucking shit!"

"What?"

"The Speaker's fucking daughter!" said the junior assistant.

"What about her?" asked Kilroy.

"This is fucking wild."

"Fucking what?!"

"Look it," answered the junior assistant, pointing to another breaking news flash, this time on Channel 3000's half-broken and early 00s-era website. The headline read: "Daughter of Republican Speaker of Wisconsin Assembly charged with overdose death of Green Bay man." The article's thumbnail was a picture of the acne-scared daughter of the Republican Speaker of the Wisconsin State Assembly looking unwashed in greasy dirty blond hair and smiling a druggie smile for her mugshot. The article within explained how the daughter of the prominent official was suspected of having sold the fatal dose of heroin laced with fentanyl to the Green Bay man on or about last Tuesday, when he then both shot up and died. While the investigation was ongoing, the article explained, the daughter had cut her hair and taken other measures to evade being taken in for questioning, such as hiding out at a friend's apartment and purchasing one-way tickets to Nashville, where her estranged Mother lived.

Back on the screen of Benyamin Abraham, the front-page headline concerning Kevin O'Leary was replaced by the newer headline concerning the daughter, as there was a mugshot, and stories with mugshots tend to get more click-throughs, and Kevin, still not under arrest, was spared that indignity. Later, the Speaker would release a statement about the horrors and tragedies of the opioid crisis and announce the forming of a taskforce to tackle the issue. In his statement, he'd reference both executive Director O'Leary and his own daughter as examples of how the crisis is not just a problem concerning the type of people most associated with drug use but had also found its way into the homes and lives of every Wisconsinite, and that immediate action was needed in stemming the tide of woe plaguing the state. The dueling controversies, one Democrat and one Republican, sort of offset throughout the afternoon, and neither side was aiming to score cheap points off the misfortune of the other. It was becoming a rare instance where partisan hackery was set aside, and both sides had to acknowledge the problem and face it head-on with some kind of action and not just sit back and throw political bombs at each other over the perceived ineffectualness of their personal political rivals. O'Leary was summarily dismissed, of course, but the party did release their own statement saying that that was done so he could seek the treatment that he obviously so desperately needed, and that they would be continuing his health insurance policy so that he might avail himself of said treatment. Kilroy tasked Jed Lucas with calling The Speaker's office to offer his (The Representative's) support and sympathies and to inquire about how one would go about being assigned to the newly created (or rather soon to be newly created) Speaker's Joint Opioid Taskforce.

Everything in Jed Lucas's experience with AA told him that he needed to reach out to Kevin O'Leary because Kevin O'Leary was a man who had so clearly lost control of his life and the consequences of that loss of control were now dire and he needed help and a friend. Everything in Jed Lucas's experience with AA told him that Kevin O'Leary would be alone and isolated and that all of the people who he thought were his friends over his twenty-plus years in progressive Wisconsin politics would be walking sideways away from him and losing his number. Everything Jed Lucas knew was telling him that a call to Kevin O'Leary now would be an act of service and would be a kindness, and he could give away what he had in hopes of strengthening his grip on what he had, and that, ultimately, he could let Kevin (the man who saw something in him) know that he was not alone and no matter what happened from here, he still had a friend, and that he could get better and that this experience would not, or did not have to, define the rest of his life. That it would be hard and there were going to be consequences, but eventually, all this would be past and could be forgiven. That he could still pull himself back from the edge, and that facing whatever was to come would be almost impossible, but that he (Jed Lucas) would be there for him, supporting him, and helping him along his way. And that even if the worst of worst possible consequences (the going to jail for a very long stretch) came to pass, it would not matter because Jed would not abandon him or kick him out, and that he (Jed) would continue to believe in Kevin O'Leary and give away whatever he had to Kevin O'Leary. Everything in Jed Lucas's soul was telling him to take his phone from his pocket and to call Kevin O'Leary right then and to tell him all these things and that in doing so he (Jed Lucas) would continue to be saved and redeemed and sober. And he did take the phone from his pocket, and he did scroll his contacts until he found Kevin O'Leary's number, but then he looked at the messages the two had been sending back and forth over the last nine months, the vague plans to "meet up real quick" at The Argus, and it rang clear as a bell in his mind that placing a call, now, exposed him, and he did not call his friend, he did not offer his support, he did not tell him that he would be alright and that he (Jed) would always be there for him because he (Jed) knew that he (Kevin) was a good person who made horrible mistakes, but that it was not too late. He did none of those things and instead deleted both Kevin's number and all the messages they'd sent each other over the years from his phone and said, "You should not call Kevin ever again," to Representative Kilroy, "because this is going to get messy and your name can't come up in the follow-up story, Phil." Then he put his phone back in his pocket and he leaned back in his chair, and he knew, absolutely knew in that moment, that he'd made a decision and taken a path that was particularly damaging and antithetical to his very soul and being, and that he would leave politics at the first chance he got.

At 5:00 on the dot he left the office of Phillip Kilroy and wanted nothing more than to go home and talk to Sophia and have her tell him that he did the wrong thing but for the right reasons, and as he stepped out of the monument to governance that was the Wisconsin State Capitol, he did not see the men approach him from behind, but he did feel the cattle prod as it hit the small of his back, and all he could think to himself was, yeah, that makes sense, before losing consciousness. He woke up later, how much later he did not know, and he was sitting upright in a chair and facing a wall-length mirror and he had the distinct impression that he was supposed to talk, that he was supposed to tell that mirror everything that was him. He had the distinct impression that it was very important that he, now, give away everything of himself and expect nothing but scorn and consequences in return. Then a man opened the slot in his door and slid some food through and said her name and nothing else.

In the weeks following the disappearance of Jed Lucas Jr., Sophia Ahrens barely left her bedroom, such was her depression. Brian, feeling the pressure of being the only responsible adult left in the unit, and wholly without his support system of both Jed and Sophia, relapsed hard on day fourteen but was able to keep it hidden for another twenty days. When he was discovered, high and incoherent, by his children, Sophia was alerted to the direness of the home situation and Brian was again forced into a rehabilitation facility and told that this was his very last chance and that Sophia was in no fit state to be dealing with any of this now.

Later, on that same day, Jed's cement room's bunk shook with the psychic shockwaves of Michael's head's explosion. After which, the sounds of harried shoes found him where he was, and stopped in front of his door, and then the schlink that told him he was about to be moved.

Everyone gets their turn in the barrel.

Frank on the town's edge stops and waits and feels

On the lip of a small rolling hill on the edge of Antigo, WI, the figure of a road-worn but otherwise fine man stands and waits with his face pointing toward where the town itself, the commercial buildings and houses, spring from the surrounding earth and congregate for protection from all the elements that would seek to harm it. It's sure to be daunting, the task. He is prepared. She has let him see the town for the first time but she has yet to let him know what it is that she expects him to do. He knows, however. Always knew. Feels it. When he first crested the hill, his feet's momentum felt to him like it would never stop. It'd been so long since he'd felt the crook of the shepherd's hook pulling him backward and back again to begin anew. He thought, then. He thought about the years and the miles and that made him angry, so, he bent at his knees and felt how stiff he was, then he crouched to alleviate the stiffness and the anger. He remained crouched for a day and a night on the lip of the hill, looking. She still refuses to speak, but he does know. He's angry she won't admit it. Angry she won't ask. Angry she just takes and never gives. Angry that that's how she was in life and angry he took it and never stood up for himself. He runs his fingers through the tall grass of the hill's top and plucks some blades and stands then, and opens his palm and lets them go on the breeze. They float toward town but fall well short as the earth's winds are fickle and indecisive. Maybe she doesn't know, he thinks, bitch.

The walking in silence and blank of thought was soothing in the years he'd done it for her. It was the stopping he'd had issues with. He felt angry Jed was there, both that day outside Portage and at his fortieth. And angry that that had happened to him. Angry that he'd waited until he was dead to deal with his life. And even then, he lacked conviction enough to deal with it, permanently. Or maybe she wouldn't let him. Maybe she felt what he felt in the moment that Jed's car flipped down the embankment and rolled into the ditch — maybe she felt what he was planning next with that rock that was actually a large chunk of rural WI HWY and she crooked him back at the moment she did because she was, is, still fundamentally incapable of letting him deal with his life his way without influence or coercion.

Maybe. Maybe. Maybe. He is alive, still. And with her.

He knows that is not true like he knows what he was made for. Made to do. This place feels like both home and not home to him, and he knows why, but only now, only after what had happened to him had happened to him. He knew it the second what had happened had happened, but it was opaque, then, not clear like it is now on the lip of the hill, and thinking about the clarity with which he sees why this feels like home to him makes him so mad. So mad that at any point he could've sought this place out and followed a trail that would've led him away from his sad life and job and wife, and toward a Mother who was both his and secretly hoping he would find her, someday. Mad that Howard and Mitzi died before his sons could know them.

On that hill, he curses both Molly and then God.

Curses Molly in hopes that he can make her feel his anger, and she will see that he is prepared, but not yet ready for what it is that is to happen here, and he'll be pulled back, just the once more, and made to start over, and the doing of what needs to be done to finish this place for keeps will be put off another six to eight months, depending. He curses God for what He did to his parents and the anger he feels then burns through him like a field renewing itself and preparing for what's still under the ground to come up and fully bloom into articulated life.

At first, Howard and Mitzi watched each other die, then Mitzi was left alone knowing she did nothing to tame Howard's suffering. Then she died of that as much as she'd died of the cancer in her bones and blood. Frank was there, in the end, and God had let him see it all, feel it all. And he'd felt nothing but low-lying anger since. That's where it was born, he knows. It's what had allowed her to do what she'd done, he knows. Does she know, he wonders, deciding it doesn't matter what she knows because nothing matters now except her anger, his presence, and the work yet to be done. Nothing matters to Frank Novinsky anymore except his anger because his anger is all she'd left him. In life first, and now in whatever this is.

She speaks, now. She speaks to the middle of his brain and she says something like I don't need to explain myself to you, dear heart, and he is so pissed, now.

You won't see home again repeats in reverb and fades away from the center of his brain, and he then hears it as if it's being whispered by the very grass on which he stands, which, the weight of himself that his feet bears did indent and bend and break, leaving permanent imprints of his shoe's shape where he has stood going on four days. He is visible from the HWY but no one stops to check on him and he never wonders why. Not anymore. Not after so much time spent outside and visible but invisible just the same. People can ignore a lot when they want to. His feet move now and he walks. The indentation where he stands will remain until the ground underneath it crumbles and falls. No other prints does he make.

But, really, you should never do that to a person

I can feel it in my everywhere and I did steal that kid's littlebigwheel but he wasn't really using it right and he could afford to ask Mommy for another and I just knew that because he looked like he loved to be loved by Mommy and she felt to me like she loved to love him too, you know? Anyway, I can't talk about what it is you brought me in here for because it's all there and not, you know? Anyway, this room feels cold and I need a blanket. Get me the afghan from my Mother's couch and I'll talk about all that. All of it. All. Of. It. She was there? Too? Yes? She is here and I am here and they are here but one is dead and you can't know what I know because it's been like this forever and a day and communication's a real bitch, you know? I've always had this problem where I sound perfectly reasonable and happy but everyone, especially here, thinks I sound angry and mad and like I want to kill, which, I fucking don't, you know? Anyway, look I can't sit in cold rooms for too long without Mommy's couch's afghan, it's cruel and unusual and I'll see you all at The Hague before this is through and once upon a time, I did steal that littlebigwheel but that was only because I needed to get to work and Frank said if I was late again, he'd fire me and I need that money. Need. That. Money. It's how I'm going to get back at them for doing what they did. Been saving for years. You can't just do that to people, you know? Anyway, she moved when I moved and they moved and we all moved, you know? Anyway, I can't see straight since like '01, or maybe '02, it's all a blur, you know? Anyway, if you give me some kind of afghan, Mommy's or no, I'll be much happier in this situation I am in and you are . . . in? You know? Anyway, the littlebigwheel was purple and pastel pink which are colors I dislike but necessity is the Mommy of inventionness and I needed the money for my plans and it rode like shit but who am I to judge, you know? Anyway, he cried when I took it and I cried later at the memory of everything, you know? Anyway, if you could maybe give me some sort of area rug for the cement floor here, I think I'd be more cooperative, you know? She is here and I am here and that's why we are all here, or no? Why am I and she and he and he and not him even here anymore? Where is the second she? Where are we? In DeKalb, this wouldn't happen. Here is godless. Here is cold and I need my Mother's afghan! Christ on a fucking cross, Helms! Christ on a fucking cross, Hargrove! If you bring me a nice oriental area rug and my Mommy's couch and afghan we can spruce this place right up. I've never came down. Don't wanna, really, you know? Anyway, and here's a thing, you know? Anyway,

Chapter Seventeen

A big square cement room
underground and isolated

THEY ARE ALL IN A BIG SQUARE cement room underground
and isolated and it is the first time they've all been in
the same room since Christmas '09. It does not feel
monumental to any of them. The body of Michael
Amadeus Greene is propped and sitting headless on
the floor of the room's SW corner. They all, except Helen, ignore him. The Bear paces back and forth. The
after spray of Michael's head's fiery explosion forms
an outline of Agent Helen Abelmen's own head (which
took the brunt of the spraying gore) on the chest of his
body's white, buttoned-down dress shirt. The room is
devoid of furnishings and is one of countless rooms at
the FPPIB complex which serve no other purpose than
to have been designed and built to hit certain bud-
getary minimums. The Bear paces and he murmurs
inaudibly even to himself. Helen stands in a kind of
silent shock. Jed has wiped her face clean of the worst
of it but still doesn't recognize her as her. As the
friend he knew. Baker strums a pantomime tune of his
own devising and hums some off-key notes. Eventually, Jesse Robinson is brought in and sits next to
Michael's headless body and clutches his knees to his

chest, and says something like, "They robbed me, you know? Anyway." No one else speaks. The pantomime tune and hummed melody has head-lyrics he does not begin singing aloud which deal primarily with the death of Mac Miller, whom he knows nothing about. The collar of the T-shirt Michael had worn is singed. The room's cement floor, cold. The room, cold.

The Bear's pacing ceases after a minute or two and he comes to rest in front of his Agent, who is standing there, in shock, looking Jed in his green eyes after her face has been wiped, and she is saying something now like, "It was so different, she is so different." The Bear sort of nudges Jed away and stands in front of his Agent. Her eyes are still on the spot where Jed's eyes were, just off and below where The Bear's face now is so that she is looking just to the immediate left of his chin and past him to where Michael's body is slumped against the wall, headless. The Bear speaks to his Agent, but really to the room.

"Years. It's been years of pointless toil in this country's government, but we are now standing on the very edge of history and we can expect no guidance from anywhere because we are the pilgrims now, the settlers treading new earth. I've known her since '67; she is the one on whom we are meant to stake our claims. This place was built as shrine to her, and now we know why. Her gift, her power, it is singular and it is unique. We are a money trap. A honey pot for spending. That's what we were always meant to be, and I was given charge of the grift, and then ignored. We have always been ignored. A line item. A column on a spreadsheet that was long-ago forgotten and left to wither and die out here, while they, back east, do the important work that people can see. We have never been seen because we were a slush fund for kickbacks and only allowed to operate to justify some of the spending. But you've all now seen what she can do when she wants to. And that's not all. You haven't seen what she can do to a person, truly, when she wants to. Frank's on the lip of Antigo, Bob says so. His head smokes now and he is walking again. He has not been pulled back in months. Something's going to happen. And she's still saying she needs all of you."

"I saw Frank nine years ago." Jed. "He crashed my car with a piece of road and then vanished and I never said anything because I was sure it was sobriety-related. My brain coming back online after so many years of anesthetization. I thought I was remembering, vividly remembering, something I wanted to forget. I thought, then, seeing him there with that chunk of highway uplifted and him cocking back aim to smash my windshield and kill me dead was my brain forcing me to face the blood shaped like a man that I saw and the trauma and regret that I felt for my role in his death, for the LSD I'd procured for her, and the resultant craziness it made of her mind. I thought, and still think, that the actions of our pasts don't ever go away, or even really fade over time. They linger on in our marrow and we carry them with us, always. We carry those actions as vivid as they were on the day when we did them or had them done to us. We can't escape any of it or change ourselves enough to make them not have happened. These pasts that we carry with us are permanent. Mistakes. Violence. Escapism. Decisions made and actions carried out are patterns made, and we can't escape them no matter how far we go or how high we climb.

"I was in a meeting a few months back on K-12 education reform. Not open to the public, this meeting. Just legislative staffers having a meeting with other legislative staffers for the sole purpose of having had the meeting so we could all go back to our bosses and say we had a meeting. These meetings, meetings for meetings' sake, happen all the time and are unremarkable. But, at this meeting, some staffer from some office I did not recognize said something about a previous Governor, some joke. It was a tired joke. One that had been made about our former Governor since he'd run for Governor. And believe me, I'm no fan of the man, so, it's not like I care what people have to say about him. But the joke has been so persistent and so pervasive, regarding this former Governor, that most of the time it just floats by on the air and I don't even hear it anymore. But this time I did. The staffer said something as the meeting was wrapping up like 'Well, it just feels good to have the education Governor now, instead of the dropout Governor, amiright?' like that. You know, because the former Governor dropped out of college. And the rest of the staffers were all nodding in agreement and one of them, some just-graduated type, said something aloud to everyone like 'Yeah, feels good to have the smart kids in charge again, maybe now we won't have to present our proposals in crayon to the executive.'

"And everyone laughed the polite laughs that political people laugh and started getting up from their chairs to leave and have those one-on-one conversations in the corridors that always happen when political people leave meetings, and all I could do was just sit there, just sit there as the joke and the resultant comment and the laughter didn't float on by on the air, but rather lingered over my head like a cloud, and all I could think was that no matter where I go, no matter what I do, I will always be dragging a me that isn't me along with me, no matter what.

"I can't outrun my decisions. I can't out-accomplish my mistakes. I can't erase how people view those decisions and mistakes. If I ever get into a position of power or ascend to a position of note, then, eventually, it will all come out, and I will just be the dropout, the burnout, the stupid kid who couldn't hack high school. And my reasons, then, won't matter. And anything I've done in the interim won't matter. There will always be someone, somewhere, in some room to make the jokes that I would never hear but would know, in my bones and in my marrow, they were making. Frank coming and smashing my window and running me off the road, he was a hallucination, but he was also an elemental truth; you are who you are, always. Trying to outrun that is like trying to outlive the wind."

"Frank's no wraith, no ghost, no reanimation. You didn't dream him up and he didn't float forth from the deeply repressed recesses of your mind. He is as real a living being as he can be. He is wrath made man. Anger tenuously contained in a skeleton's cage and wrapped in flesh. He is what she made him. He is the instrument with which she will paint her will on this earth. And, she's not through. She refuses to be the sum of her mistakes and decisions. She feels she can live and be happy, here, with you all. She has communicated to me, alone, in the small hours when this place is empty and I should be lying next to the loveliest of lovely women who has spent decades taking care of my every need, that she wishes to reverse the course of her own life and the lives lived adjacent to hers and to arrest them there when she was happy. When everyone was happy. She can make an anger-Golem to spread her wrath. She can make the opposite of you all to safekeep her happiness. She will not take no for an answer, I'm afraid. We are out of options."

The room falls silent as The Bear's words float over them all on a breeze from the ceiling's exposed ductwork, and no one moves or even breathes. Helen Abelmen's eyes have yet to move and continue to look just beyond The Bear. Michael's weight shifts and his body slumps over onto its side and rolls a little, and there is a wet thwacking noise as he falls into his new supine position. The blood puddle he's been sitting in breaks its surface tension and runs. Jesse lifts Michael's legs and rests them on his lap and rubs the corpse's calves and says something like, "There, there, you know? Anyway." Baker stands and walks to Jed and puts his hand on his shoulder and comforts his friend as best he can, but it doesn't feel right to either of them; too much has changed, too much has not. The door to the large empty room is metal and locked and it breathes deeply, distending inward upon exhale. Helen's eyes move from supine Mike and fix on the door's movement. The whole room quakes briefly. "She's waiting," says The Bear. "She's waiting."

Excerpted from Interpersonal Interrogation and Statement Aggregation of one Michael Amadeus Greene: **/**/2019

UNKNOWN: "Your wife, where is she now? Do you even know? Do you keep in contact with her at all?"

MAG: "God, I haven't spoken to Helen, in what, in like eight years. I couldn't tell you where she is if I wanted to. For all I know, she remarried, had a couple of kids, put on a solid twenty, and is living out the whole domestic thing somewhere in like Indiana."

UNKNOWN: "What was said the last time you two spoke?"

MAG: "That's interesting. You've been divorced, haven't you?"

UNKNOWN: "Mr. Greene, if you'd answer the question, please."

MAG: "No, look, I've been here for like God knows how long and you assholes have kept me locked up and not told me shit. Then I'm dragged into this room and you are asking me about some decade-old shit that has to do with some gaslighting crazy person that I don't even know anymore. So, indulge me, you've been divorced, or no?"

UNKNOWN: "Yes, I've been divorced."

MAG: "See, shit, I knew it. You ask any person what was the last conversation they had with their wife, like that day, and probably a good chunk of them won't know or remember. They'll know generally what it was about, but they won't know what was said. The words. Exactly. But divorced people, know the words. They know the words and how their ex was holding their arms when the words were said. They know the facial expressions and the little tics and what the body language was communicating. Ask any divorced person what was the last thing their ex said to them during the divorce process, like standing there in the courtroom when the thing was finalized, I mean, and they'll know exactly what that bitch said when she dropped the hammer once and for good. If they have like a custody thing because they had kids, then the relationship and the interactions largely can go back to being forgettable, and the slights and the grievances can just keep on piling up more or less anonymously, much as they did before the Big D, but if that was the last time they spoke, at the proceedings, then those words are etched on the brain, they have their own special place where they live forever. It's like especially true for the partner who didn't ask for the divorce. Only a person who's been divorced would ask a person a question like that, 'what was said?' not, 'what happened the last time you and the ex spoke?' which is a much easier question for most people to answer a decade on."

UNKNOWN: "So, what *was* said, Mr. Greene?"

MAG: "We don't have to do this."

It was a bar fight

In the ensuing weeks, The Callaghan Collection faded from the collective memory of the employees at Capitol Capital. No one mentioned it much anymore and to make matters worse, Michael was actually in a bit of a slump. He was still bringing in the dough, but it was picayune shit and in drips and drabs. Betty Von Trier only used the parking spot once and then never again, and then, finally, one day, Michael arrived at Capitol Capital and the markings designating the spot her spot were gone. Last week he brought in $2,000, total, which was the lowest for all collectors. He'd fallen off the mean, hard. His system was broken, or at least not working properly anymore. She'd dropped the papers on him the night before at the mostly empty apartment that they'd once shared, but now didn't, and she'd told him that once he signed them that the state would make them wait six months before the divorce could be finalized.

He scanned the stack of papers on his desk's top and he found nothing there that jumped out to him or looked promising. Nothing looked promising anymore. In a file marked Marcus A. Allen he found a story of a man in debt to Dick's Sporting Goods to the tune of $15,000. The debt was incurred when Marcus A. Allen opened up an in-store credit card at a time when he was particularly flush, had a great credit score, and plenty of assets, and he'd used the credit card to completely outfit himself with top-of-the-line hunting gear — shotgun, long gun, five different Blaze Orange camo sets, three different kinds of deer stand, four duck blinds, and just like a fuck-ton of ammo.

His wife was pissed when he got home late because she'd been waiting at their apartment's door with the papers and he'd *promised* he'd be there right after work and afterward, he couldn't eat or sleep.

He picked up his phone and dialed the first number on record for Marcus A. Allen, a home's landline, and the receiver, which he scrunched between his shoulder and ear, screeched and whistled and informed him that the line had been disconnected.

Betty Von Trier was ignoring him at the A8 Chinese Buffet and Carry Out and he did not know why, and he also had to give his key back.

The cellphone on record was also disconnected — a robot had told him as much when he tried it. Looking through Marcus A. Allen's file, Michael had to wonder about the kind of person who goes into that kind of debt starting what was clearly a new hobby. What kind of person torpedoes their life and financial stability for the dopamine rush of something new? The high of the swiping of a card and the feeling one gets when holding something expensive and new. He was that kind of person when he really thought about it, but he'd always been in check. He wondered what would happen if he let go, now. Like what would happen if since he was going to be single again, he just let go, said fuck it, spent freely, lived freely. Didn't let anyone or anything dictate what he thought of himself and just did whatever it was that would make him happy.

She'd stipulated in the divorce papers that she dropped on him that he could keep his car and she would keep hers, but that she got the bulk of the furniture, which was already at her apartment anyway — he'd made her write in that he got to keep the television regardless of whose Father had purchased it as a wedding gift.

Marcus A. Allen worked at Epic Systems in their Software Development Department, according to the file. It was possible that he still worked there, thought Michael, but all evidence was pointing to the contrary. He dialed his phone for a third time and asked the person who answered if he could speak to a Marcus A. Allen and was told that he was, in fact, no longer with Epic Systems and thus no longer getting the legendarily large Epic Systems salary. Michael knew what had happened to Marcus A. Allen. Knew it in his guts. And it wasn't a unique story or circumstance. It had happened to a lot of people.

There was no point in pursuing Marcus A. Allen any further. He couldn't pay. Not yet. Marcus A. Allen would be somewhere, right then, quietly trying to piece together just what had happened, what had gone so wrong, and actively wondering how he'd fix it all, and then later, how he could make sure that it never happened again. And he would maybe succeed — in putting his life back together, that is. He'd get a new job, he'd find a new place, he'd probably meet a new woman and get a new wife, and then, he'd build back a solid base for a life that was turbulence-free from here on out, and then, at the moment when it was all going right again for Marcus A. Allen, he'd fill out some application for some credit card, or a home loan, or car financing, and bam, he'd be denied and Michael's company would get a ping, and his new contact information would be conveyed, and Michael would have a fresh lead on Marcus A. Allen and begin his (Michael's) campaign of harassment over the old $15k he still owed on the hunting gear that was long ago hawked, because you are never free, Marcus A. Allen, it always follows.

When everyone else has forgotten, and life has moved on, there is always a Michael A. Greene who hasn't.

He had to set strict appointments to see Betty Von trier now, and another Capitol Capital employee also had to be present in those meetings for the benefit of everyone involved, or so he was told.

A few days after he was presented with the divorce settlement papers, he found himself entirely disinterested in the manila folder on his desk's surface and instead stared forward, at his screen, and held his hands in his lap, and did very little else until lunch, which consisted of a single tuna sandwich and a single pickle spear that he ate at his desk. The office was empty over the lunch hour, so he had the place to himself and he did weep openly, for a time, while eating his tuna sandwich. Once divorced, in six or so months, he couldn't help but think he'd not be a particularly desirable catch and privately he thought that he'd fucked up the best thing he'd ever have in Helen Abelmen. But then again, she wouldn't even change her name, so, how committed could she have been? His face was puffy and bloated after lunch, and one of the other guys said he looked like he could use a drink and invited him to the TGIF after work and Michael accepted.

After the invitation, the afternoon crawled. He did no work, made no calls, and Betty Von Trier kept looking over at him as he sat and did no work. She did not approach him to talk or send her personal best friend and "office wife" Nancy McNally over to set a time when she (BVT) wished to see Michael in her office. He convinced himself it was just a joke that had gone too far that had made everything weird. Around 4:00 P.M. he considered what he was going to do next, living arrangement-wise, because without the continued support, which would surely be cut off in the coming weeks as they hammered out the final details of the final settlement and he signed the damn thing, which he'd not consented to do on the night he was presented with the papers, even after she'd agreed that he could keep the very expensive TV that her Father had purchased for her, he could not afford the two-bedroom unit in the new development on Madison's west side.

His desk phone rang and he ignored it. When Michael was in his early twenties and working at the Antiquated as a server while he attended the UW, he'd had an apartment on Doty Street, a one-bedroom, which cost $500 a month — all utilities included. He assumed something like that was more expensive now. But the place was a shit box, so he assumed whatever they charged he could still afford it, even if his collecting never got back to where it was pre-apartment divorce settlement meeting. His desk's phone rang again and he picked it up and Kevin Hollister was telling him it was 5:00 P.M. and quitting time, and that he had to take a wicked shit but would meet Michael at the bar at the TGIF for a drink, but apologized as well because since Kevin had invited Michael out for the evening, Kevin had subsequently spoken to his own wife who needed him home as close to after work as possible because the kids had been just impossible that day and she (the wife) could use a break, so, he (Kevin Hollister) should be tending to his own affairs and not worrying about the affairs of others, on this particular day, or so said the wife.

Michael understood.

At the bar, he ordered a martini with four olives and light on the vermouth, and he stared up at the TVs on the wall above the bar and watched the CC of Sports Center appear and disappear with the moving of talking heads with impeccable hairdos' mouths. His cellphone buzzed once and he ignored it and continued reading the CC's scrawl but not taking in what was being said. It was off-season for football and he'd always found baseball's early-season machinations too boring for words. He *should* root for The Brewers, or at least pretend he did, but he didn't. When pressed by a friend or colleague on what team he did root for (in baseball) he'd demure and say he just wasn't a fan of the sport in a general way. But that wasn't entirely true. Michael A. Greene rooted for The Cubs, but only if they made the playoffs, and only because he enjoyed the idea of them finally winning another World Series and the spontaneous joy that would cause in his general geographic area. He enjoyed the idea of The Cubs winning and the people of Chicago experiencing something rare, something great, and at no real cost to anyone else. It's not often that a whole lot of people get to feel that good and have it not be at the direct expense of a whole other group of people. Sure, there are the opposing teams' fans to consider, and M. A. Greene did consider them, but he had concluded that, ultimately, the very fact that they were beaten by The Cubs, who hadn't won one in so long, would almost negate the fact that the opposing team and their fans really wanted to win too. And they (the opposing team and their fans) would be swept up in the moment, too, and experience a kind of begrudging joy that could be summed up by the players and their fans expressing the sentiment with the phrase "If we had to lose, I'm glad it was to you."

His phone buzzed again and he checked it and Kevin Hollister was not coming, after all. He decided he would stay anyway, drinking martini after martini and watching Sports Center and reading the CC scrawl. The martinis were probably the reason that he didn't notice when she sat down next to him, not until she said, "My ex couldn't take his eyes off that damn show either."

"It's the underlying condition that plagues the gender and makes us assholes, I think. It's not our fault, you see. Sports Center is the malignancy at the center of our existence."

"So, it's the watching and rewatching of Sports Center every day, multiple times a day, that makes you all the way that you are?"

"Absolutely. It's a whole conspiracy against us, Sports Center. Makes us ignore our wives and children. Get upset at the very presence of the other human beings in our lives because they want to take our attention away from sports and Sports Center."

"My ex would agree with that."

"So would mine."

"Jane," she said, extending a hand that had that distinctive just-stopped-wearing-her-ring white skin on the hand's ring finger.

"Michael," he said back, taking her hand and giving it one of those informal and soft half-shakes that men give women who aren't their colleagues. The last time he touched a woman who was his colleague he'd given her an unsolicited hug by the water cooler and thanked her for all the support she'd given him over the last few weeks and said he'd wanted to repay her with a nice dinner out, anywhere she wanted to go.

"Well, if your ex is anything like me, she probably didn't actually do much to help the situation, just sat there quietly, stewing in her own discontent with the relationship and wondering, internally, why you wouldn't just change and she could stay exactly the same and then everything would be fine, instead of just admitting that you both had probably made a mistake, all those years ago, and just moved on in a friendly and healthy way, one which would've saved the both of you some trauma, in the end."

"We just met, Jane."

"Exactly what my ex would've said just now."

"Yeah, I suppose it would've been easier on everyone involved if one of us would've just said, 'hey, you know what, I think we were good in the beginning, but something broke along the way or was never really there in the first place, and now it's time for us to move on. No harm no foul.' But instead, what do we do? What does anyone do? They let it drag on and on, getting angrier and more bitter, until, finally, they themselves force the issue in a totally volcanic explosion of repressed emotion at all the perceived slights they've endured. Or, they force the other to do the same, and can still leave, but now they get to feel victimized, present themselves to friends and family as victims of the whole thing. Put upon. Done wrong."

"We just met, Michael."

"Yeah, I suppose. But wouldn't it be cool if we just met, and just made a deal to like make a go of something new, together, knowing nothing about each other, and knowing full well that it could end horribly, down the line, if we let it, because our track records would indicate that we are both capable of going nuclear in relationships, and just made a deal, here and now, that, like, we'd just tell the other at the exact moment something in the relationship stopped working, and the other could decide, at that point, if that issue was something they could work on to change, or if it was a dealbreaker, and then, if it was, a dealbreaker, we'd both walk away happy in knowing that we got to experience something good that made us both happy for a while, but that we also got to cut and run before it truly made us unhappy. Wouldn't that be something?"

"I think that's just called a mature relationship."

"I think you're righ–" The first punch came from behind and caught Michael on his ear and he spun around from the force and the shock of it. The second punch followed closely. The man doing the punching was obviously practiced in punching and Michael felt his left orbital bone crunch and go all bag-of-sand under his face's skin. He raised his fists in a defensive posture and threw what he thought was a forceful counterblow but was only a weak and feeble and pathetic attempt, which also left his face exposed, again, and the third punch caught his jaw hard and Michael felt his brain bounce against the inside of his skull and everything just gave out from underneath him.

Falling clean off his stool, the back of his head bounced hard against the floor of the TGIF. Just before he lost consciousness, he heard the man say, "What the fuck Jane, it's only been a week."

The ammonia stink of the smelling salts woke him, and he immediately touched his face, which felt like a pillow stuffed with broken glass. He began to cry, then, and Jane was gone, and he was asked if he thought he required an ambulance, to which he said no.

The world reacts to Baker Thomas II

A Big Mac for Miller
Too Soon Radio
5,897 views – 02/01/2019   SUBSCRIBE

Dereck François   9 months ago
Ahh, see, do you see, this is what is feared with any performance artist when they are conceiving and practicing their concept. The artist (here Baker Thomas of Madison, WI) has overplayed his hand and is now seeing serious diminishing returns, which may be the point, I think. I must confess, when Mac Miller died and there was silence from this channel, I was excited because I thought that Baker, who is an artist I had greatly admired, did not take the bait and was instead waiting for a more low-rung death in the world of celebrity — think a Hulk Hogan or like a Snookie and J-Wow. But instead, what he was doing, I think anyway, but I guess the world will never know for sure (more on that later), was testing the limits of the general public's capacity to care as well as their attention spans. Essentially holding a mirror up to our current pop-culture zeitgeist which is dominated by flash-in-the-pan

scandal and mourning and celebration played out live and intensely on social media, but then fades just as quickly and is forgotten about and moved on from. In the case of celebrity death, you will see a resurgence in performative emoting on Twitter and Facebook and on the listicle-sites like Buzzfeed on the anniversary of the death, but other than that, there is no staying power, attention-wise, anymore. What I think Baker has done here by releasing this song (which is by all accounts a huge step down from The Verne Troyer Blues and kind of crass if I am being honest) is asked us all the question, do you still care enough to hate me, this many months later? And the answer seems to be, no. He's also, I think, playing a much more dangerous game with his art and also asking, do you still care about me? About my concept? Do you trust me enough to follow me on this path knowing it will only lead you to frustration and to ultimately not knowing why I do what I do? And as the numbers have borne out, I think the answer is also no. Putting aside the content of the song itself, which is vulgar to the point of absurdity, let's think about the actual construction of the concept itself. When VT died and the song went up within hours, it was the first such tribute on the scene and obviously done in a humorous way, which was as if by design, intended to offend but was mostly innocuous — content-wise. But it was also sincere, that much could be seen from the earnestness with which Baker presented the music. The shirtlessness. The shabby couch. The obviously shitty apartment. All of which illustrated a life that was unenviable, regular, without note. It was painful because it was so obvious, as demonstrated by his obvious talent with his guitar and his voice, that Baker Thomas wanted to be a star in his youth, and that now he was fading into early middle age and nothing had panned out for him. He was like that cougar stalking the bar long into her fifties with her shoehorned butt testing the integrity of her jeans' fabric and looking more pathetic than sexy. His friends all probably privately pitied him. In that sense, it was a perfect tribute to the subject at hand, Verne Troyer. Not that the subject at hand was particularly pitiable, but rather that that's how the world saw him after his time in the sun during the Austin Powers years. But here we are, months later, and he's made us wait and wait and wait only to then present us with something so vile, so mean-spirited, so unapologetically 2 Live Crewian, that he is daring us to spin ourselves out in a self-feeding orgy of outrage. Daring us to make him go viral again, but only after all the algorithms have cooled on the death of Mac Miller and everyone's already forgotten. I wouldn't have even known of this song's existence had I not subscribed to the channel. In the end, when I really think about it, the fact that this song has not taken off, not done the numbers as it were, probably, ultimately, proves Baker's point. No one cares. Not really. And in that sense, the art was successful. Congratulations everyone on being exactly who he thought you were. And now this. What does his own death say about us? What does it say about him? Was it part of it? Are we now supposed to react in the way he would've? Or, and I think this is what he was hoping, do we react with sympathy, kindness, and love? Do we demonstrate, if only to ourselves, internally, that we are capable of empathizing and feeling bad for a guy who trolled us and probably won, in the end? All I know about Baker Thomas and his art is that it was probably saying something none of us truly understood at the time, and the way he did it would ensure that no one would ever really care. It is a sad day indeed. RIP Mac. RIP Baker. May the next world be kinder to you than this one ever was.

Killian red   8 months ago
Fuck you, you French fuck.

In the room no one ever called a cell, the party ends

The cold cement radiates heat when she looks at it long enough in one spot. The walls wobble and breathe with her aftershock. Her bunk floats two centimeters off the ground. Her toilet runs a continual flush but the bowl is dry, just the noise. Her sink has disappeared with Michael's head, but no one notices that. She is silent. So are They. She looks down. The cement where her gaze falls is orange-glow. The Bear adjusts his tie. He's worn exclusively black ties since 1986. She looks up with her head but her eyes are still directed down, at the spot, which now glows a deep red at its center. Her hair no longer auburn streaked in white, but rather white streaked in auburn. They can all see the tops of the whites of her eyes, and they all feel nothing in that moment. Every one of them is blank. They can't think of anything they'd want to say even if they could speak. Helen Abelmen looks at The Bear because it is less disturbing to her than looking at Molly, and he, very suddenly, looks very old and enfeebled, like the effort it takes for him to stand is more than he can bear but he does it anyway out of respect for the woman at whom he is staring with a mouth agape with awe. Something special is about to happen. Something special is about to happen. This, they all feel. No one thinks it, though. Feels it. The room is cold now. The room's coldness goes unfelt and unremarked upon. Her eyes rise to sit forward in her head and Helen is in her gaze, and Helen then feels warm. She feels the cold leaving her. She smiles. She is happy. She feels a love. A CD's jewel case is suddenly on her bunk, or they all just notice it has been there the whole time, and on it are white lines of cocaine. They all think the word "partake" simultaneously. Jesse Robinson approaches her but does not partake in the drugs because they are not for him, and her warming eyes fall on him, and he articulates clearly for the first time since August 2001, "Molly, how I've missed you. You were always so kind to me." Then his own eyes roll down to the floor's red and he is silent once more, but by choice. Baker Thomas is alone in being seemingly unaffected by all of this, awe-inspired-wise. There are, however, silent lyrics in his head, but those aren't consciously thought, more like the muscle memory whisper of something that it is imperative he remember. Background only. Molly raises a hand, and one finger of the hand, and she curls that finger indicating Jed Lucas should approach to partake. He does. And he, too, feels happy. He remembers what it all was about, what it all had felt like, what his oblivion had meant to him, and for that reminder, he thanks her directly in her ear and he kisses her cheek and she, in turn, places her hand on the side of his face and says nothing to him, but in her saying nothing he understands something elemental about himself and what he can and cannot escape, and in that knowing, that real and true knowing, he now knows what peace is. Internal peace. And he puts his struggle down. He lets that go. He is done play-acting. She uses her hand on his cheek to guide his face up, and he understands who he is. The Bear approaches uninvited and the weight of himself becomes too much for him and he needs to immediately sit, then lie. He crumples to the floor at her feet. Age is there, in that room. The thing he's raged against is present and there is nothing he can do about it anymore. His skin sags and dries and cracks where once it was fresh and taut and radiant with the vigor of undeserved youth. She places her bare feet on his chest where he lies. The weight of her feet is not held by his sternum and her feet sink into his chest and she can feel the weak and slow beating of his heart through her feet's callused bottoms — feel the soft sack of one lung. Her feet sink still further down and her ankles touch rib bones exposed through the skin, and she comes to rest on his spine; the heart still pumping, she can feel, but barely. In his face is confusion and she whispers down to him, and he, too, understands his very nature and what he's accomplished and how rare and good it is, and how he's never known, and still longed for more, and how that longing has left him, ultimately, deprived of the life he'd actually had for so, so long. He has regret, then, for what should be but isn't. "I saw you, though, I saw," he croaks. She bends at her waist, sitting on her bunk, and she leans so forward that all present think she might fall, and she kisses his forehead and she says, "I know," and her tongue punches his brain and he is then there and not, and she is so there that everyone in the room hurts for the loss of him through her, and in that moment, he sees, really sees, everything he needs to know about the universe and its secrets, and he dies in a kind of joy that no man ever gets to feel, but he does, he does. His body will not cool. His soul will never leave that place. He will linger on and on and on, because she has given him what he's always wanted: to know how it all worked. A rumble begins from the floor's red. The eyes still on her are unconcerned with this. They are the placid and contented eyes of cows knowing the feed will always come. The nourishment. Baker's fingers strum uncontrollably and subconsciously, and there is nothing she wishes to do about that, nothing she wishes to lift from him, nothing she thinks will benefit him from knowing. He makes to approach, but she holds her hand up and she smiles and he feels an absence of discontent but he does not feel what the others feel because she has denied him an understanding of himself, because if he understood himself, truly understood himself, then he would feel only despair and anguish, and she knows he has enough of that coming, soon. The floor's rumble spreads from the spot which still glows and the cement cracks a large, sharp, and loud crack and she stands, feet still in The Bear, and she holds her arms out as if she means to embrace all of them, and in that moment, the ceiling too cracks and stone falls but none strike true. Helen's smile grows and grows and grows until she is all teeth and laughter. Molly makes for her and they embrace and thunder claps and white comes over them all, and then they are all gone from that place and in a place of nowhere.

White floor.

White walls.

And a nothing above that went on forever.

Weightless.

Burdenless.

Selfless.

Soulless.

Thoughtless.

Void.

No anger. No fear. No invasive thoughts. Nothing on nothing on nothing. All content. All neither happy nor sad. All moon-eyed. She holds it all together, rotating at the nothing's center. Useful. Exerting maximum effort. Hands outstretched and fingers splayed. The Bear rotates near her floating feet, having detached from her. Her face a mask of concentration. No telling how long they've been there. White streaked with auburn hair floats about her head. She says nothing. Holds nothing back. All is right and all is wrong. She thought she could but she can't, in the end. She thought she could but she can't, in the end, hold them all in that place where nothing can touch them and nothing can hurt them and everything that they have known and have experienced is nothing anymore and does not matter because this is a place where she makes the rules, she decides what gets through and what does not, where she can undo what was done to all of them. The explosion comes slowly like fog rolling over a hill in the dawn's cold on the exact day when late fall turns early winter. It, too, rolls. Rolls from her and into that white and blank world of contentment and touches them all with its heat and its extreme energy, and one after another their eyes regain themselves, their thoughts, their memories, their experiences, and they are again; and they see the devastation that is coming from her in the center, see what it will do. She looks at them all and she smiles. "It's okay, it's all okay, we are all okay."

They all stand around the crater where The FPPIB was once buried but is now just a hole, and she is gone and the smoke is rising and none of them know exactly what she expected of them, moving forward, but they all know, in their guts, that they must move forward as if all of this has really happened and also as if none of it has.

Cleaning up a life

The TV in Baker Thomas' apartment played the *7th Heaven* main menu with its accompanying loop of theme song. The noise faded into the background the longer he was there and after a while, he did not notice it at all. He didn't know what was more embarrassing, the circumstances, or the DVD. The story was what it was, but he thought he knew better. He thought he knew what Baker Thomas would've wanted, and it did seem like it was his place to make that happen. That and he somehow thought this way was better, for Baker's family and all.

His second song *had* come out, and that was all that was important to him.

He was there because Baker still had the things in this apartment that Jed wanted and Baker would sell to him; that was it, the only real reason. And, also, the door was open so he could let himself in upon receiving no answer to his knock. They had not remained friends, afterward, but now that he was in the apartment, a deal was a deal, and the two men had had a deal, if only once upon a time. Upon the death of one, the other would do their best to clean up the other's apartment before any family could arrive and find things that they ought not to be finding.

In recent years, it wouldn't have mattered much (finding-things-wise) if Jed had died unexpectedly because he'd cleaned his whole act up and was (past tense) living the family life. His phone buzzed in his pocket and he checked it. A text message with some urgent business Rep. Kilroy needed him to look into. It could wait, he thought. It could always wait. A quick search of the apartment netted Jed Lucas a handful of Xanax, a quarter ounce of weed, an eight ball of coke, three bottles Jack Daniels, some Oxy and assorted other opioids, and the kicker, a gram and a half of the white pony.

He removed the old porno mag from where it had fallen, at the feet of Baker Thomas as he hung purple-faced from a pullup bar he'd hung from his bathroom's doorjamb for that exact purpose. The belt around his neck was of braided leather. His shoes were still on, pants and boxers pooled around them. He must've uploaded the video and then come to do this. He must've been pleased with himself. He would never know.

Jed Lucas thought about fabricating a note to sell the fiction of what he wanted the cops and everyone else to think had happened there, but he knew that that was a risk as he had terrible handwriting, and Baker, he knew, did not. Also, Baker was a lefty, and he a righty. He was unsure what kind of difference that would make. Anyway, most leave no notes at all, that's just a cruel fact of suicide. Jed thought that he knew why, too, and it was because he thought the suicides thought no one would really care why they did it.

Baker hung and was cold to the touch. He spun slightly after Jed checked his pulse. There was no piss on the ground. The magazine that Jed had placed in the bag with the drugs and drug paraphernalia was a *Hustler* of mid-nineties vintage. He wondered how many times Baker had used it for this purpose over the years. He wondered how much longer he could keep himself in check. The bag weighed heavily in his hand. Molly Duch had shown him his truth, and, in that truth, he was happy and content and still, miraculously, consequence-free. Others, just as was true before he Came In and Surrendered, were still not so lucky.

The *7th Heaven* theme song began anew. Jed left his friend where he hung and did another sweep. He netted an additional eighth of an ounce of marijuana and found (under the bed as was customary of adult males of their old-millennial age bracket) a stash of pornographic magazines and VHS cassette tapes dated between 1987-1999 — no DVDs. He put the pornography and additional marijuana in his sack of embarrassing shit and then he ejected the *7th Heaven* DVD, collected the rest, and added those to the sack as well. He put everything in the trunk of his car before reentering the apartment and calling the police, Baker Thomas still rotating slowly from his touch.

Let's walk together

Frank Novinsky takes five steps total from the lip of the hill when he feels her presence behind him. She is here. She smells of smoke and love. He fears her. It is the first thing he's felt that isn't anger since he began walking and repeating the walking. He sees through her eyes her seeing Antigo, WI. His fear fades with the touch of her hand on his shoulder, which he also sees (her reaching out toward him) from her perspective. And then the fear is gone and the anger is gone and he feels her nothing, her calming nothing. "Let's walk together, dear heart. Let's walk together."

Excerpted from Interpersonal Interrogation and Statement Aggregation of one Jesse Lee Robinson: **/**/2020

HBA: "Do you know where you are?"

JLR: "Yes, Helen, I know."

HBA: "Can you state it, for the record?"

JLR: "Langley, VA."

HBA: "Can you articulate for the record what happened to you?"

JLR: "Only after, I think, before then it's vague."

HBA: "But can you tell us what you do remember."

JLR: "The first clear recollection I have of 2019, is walking toward her. And telling her something nice, but I don't recall what."

HBA: "Then what?"

JLR: "Then I was home again. Back home."

HBA: "Where? For the record."

JLR: "I was at my Mother's house, in her kitchen, she was crying and saying how she missed me, asking me where I was, then saying to never mind that and she was just so happy I was back, and she was hugging me. And then I slept for two days, she said."

HBA: "Do you remember anything else from inside The FPPIB?"

JLR: "No, not really. But that's not entirely true, because while I don't have recollections of actual events, or what it was like, or what I was like, I do remember laughing, I remember vicious laughter, directed at myself from well-appointed men, mostly."

HBA: "Do you know who was laughing?"

JLR: "No."

HBA: "Would you like to?"

JLR: "I think I would."

HBA: "It was Bob and Bill, mostly, but the others too."

JLR: "Did They get sent somewhere nice too?"

HBA: "No, Jesse, They didn't. No one else did. Just you, me, Jed, and Baker."

JLR: "Where is she, like right now, where is she?"

HBA: "We don't know where she is."

JLR: "Was it bad?"

HBA: "It was covered up, but yes, it was bad."

JLR: "I hope she's happy, wherever she is."

HBA: "I, I mean, we here, don't believe she exists in the same sense that you and I do. We are not sure she has the capacity to feel anymore. We think, what I mean is it is our best hypothesis, that when she did what she did, for us I mean, she transcended our reality and exists on the same wavelength she sent Frank to. She both exists and doesn't. We still think she can be dangerous but are unconvinced that she wants to be, dangerous, that is."

JLR: "Are you looking for her?"

HBA: "That pursuit died with The Bear."

JLR: "Who?"

HBA: "That's unimportant."

JLR: "Oh."

HBA: "Jesse, can I ask you something personal? I mean like a question driving at the internality of what you have experienced over the last twenty years?"

JLR: "Shoot."

HBA: "Who do you blame?"

JLR: "What do you mean?"

HBA: "I mean, we have all the testimony from The Bunker, it was streamed back here, we know pretty much your whole story, how you ended up where we found you. How you ended up at The Antiquated, so, who do you blame? I mean, for all of it."

JLR: "I chose not to blame. I have been told what happened, a few times. But I can't seem to internalize it, to make it a part of me. I can't make the past a part of me moving forward. Something in me won't let me. I think she put that part there when she touched me and brought me back, brought me home. I don't think she unfucked me, as such. I think she made me unable to be fucked, get it?"

HBA: "Kind of."

JLR: "So, I don't blame anyone because blaming someone would mean I've re-internalized my life up until now, and in doing so would remember, and in remembering would re-experience, and I really don't want to do that, at all."

HBA: "What do you remember? From before her, and before you ended up back at home."

JLR: "Nothing."

HBA: "What of your time in Madison?"

JLR: "Nothing."

HBA: And how do you feel? Like right this very minute."

JLR: "Happy."

Scott Mitchel May is the author of the novel *Breakneck: Or It Happened Once in America*, the collection *Dekalb, Illinois is a Paradise What Eats Its Own*, and the novelette *All Burn Down*. His fiction has appeared in *HAD*, *W&S*, *Rejection Letters*, *Maudlin House*, *Bull*, and many more fine publications across the internet. His essays have appeared in the craft anthology *How to Write a Novel* from Autofocus Books, *Trampset*, and *Jake*, and have been nominated for a Best of the Net and a Pushcart Prize. He was a shortlist finalist for the 2022 Santa Fe Writers Project Literary Award for his unpublished novel *Bridgeport Nowhere* and won the 2019 University of Wisconsin Writers' Convention Poem and Page Competition in the category of literary fiction for the same. He holds a GED from the Wisconsin Department of Public Instruction and a BS in English Literature from Edgewood College.

DEATH OF PRINT

An imprint of Malarkey Books

Consumption & Other Vices
Tyler Dempsey

Drift
Francis Top's Grand Design
The Ghost of Mile 43
One More Number
Craig Rodgers

The Sun Still Shines on a Dog's Ass
The War on Xmas
Alan Good

deathofprint.press / malarkeybooks.com

Milton Keynes UK
Ingram Content Group UK Ltd.
UKHW010802220224
438165UK00004B/118